Geeta Rahman at Championship Point

Geeta Rahman at Championship Point

A Novel

SASKYA JAIN

SIMON &
SCHUSTER

London · New York · Sydney · Toronto · New Delhi

First published in India by Simon & Schuster India, 2021

This edition published in 2021

1 3 5 7 9 10 8 6 4 2

Simon & Schuster India
818, Indraprakash Building,
21, Barakhamba Road,
New Delhi 110001

www.simonandschuster.co.in

HB ISBN: 978-93-92099-29-8
eBook ISBN: 978-93-92099-34-2

Typeset in India by SŪRYA, New Delhi

Printed and bound in India by Replika Press Pvt. Ltd.

FSC
www.fsc.org
MIX
Paper from responsible sources
FSC® C016779

Simon & Schuster India is committed to sourcing paper that is made from wood grown in sustainable forests and support the Forest Stewardship Council, the leading international forest certification organisation. Our books displaying the FSC logo are printed on FSC certified paper.

For the Cs, little F and the JJs.
And for D II/11,
where I learned the rules of
life and badminton.

That one, I say and point at the red Jonex ISOMETRIC badminton racket inside the glass cabinet.

The parent cadre, also known as Abba, continues to knead the seam of his purple khadi kurta.

You already have a racket.

Usually, when the parent cadre states a fact, it is not permissible to answer back. But today, February 1, 1993, I, Geeta Das Rahman, have special answer back rights.

My racket is so old, Abba. It negatively impacts my hand when I play. And sometimes the whole shuttle gets stuck in the stringing and I lose a point pointlessly!

I glance at the parent cadre to see if he noticed my employment of wordplay. He didn't. I turn towards Vijay, salesman at Ramji Sports N Games and also my personal friend, because whenever we come to Khan Market I create an opportunity to go look at the new rackets and equipment in his shop.

Uncle?

Having to call grownups Uncle and Aunty outside of my head is my Public Grievance # 4.

Uncuuull!

Vijay seems hassled when he finally turns. Behind him an Aunty in the latest sari-and-sneakers fashion is waving a broken antenna at him.

Since I'll be asking him for a discount soon, I adopt my high sugar smile, tilt my head same like the I-love-you-Rasna girl and point again.

Uncle, show us the ISO, no?

Instead of the red Jonex, Vijay lifts the red and silver Yonex from the top shelf and hands it to me. I let him, because maybe if the PC hears the price of the Yonex first, he'll be happy to settle for the Jonex, which is fine by me: same new shape.

Plus, as a bonus I'm getting to hold the Yonex now. The racket is light in my palm. The grip is smooth black tape, not dissolving terry cloth with chipping wood peeking out from under it. The stringing leaves a chequered mark on my thumb and doesn't give in when I bounce the base of my hand against it. The sound this makes is simple but also not.

Same like a knot tied around a government file, I say out aloud for Abba's ears, because as a Director at the India Trade Promotion Organisation the parent cadre is an expert of files. But Abba's eyes are examining me instead of the racket.

And I don't get to untie them today because I played games all day long as a boy.

I have not yet recruited the right words to tell the PC that when I'm on court I'm not playing games but just being myself, so step number one is to make Abba understand that I can also be an expert, maybe not of government files but definitely of feathers and strings. I breathe in sharply and widen my nostrils the way Mummy always used to when she was about to say something important.

Did you know, Abba, ISOMETRIC means of or having equal dimension? My old racket is same like an anda, oval, but this is ISOMET—

It's a pompous way to say circle, Geeta. You should understand the meaning of words properly, then you won't fall for such big companies' cheap tricks. That's exactly why I gave you the dictionary.

Actually, sir, kya hai na, ISOMETRIC ka matlab yeh ki it equalises the length of the main and cross strings in the string-bed, so sweet spot ko jo kehete hai enlarge ho jata hai for more accuracy, consistency and speed. It's the latest model, sir. From 1992.

This makes Abba initiate his snorting laugh.

Typical! In India, the latest model is always one year old.

Vijay grins. But that's about to change, no? Goodbye, socialism. Welcome, Dr. Manmohan Singh!

Inviting in MacDonald is not going to save this country. The riots—

Which MacDonald? The farm one? I interject quickly to stay in circulation but Abba remains focused on Vijay.

That's just politics, Uncle. The riots will pass and then everyone will forget about Babri Masjid, and all will be as before.

Last night, one Hindu boy and two Muslim girls were attacked in separate incidents right here in Delhi. It's the soul of our country that's at stake, Vijay. Don't get distracted by a slab of meat. Young people like you must take an urgent interest.

I have an urgent interest! I say loudly to conclude Abba's

lecture and remind him of our one-point agenda for coming to Vijay's shop.

Vijay breathes relief. So shall I pack the racket, sir?

More moments pass before Abba finally turns to me, and I, too, breathe like Vijay.

For her purposes the old one is perfectly fine.

But it's my birthday, Abba! I say, because a very unsettled feeling has begun to spread in my stomach: we have not even started talking about the price of the Jonex and the parent cadre has already said N-O.

And you promised last time ki next time for sure!

Because the PC and I agree that childish children are the pits, authorisation is not hereby granted to myself to cry or stomp my foot.

Come on, Geeta. You're twelve now! At your age I was teaching myself English with the help of Eliot and Yeats. You can have a new box of shuttles from here but not the racket. And then we go to Bahri Sons and you can pick out as many books as you want, special birthday treat. Happy?

I swallow the karela that's lodged in my throat and nod, even though I think that promises should not be exchangeable like wrong sizes or broken antennas. But even more than the racket, I want to like reading the books Abba buys for me, because then I will be better in my studies and get admission in a good college like St. Stephen's and pass the Civil Services Examination and join the Government of India, just like the parent cadre.

See, that's what I like about you growing older. You listen and understand what I'm telling you.

I swallow the second karela and nod again, though this time I find it easy to smile because of what the parent cadre has just said: In Abba's eyes I'm getting better at being Geeta!

Vijay, how much are the shuttlecocks?

One-ninety-five, sir.

What?!

Best quality, sir.

What other qualities do you have?

You want feather or plastic?

Feather!

Don't shout, Geeta.

Feather, there's a box for one-twenty-five, one-sixty-five or one-ninety-five, depending on their grading.

You mean, how good they are for fleecing people?

Si-i-i-r, Vijay says, chuckling but also not.

We'll take the one for one-twenty-five but only if you give us a discount. It's her birthday, after all.

Vijay gives Abba a helpless smile, which also contains a sigh. I examine the hole in my shoe through which I can see my brown sock. It's official: Abba's comprehensive and integrated opposition to my topmost favourite thing in the whole wide world is my Public Grievance # 1.

Sir, the margin is too small for discount.

Fine, but then you'll lose a customer.

I can feel Antenna Aunty trying to encroach on our circle from behind with the help of her namesake and I step aside to let her in, because civil means of or relating to ordinary citizens and their concerns, so this is good practice for the CSE.

Feeling for the tube of shuttles inside the brown paper bag as we leave the shop a moment later, I think that maybe the parent cadre's wish that I should join the civil service should also be my wish, because then I can always live in Kaka Nagar and play badminton forever, first as a girl and then as an Aunty: during the day I will serve in the office like Abba, and in the evening I will serve on the court like Geeta.

We have engulfed most of our kulfis to maximum effect when we turn from the main road into Kaka Nagar on our way home from Khan Market. Though a kulfi also has a handle, we must nota bene that it is not a badminton racket as per prior birthday promise. Abba is pinching his kulfi stick between his left thumb and forefinger while his other fingers are gripping the steering wheel. He is trying to lick the last chunks of the ice cream but they are beginning to drip into his lap. He catches the drops with his tongue as he steers the car into our side street, changing the gear with his other hand. This makes him giggle, so I, too, have to do the selfsame, because even though on the inside I am still angry with Abba, the only thing worse than that is when he is angry with me, and right now his eyes are looking at me very happily.

You know when I first met Mummy, that's how she used to change gears.

I sit up a little straighter in my seat, which helps you remember important things thoroughly and in full later. Eating kulfi?

This makes Abba smile even more. No, silly. With her right hand, reaching across her lap like this.

I quickly demolish the rest of my ice cream. What was wrong with her left hand?

Nothing, but she felt that was the better way to do it. She always complained back then that we drive on the left side in India just because the British do, even though most people are right-handed.

This knowledge is circulated with a renewed chuckle from Abba.

So why did she stop changing gears like that?

I guess it was too tedious to keep up. As you know, her love of driving trumped everything else.

An Ambassador toots at us as we pass. All my anger has been smashed out of court with Abba's words, because it is not possible to be upset with him when he is telling me stories about Mummy.

Show me again, Abba.

Instead of continuing straight to our building, Abba begins a lap around Kaka Nagar, which is made up of about fifty identical grey-white matchboxes split into four flats each: ground floor flat always with garden and first floor flat always with rooftop terrace. The shape of Kaka Nagar is same like a very big triangle, which is filled up entirely with our matchboxes. But there are also small parks here and there, and the market with the Safal shop, Bird Aunty's clinic that I visit often, including yesterday, and, of course, the Club House. To be assigned housing in Kaka Nagar, a parent cadre must at least be having Abba's rank of Joint Secretary, Government of India, which is one whole rank above the Under Secretary and only two ranks below the Minister.

Abba changes gears once again with the right hand.

You're doing it wrong, Abba. With her left hand at least she would somehow swerve the gearstick with the base of her palm, not with the fingertips. Like this.

Abba lets me show him.

You're right, he says and promotes his smile to wide grin. Do you remember how instead of just walking she would take the car out again to the Safal shop if we forgot the onions?

She forgot them on purpose, Abba!

He brings the car almost to a halt as he goes over a speed bump.

I'm still jealous of how she felt so at ease behind the wheel. I'm always scared something will go wrong.

She would keep the window rolled down and put her elbow on the rim, and you would tell her not to do it.

Abba chuckles.

Spoilsport!

That's exactly how she would say it! With that mocking lisp!

Where was the scar, Abba? I ask, even though I know the precise location.

Abba lifts his arm and runs his finger across his elbow. I find the same spot on my skin and trace a line with my fingernail.

She was a rebel through and through.

A rebel, I repeat. I will find that little part of Mummy in my dictionary later. Mummy was just steering the whole world in the right direction, Abba.

I watch the parent cadre drive his hand across his hair and blow air through his lips. He shakes his head gently at the windshield.

That's right, she always said that. Right until the end. When she was wheeled around in the hospital bed. She thought she was being terribly funny.

Abba turns his face away from me, but I know that the hand on his cheek is engaging in invisible wipeage of tears.

Hard to believe it's been eighteen months already, he says to his window.

I swallow the water that is gathering in my eyes. Eighteen months and three days, Abba.

He looks at me. His lips are shaking ever so slightly. That's right, jaani. Eighteen months and three days.

We pass the red letterbox, which is being emptied by the postman. The hatch appears to be jammed, and he is fiddling with the key.

Abba clears his throat as if there are still some words stuck inside that he needs to get out. He turns back to me.

Shall I tell you a secret?

Although Abba must know the answer to this question, I nod to make sure, because it is not very often that I am the recipient of new information relating to Mummy.

Sometimes, when I feel down, I go for a drive alone and I talk to your mother, and that always cheers me up.

And Mummy can hear you?

Yes, of course.

And she replies also?

Yes!

Really, Abba?

To me her voice is clearest when I drive and talk to her.

As a birthday gift it is a more than adequate compensation for the racket to find out about a direct intercom line to Mummy.

Can I come with you next time you feel down and we can talk to her together?

I'm afraid it only works when I'm alone with her in the car. You see, her voice is not loud. You just hear it deep inside your heart.

Abba glances at me and looks worried.

Now I've disappointed you. See, that's why I didn't tell you earlier, because you'd feel left out.

We could still try!

You know what? When you're old enough to drive yourself, you can also talk to her like that.

How many years until then?

Six.

Six is an abundance of years.

It's not that long, really.

Our round of Kaka Nagar is almost complete. Abba turns the car back onto our street and our building comes into view. I would have liked to continue my inquiry but a truck is parked in our space, and I can see Abba's eyes getting distracted, so I, too, take a closer look.

Each matchbox house in Kaka Nagar is cut in half by a staircase that goes up to the two first floor flats. Our parking spot is in front of that staircase, to the right of which is the white metal gate to our flat, which has the biggest lawn and senior-most mango tree in the whole colony. But our flat is special for another reason: The flat on the bottom left just next to ours is the Club House, with the badminton court in lieu of a garden and table tennis and carom boards inside the rooms of the flat. Once a year, the Resident's Association organises a tournament, which I have won three times in a row for my age group.

Right now, labourers are carrying sofas, chairs and boxes up the staircase and their truck is blocking the spot where our Maruti usually sleeps.

The New Khuranas have arrived, Abba says cheerfully to help me forget his tears. He gets out of the car and I follow him. The Old Khuranas moved back to Amritsar last month, because Mr Khurana retired.

The parent cadre often says that we Indians don't understand the value of time and this makes him angry, but he also has a soft spot for all truck drivers and peons and delivery boys. He says they still have some poetry left inside them, unlike those English-speaking imbeciles that are his batchmates. I didn't ask Abba how you can swallow poetry and it also took me a long time to find imbecile in the dictionary, because m can sound a lot like n and s can be spelled with a c.

The truck driver says that upstairs a family called Bhabra is moving in, from Delhi only. Husband IAS, UT cadre, they say he had to leave his previous posting because of some money scandal. Wife's the modern type (short hair; big bindi; full-time job) and, Sahab, she's ten-plus years older than him! Troubled marriage of course (single child). Child is a daughter, age fifteen, same hair as mother. Then he says that riches (two colour TVs; suitcase full of shoes only for the Missus; imported machine for washing clothes!) don't automatically lead to happiness, which makes the truck driver look hopeful and Abba look pleased with himself.

But only for a brief moment. Then Abba's eyes become cloudy again. Saleem Uncle walks past him in his badminton whites and touches his fingertips to his nose in greeting, which Abba then does, too. Saleem Uncle is the boss of the Tilak Marg Police Station, which is maybe why he always looks at Abba like a schoolteacher at a misbehaving boy.

Abba has been trying to avoid him, because Saleem Uncle invited us to his house recently, and Abba decided at the last minute to bunk.

All well? Saleem Uncle asks as they shake hands.

Bas, badhiya. Abba replies to the corners of his eyes.

I have launched an official complaint.

Abba's eyes widen as they fly to Saleem Uncle's, who is not looking back at Abba but at the enormous ditch that has been dug into the street in front of our building. Now the people of Kaka Nagar can only continue on foot or by bicycle on the narrow strip of road left over on one side of the ditch. Cars have to turn around and go back the way they came.

Good, good. Complaining is always good.

It's the municipality again. Thieves! Trying to make a buck with some bogus repairs. They've been at it all week and I don't see any pipes being changed. You live right here, Rahman, how come you didn't bring this to my notice immediately? Don't you think about Geeta's wellbeing? This pit is just an invitation for all kinds of mischief and who knows how long it'll be here now.

Abba's tongue is busy gathering spit from all the folds inside his mouth as Saleem Uncle continues with his speech. I extend my neck slowly to escape Saleem Uncle's notice. When I came home from school yesterday, the ditch was still being dug. Today, the hammers and drills are silent. It's as if the CPWD workers cut out a room-sized piece from the street, ate it like birthday cake and then went home.

But the street is just the top layer—the icing. The walls of the underground room are neat brown mud and at the far end there are steps moulded into it that would make it substantially unchallenging for anyone to climb down into the underground mud room.

So keep an eye on this for me, Rahman. You poets need to start taking your heads out of the clouds.

I wonder if, because he is a cop, Saleem Uncle has noticed the lines of sweat now marking the dark circles around Abba's eyes.

You probably don't even read the newspaper, but take it from me and my boys on the streets, these are bad times. You and I, we are one family under Allah's merciful gaze and we need to look out for each other now.

Abba swallows a lot of spit and forces a smile. We say bye and Saleem Uncle turns to go. Abba unsmiles his face. Saleem Uncle stops and turns.

We missed you at our qawwali, by the way. Again. If I didn't know better I would think you don't like coming to my house.

Abba's eyes widen one more time. What are you saying, Saleem Sahab? My Geeta was sick, vomiting all evening. Food poisoning.

I am not aware that I was having food poisoning on the occasion of Saleem Uncle's last qawwali, which he organises every few months and which we went to only once last summer. Saleem Uncle was playing the harmonium and singing, and another man was playing the tabla, and we all sat on white sheets on the floor and clapped along and ate what felt like a whole tree of the best mangoes. It was therefore fully enjoyable, but Abba informed me afterwards that in this day and age he is always suspicious when music and poetry are used for religious purposes, be they bhajans or qawwali or hymns.

Of course. Good to see her back on her feet.

Khuda Hafiz, Rahman, Saleem Uncle says again.

Khuda Hafiz, Saleem Sahab.

I know Abba will mutter under his breath when Saleem Uncle is out of earshot.

Bloody holier-than-thou arse of an ape. Thinks he's the bloody Ayatollah, going around Khudahafizing. What does he know about poetry? The only book he reads is the telephone directory. How dare he talk to me about my daughter's wellbeing!

Turning to me the parent cadre says, Next time we'll just have to go to his stupid qawwali and clap our hearts out like monkeys. Don't let me make an excuse again.

As we enter home, Abba unlocks the brown letterbox next to our door that reads in white, hand-painted font *Mr Akbar Rahman & Mrs Sakshi Das Rahman*, and, finding it empty, he says, Go take birthday blessings from your grandmother before she, too, gives me a scolding.

He sounds as if he is crunching each word between his teeth. Abba always says that people like Saleem Uncle or Naniji hold on to religion because they are afraid of facing life on their own. Of course without religion Abba is just afraid all by himself, because he would never dare tell Naniji not to bless me in a religious way.

I quickly allot time to supply all the plants with their specified quantity of water as per my post-school routine before finding Naniji as always sitting cross-legged on her cot with her back resting against the thin pillow and the wall, holding on to her bead necklace. Naniji's mouth has an excess production of spit, so she has developed a habit of scraping her lower lip dry with her upper teeth or her fingernail before swallowing. This makes her look permanently hungry and a little wolfish. But the rest of her looks sufficiently Nanilike with grey hair tied into one medium-length, thin braid and her earlobes so long and soft that Naniji could probably use them as earplugs if she wanted to.

The television in the corner is on, shooting silent images of gods and gurus at Naniji.

I've been waiting for you, she says. Because as a special birthday treat Abba took the afternoon off and picked me up from school in the car so we could go to Khan Market together, I have not seen her yet at all today. Naniji tends to sleep in, because of her insomnia during the night, so I usually leave for school before she is up. As always, there is a degree of reproach in her voice. Abba says it's her way of speaking, because she grew up in a different time and that I mustn't take it personally. I asked Abba if this means that she would be automatically friendlier if she suddenly knew how to speak English but Abba just laughed at me and called me Little Colonial.

Today is your happy birthday. I hope you have a long and healthy life.

I know Naniji is thinking of Mummy as she says this, so I say, Definitely, Naniji. Inordinately long and healthy.

That's up to God to decide.

I want to ask her why God decided that Mummy's should

be a short life with a long illness, but as a general guideline you should only ask a question to which you want to hear the answer.

Because Naniji will have a present for me, I try to steer her Mummylike in the right direction by spreading Abba's gifts on her bed, even though I know what she is going to say.

Books and sports! Where does your father think all this reading is going to lead? Thick-thick specs you'll be wearing and dark brown and cracked like an old cowpat you'll be from playing in the sun all day long.

No, Naniji, I'll be clever and strong!

And unfit for marriage or childbearing.

In the distance, the tyres of a bus are screeching to a halt.

Naniji, don't you want to give me my birthday present?

She sighs, reaches behind the pillow and hands me a small pouch of red velvet. I pull the strings to open its mouth. Inside is a silver pendant in the shape of a bow stretched to its limit by an arrow.

I got this made for your mother when she was a little girl, and now I want you to have it. Naniji produces a piece of black string and I let her tie it around my neck.

What is it, Naniji?

All I want is for you to understand.

Understand what?

Did you know that Ram shot this very arrow through seven palm trees at once, only to prove to the monkey king Sugriva that he was fit to fight Sugriva's enemy and brother, the mighty king Bali?

No, Naniji.

Can you do that with your featherball?

Shuttlecock.

Can you?

Not yet, Naniji.

Ram was desperate to find Sita.

Why?

Naniji is forever seeking opportunities to tell me her religious stories, which I know by heart, but she secretly likes it when I pretend that I've never heard them before, because then she feels like she's teaching me something.

Ravana abducted and carried her off to Lanka. That's why Ram agreed to help Sugriva in the first place, so that Sugriva would help him in return. You see, Geeta, life is full of difficult choices. Some might say Sugriva was the aggressor and Bali was innocent, and that Ram should have fought on Bali's side against Sugriva. Like with most things, there is no clear answer. Yet Ram had to make a choice.

Is that why he let them destroy the Babri Masjid? Abba says—

Don't blame Lord Ram for the actions of people, Geeta. Your Abba should know better than that.

I decide to drop the question to discourage further anti-Abba sentiments.

So what happened to Bali?

Ram killed him.

Why?

He had to.

Why?

Because he had promised Sugriva and was dependent on his help to find Sita.

He killed him to save Sita?

That's one way of putting it.

I look down at the pendant around my neck, imagining how girl-Mummy looked down at it once upon a time. In such a situation, does a rebel through and through tilt her head to one side or keep it straight?

Naniji? Would you have killed Sugriva to save Mummy?

Ram was a god, Geeta! We are not gods.

But we get sad just like them when someone is taken away from us.

That's why we have our faith, you see. That's what I want you to understand. You don't have to come to the temple with me, and you don't have to pray, but there will come a day when you will realise that your spirituality is the only thing to save you from dying alone.

I want to tell Naniji that this is a para—, para—, a contradiction in any case, but because I don't know that word in Hindi, I say, Now you've made me sad, Naniji, and it's supposed to be my happy birthday.

But that's what life is! Happiness is finding that single drop of water in an ocean of sadness.

Naniji's ideas do not sound promising, so I ask, When she was a girl, did Mummy wear the pendant around her neck in this exact way, with a black string?

But Naniji is already reaching for my face and clasping my cheeks, kissing each one as she says, Happy birthday, Geeta! Now run along and let me watch my serial in peace.

As I slip out of Naniji's room I think that at least she did not ask me again to come with her to the temple, where last time I had to sit beside her for a period of infinity and listen to the pandit chant. The chanting is not a Public Grievance per se, and Abba says it's no different at the masjid, but unlike in school you can't even raise your hand in between and request to go to toilet for a free break. At the end, Naniji made me touch the feet of all the pandits and since then touching anyone's feet, no matter how holy they are, is my Public Grievance # 5.

In the kitchen the parent cadre is stirring two spoonfuls of sugar into a cup of tea.

Bhabra! Definitely Punjabi. Trust them to be too stingy to provide even tea to those poor labourers because—what's that?

Naniji's birthday present. Mummy used to wear it around her neck same like this, with a black string.

The tea inside the cup he is holding spills over the rim as Abba laughs.

Did Naniji tell you that particular mythology?

Because I don't understand what Abba is trying to say, I invite him to explain by blinking at him multiply.

Mummy refused to wear the pendant. She was a stubborn child, just like you, and she told her mother that she will not wear a murder weapon around her neck.

Because Ram could have talked to Sugriva and Bali rather than killing Bali without prior notice?

I guess. But I asked Mummy: which one makes the better story?

Why is that important, Abba?

Because that's what religion is. A compelling story.

That's all it is? A good story?

Compelling doesn't just mean good, Geeta. It means something so powerful you simply can't resist it.

Like jumping in puddles?

No. Like all the izzums. Patriot izzum. Fash izzum. Race izzum.

What's an izzum, Abba?

It's an oppressive practice legitimised by a lot of hot air. It's a way to bend a story any which way you need. It's why this country was partitioned. It's how they got the Babri Masjid demolished.

Abba hands me the steaming tray. Now go and take this outside.

Although I can tell Abba is still in a tense mood because of (a) Saleem Uncle and (b) Naniji, I decide to take the risk.

Can I go play afterwards?

Don't you want to read your new books?

Mistake.

I'm dying to, Abba!

So, then?

I'm saving them for after dinner.

Abba looks at me, sighs. The good mood is out.

If only your mother were here to tell me what exactly I'm doing wrong.

Somewhere in my throat a volcano of tears is beginning to bubble. I try scraping my upper teeth over my lower lip to dry myself out. Then I swallow.

Please don't be angry, Abba.

I'm not angry! Don't make me out to be some kind of a monster, Geeta. I'm not doing this to torture you. I want you to develop an interlicked so you can have a fulfilled life, is that such an unreasonable thing for a father to want for his child?

To be on the safe side, I shake my head at the floor and say nothing. Behind my back I am spelling i-n-t-e-r-l-i-c-k-e-d into the palm of my hand with my finger, which is how you remember things to look up in the dictionary later.

Reading should not feel like a chore to you, Geeta. It should feel like a hunger that needs to be satisfied.

But I love reading, Abba! Especially the books you buy for me.

Abba just looks at me with tiredness accumulating in his eyes.

To help Abba revert his mood back to how it was in the car on our way home, I ask, When I read is Mummy watching me?

Yes, jaani.

Is she always watching me or only if I do something special?

Always, baba. Abba sighs again and then it's there—the tiniest smile in the whole wide world. A moment later it's gone.

Go play, Geeta, but be home in time to help Naniji with dinner.

After delivering the tray to the labourers I step onto the small road that holds all of Kaka Nagar together like the string around one of Abba's files. I'm not supposed to go on it alone but now I'm walking along the outer side of the Ashoka hedge that surrounds the Club House grounds. The steps leading down into the mud room appear to have been built specially for me, because clearly nobody else has contemplated their usage.

Once I'm inside the mud room I pop open the tube and pull out a perfect new shuttlecock. On the main road, which runs parallel to our narrow side street down into which I have climbed, an auto rickshaw is coughing past: trrrrr-tr-tr-tr-trrrr-trrrrrrrrr. I look up following the sound and see nothing but blue sky.

I used to really like reading, though now I much prefer watching TV with Naniji on Sunday mornings. Sometimes I even think that hitting a shuttlecock is a bit like being Krishna and spinning your chakra to slice off your enemy's head. But maybe the problem is that when I read the books that Abba buys for me now—which are never like Famous Five or Matilda anymore—he asks me questions afterwards to which there is a correct answer and an incorrect answer, and mine is never the first.

Thack!

Unlike the courts above ground, there is no wind or even draught here to steal points away from me, and the shuttle lands exactly where I want it to land.

And of course I don't want Abba to think I'm a failure in life, which is how he describes most people. When I was younger and less informed about word spellings, I thought Abba was saying failyourownlife. I still think of it that way, because it reminds me of the fact that Abba knows best. If there was a Concise Abba English Dictionary, it would be there on page 1: failyourownlife.

I pull out another shuttle by its bald cork head.

Thack!

Perfect serve.

And so I decided recently to take matters into my own

hand: I have started taking a page here and a page there from the files Abba brings home in his black attaché. Because if I am to become same like Abba through reading and Abba feels I am so much behind, then shortcut is the only option: better just to read what he is also reading.

Thack!

Each new shuttle feels soft against my cheek.

Thack!

More of my arm disappears into the tube with every serve.

Thack!

Thack!

Thack!

Out! Service over!

I look up and back and more back and see Faraz's head dancing above mine like a cartoon genie. Faraz is Saleem Uncle's son and he wears round specs like Gandhiji but with the hair of Aamir Khan singing "Papa Kehete Hai". Faraz was also the very first person I met in Kaka Nagar, when we were brand new in the colony and I was about six or seven. Faraz is also easily found in all of Kaka Nagar as of yesterday because of his bright red Power trainers that would have matched my Jonex ISOMETRIC 100%. Right now he is grinning at me the way he always does, sideways.

So this is where you've been hiding, Smalls!

Come down, there's absolutely no wind here!

No, ya! My shoes are too new.

A red sole appears and waves at me under Faraz's chin. Specks of sand land in my eyes and I rub them.

Come up, ya. I still have a match to win against you and you know I have to be home by six.

Faraz's head disappears. I collect the shuttles that look like birds shot out of the sky and stuff them into the tube. As I jog up the eighteen mud steps, their corners begin to crumble under my trainers, which are already so dirty that a mud coating might even improve them a little.

I slip into the Club House through the gap in the Ashoka hedge.

The Greek Chorus is already assembled vacantly on the sidelines: Angad, Short Ratan, Tall Ratan, and, of course, Shipra. Faraz calls Shipra Shipwreck, and it would almost be a mercy if that would somehow happen to them all.

Shipra giggles at everything Faraz says and then sticks out her lips at him like a hungry giraffe. But Faraz is too smart—he wouldn't be my friend otherwise. And I am his friend, too, because I'm the only one in all of Kaka Nagar who can make him run for his points and beat him on court, even though I'm only twelve and he's seventeen. My anti-liking for Shipra started when Tall Ratan was still new in Kaka Nagar and I heard Shipra talking about me through the open window in the table tennis room. She said: Mozzie father, Hindu mother, dead but, so the Nani lives with them and Papa says he probably forces her to eat meat and share his bed now as revenge for Babri Masjid. True or not, bottom line is: avoid.

Abba, of course, is pure veg, just like Mummy was, though Naniji will sometimes ask for meat for her health and my growth, but I think she just likes the taste. Abba's so-called journalist friends tease him and say that his wife turned him into a good Hindu and that he should either eat the tikka or start wearing it on his forehead, which personally

I think makes zero point zero sense. But Abba says they are all hypocrites at the end of the day: if their daughters brought home a Muslim boyfriend they would all bloody lose it. Lose what? I asked him, but Abba did not tell me. Bottom line is: The Greek Chorus is my Public Grievance # 2.

Briefly, I imagine Faraz stepping onto the court to sing Happy Birthday, but I decide not to tell him, because then he will ask When is the party, Geeta? When are you taking us out to eat, Geeta? And the parent cadre says that children's birthday parties are exercises in human imbecility.

Twenty minutes later, Faraz shows me an unnecessarily broad grin through the net.

Wide! Mmmmatch point, Smalls!

He is teasing me because the score is 14–13, and he doesn't want to lose to a twelve-year-old girl with the GC watching. I make a farting noise in his direction.

Faraz raises the shuttlecock. He produces his standard high serve, and I have to run backwards to return it. The high serve is a mean shot, because it can be out or it can be in but you would have to keep your eyes on the sky and on the floor at the same time to make an informed decision about whether to return the shuttle or let it drop. To be on the safe side, I shoot it deep into the corner of Faraz's court, far enough, I am hoping, that he cannot smash it. He can't. I swing my racket back almost to the heel of my shoe but touch the shuttlecock gently, making Faraz race to the front of his court.

My serve!

Pure fluke, Faraz says, but he is breathing hard.

Unlike Faraz I don't have a standard serve. I take a step back to make him think I am serving high but instead I whip the shuttlecock just over the net, aiming a little lower to take the small breeze into account. The shuttlecock flies back and forth like a cartoon grenade that neither Tom nor Jerry wants to hold. Who knew that it could be so easy to make Faraz run! He returns to the back of my court, I lift it even higher and—he leaps to smash!—but I return it! Faraz lifts the shuttle and I drive it into his thigh.

Ha! 14-all!

Keep blowing your own trumpet, Faraz says, and you might run out of air.

I'm not the one who's out of breath!

I decide to try out a high serve, just to confuse Faraz and surprise him, who, impatient that he is, jumps to smash. Into the net.

15–14! Match point! I glance at the Greek Chorus, who have stopped chatting and are paying us their full attention, so I say, I think someone is going to lose to a twelve-year-old girl today. I refrain from adding: a twelve-year-old girl with a deficient racket, because last time the Greek Chorus cracked jokes for an entire afternoon about the parrots living in our house and picking holes in my shoes.

I collect the shuttlecock and position myself behind the service line. I watch Faraz wet his lips. Our eyes meet. The slap of string against cork echoes in our joint ears. Faraz plays deep into my forehand corner, which leaves me no option but to play a high shot in return, and Faraz is there to drop it on the other side of my court just beyond the net.

Service over, Smalls!

Though Faraz is smiling at his Greek audience, he is flicking sweat from his temple like relieved people do.

I have to return Faraz's serve at an awkward angle, because my thumb has got caught in the torn terry cloth of my racket handle. I would have demanded a replay but I know the GC will laugh at me behind my back and in front of it, too, if I draw attention to my disintegrating racket. So I let Faraz convert my wobbly return into a backhand net shot that zips across my court like an excessively angry bee. I run as fast as Geeta's legs will allow and even manage to lift it across the net but Faraz follows it up with an easy-peasy smash.

Ouch! I rub my thigh where the shuttlecock hit me.

15-all.

My sixth sense informs me that everyone is rooting for Faraz, so I don't deign to look at them. I make a promise to myself: I will win the serve back with the next point.

Faraz raises the shuttlecock. I stay where I am, not wanting to give away my prophecy of how Faraz will serve from moving a few steps to the front or back of my court, but I am secretly betting that it will be another high one. It is. Utterly butterly prepared, I leap into the air and intercept the shot a little earlier than Faraz expects and smash the shuttlecock at his confused feet.

Service over! My serve!

I scoop up the shuttlecock with my racket and a second later it is in the air again. As he returns the serve I feel the small breeze growing, so I hold back a little to control the drift. Too much! Too much! The shuttlecock falls steeply on my side of the court, without even touching the net.

Faraz serves deep into my backhand corner, and the shuttlecock sails. Keeps sailing.

Out! Out! Out!

In!

Out!

Faraz jogs over to my side, where the shuttlecock is resting just beyond the back boundary.

It touched the line and bounced. I saw it, Smalls.

Because I didn't see it, there is a chance that he saw wrong.

No, it was out the first time.

It really wasn't, Smalls.

What's the score? Shipwreck calls out from the sideline, and Faraz and I both turn to look at her.

Still 15-all, he says. I just won the serve back.

No, you didn't!

How boring, says the Greek Chorus.

Faraz sighs. From the way he is blinking at me slowly I can tell that he thinks that I'm trying to cheat.

Okay, Smalls, let's just call it a tie, shall we?

Little does he know that Geeta never cheats!

No! It's not a tie. It's 15-all, my serve.

Now Faraz's pout is converting into a grin.

Tie is my best offer.

That's cheating, I say.

Faraz drops his head and looks at me over the rims of his spectacles.

Here is my best offer, I say. We say it's a tie for now and play one more game, and whoever wins that wins the whole match.

The Greek Chorus titters and nudges Faraz to agree.

Faraz's eyes flit back and forth between me and the GC

before he says, In that case, let's raise the stakes a little. Winner doesn't just win the match.

A very exciting idea presents itself to me and I tell him, Ya okay, if I win, we trade rackets for one whole week!

Sure. Done. And if I win?

You can have one of my new shuttles?

I check inside Faraz's eyes whether I can get away with just lending it to him. For one week?

No.

Faraz is giving first the Greek Chorus and then me his amused look.

If I win, every day for the next one week we'll write on your forehead in Shipwreck's lipstick: 'Faraz is the best'.

This makes the entire Greek Chorus laugh, which is the sound squirrels would make if you tied their tails in a double knot.

I wish the new girl were here to witness this! Shipra points her finger up at the Bhabra's flat and adds loudly, When is she finally going to make her appearance?

I allot maximum annoyance to the thought that soon the Greek Chorus will have one more member. I glance up to D II/10 and nota bene that the curtains in the window are shaking, which usually means there was someone there a moment ago.

Done! I shout to Faraz, who makes the thumbs-up sign and announces to the Greek Chorus, Ladies and Gentlemen, welcome to the highlight of the day!

I roll my eyes at Faraz.

Coin toss for the serve?

He nods and pulls out the rupee he always keeps in his pocket for this purpose.

Heads! I shout, before he can demand them for himself. The coin spins through the air and tumbles into Faraz's palm, who slaps it onto the back of his hand.

Heads, he says and throws me the coin, which I manage to catch only because I let go of my racket.

Keep it. For good luck. Because you'll need it.

I pick up my racket. The sweat between my nose and lips is coming alive and I wipe my mouth on the sleeve of my t-shirt.

No, I don't! I shout back. Because I have expertise!

And a forehead waiting to be inscribed.

I throw the coin at Faraz. It hits the ground and bounces towards him. He stops it with his foot and returns it to his pocket, grinning and a little startled.

And like a flame exploding at the end of a matchstick I am fully Geeta again.

Love-all. Play! I shout and glance up at the Bhabras' window again. Maybe I just made their heads turn with my voice.

I open my fingers and hit the shuttlecock hard.

Vicky Bhabra steps out of the bathroom, the smell of whitewash in his nose and a moist towel in his fist, ready to be lassoed around his waist should anyone surprise him. And surprised he is. Not by Anjana or Sitara, or the new maid whose name he will definitely not memorise for another two weeks, referring to her instead by the name of their old maid like a generic brand, the Xerox and Tipp-Ex of servanthood. No, what catches him unawares is hearing the three most important words in a man's life—Love! All! Play!—followed by the rhythm of catgut hitting cork. Of course he had been dreading exactly this: the wonky, out of tune play of talentless children with cheap rackets that would add insult to his long-standing injury.

Because if Vicky had known that their new flat was directly above the colony's badminton court, he would have bribed someone to allot them another one. He would have gone himself to the officer in charge instead of sending his PA, would have slipped the package under the table into the man's lap, making sure its bulk landed squarely on his uppermost thigh, a touch he had added to his routine once Vicky realised that he had learned to tell the rough amount inside brown paper envelopes from the weight placed along the axis of his own groin.

But he had been innocent of the flat's exact location in Kaka Nagar when he had signed the papers and hired the packers and boarded the train to the city of his birth. It all went back to Vicky's immediate superior at his previous posting in Chandigarh, a lanky Pune cadre officer named Atre and the only man in the entire department not to wear a vest under his shirt for a pathological lack of sweat, a condition Vicky put down to him being either a god or a devil—the latter proving to be true when the officer revoked their erstwhile friendship after they watched the orange hordes streaming towards the Babri Masjid on the evening news and Vicky joked that you knew the country was going to the dogs when the carrots themselves turned out to be the sticks, which resulted in a heated argument culminating in Atre storming out of his own house. Vicky had already told Atre his whole story, unfiltered and bitter, and so, while most officers would have cut off their wife's pinky for a transfer to the capital, Atre correctly identified Delhi as Vicky's punishment posting, for funds that Atre as a matter of honour personally misallocated for this very purpose.

Atre had done his utmost from Chandigarh to house them in one of the crammed smaller colonies by claiming that all the flats matching Vicky's rank were currently occupied, but Vicky got Kaka Nagar anyway. All it took was one very thick brown paper envelope. Yet when Vicky stepped into this flat for the first time, he quickly discovered that not only is it located above the badminton court, the master bedroom overlooks it. Vicky realised his mistake: the brown paper envelope had been so thick that the housing officer thought this was exactly what Vicky and especially the missus desired: the flat directly above the Club House, the latter being the natural harbour of any government colony, from where its gossip travelled to and from the entire area.

So here they are, shifting into D-II/10. Earlier that day, he dispatched the truck driver, who was moving their things, to Lajpat Nagar Market to procure a single bed and mattress for him, which he set up in the narrow hallway connecting the kitchen with the living room at the other end of the flat, forcing the maid to crab walk past his refuge with the tray bearing tea. But this was much better than waking up to the taunts of a shuttlecock fallen into the wrong hands.

This is how badminton fills Vicky's ears against his will when he steps out from his evening bath into the landscape of moving boxes and suitcases in the master bedroom. But, contrary to his expectations, the rhythm he hears is pure, snuffing out the tangled web of office, family and personal drama occupying his head in one clean stroke, followed by another and another and another. As he enters deeper into the rhythm he is visualising, he notices that it is every alternate shot that reveals the more unique intuition, one of the two players obviously the more gifted. The shots are punctuated with a boy's exclamations.

The grip of Vicky's fist on the new Bombay Dyeing towel softens slightly as he stands still listening, eavesdropping on his player's initial impatience, which costs him a few points, steadying his pace only towards the end of the first half. The second half is a euphony of long, complicated rallies reflected in a score that climbs slowly and not in clear favour of any one player. A cheaper, thinner towel would have dried by now, but this one is still heavy with moisture when Vicky flings it onto Anjana's bubble-wrapped bed and the score stands at 14-all. He pulls underclothes, t-shirt and sweatpants from his suitcase and, in his hurry to get dressed, leaves it not just unlocked but wide open, and the maid (whose name is Leela) to wonder a little while later whether the Sahablog will notice if she borrows one of Vicky's imported pairs of multi-coloured socks for her lover to wear on their next rendezvous.

Vicky bursts into Sitara's room, ignoring her self-drawn PLEASE KNOCK BEFORE ENTERING sign that already hangs laminated from a pale blue suction cup hook meant for damp bathroom towels. Anjana is still at work, of course. They've been in this city for barely a week, staying at a guesthouse until today, and even on the day of their move his wife prefers her new job to setting up a home for her family.

Come with me, he orders. We're going downstairs. You should meet other children, make some friends. Oh, and bring your racket.

He hopes to catch Sitara off-guard with his sudden entry and casual tone, but he is many years too late for that. She gives him the look he has come to abhor: a calm, unblinking stare. He would prefer rolling eyes or an upturned nose or any other age-appropriate response to this particular form of arrogance, which makes him feel for a brief moment as if he, and not his teenage daughter, is the impulsive and unreasonable one.

Firstly, you didn't knock, she notes and returns to what Vicky has come to see as the chief weapons of her passive resistance: colour pens and paper. Secondly, those children downstairs seem pretty daft. And, thirdly, I'm definitely not interested in playing badminton with you.

Vicky, of course, expects this response. The last time Sitara played a match against him was almost two years ago, on April Fool's Day 1991, when she told him that she used to enjoy badminton until he, as she put it, took all the magic out of the game with his drills and workouts and tournaments. He knew right away that she wasn't joking, never mind the date. It still makes him angry—the fact that his own daughter, who has—had—the potential to be a great champion, could not see that he had only just begun to put the magic in and that she herself was the disenchantress with her eternal sullenness and yes, he is willing to say it out loud as her father, *difficult* personality.

But right now he is anxious that the game will be over by the time they make it downstairs, and that his badminton wizard will have slipped through his fingers and gone home. He knows from his daughter's failed championhood that his zeal can be overwhelming to a young person, needs Sitara there for him to look fatherly and inconspicuous, so that he can observe the boy's play without frightening him away, to judge his level more precisely and identify his gravest faults. He will not make the same mistake again. Sitara will compensate for her inadequacy by being his alibi.

Good thing he didn't have their flat changed to another. Maybe Atre was some minor god after all.

If you come with me now, right now, with your racket, I'll buy you the most expensive set of colour pens on the market. Imported. From a fancy shop in South Ex.

Sitara looks up and blinks once, slowly. You can't bribe me.

Vicky wants to smile. So there is still a little remnant of innocence left inside her. He has heard these words before and knows from experience that they are never true. Sometimes it's just harder to find the right price. And sometimes the Reluctant Bribee just doesn't want to hear the words I'll buy you_______________when s/he accepts his/her inducement.

All right, he says, drumming the tips of his fingers against each other. Come with me now, with your racket, and you can do the photography course. And you can have your own camera, too.

He knows that the camera is unnecessary. He'd overheard Sitara beg her mother to be allowed to do the forbiddingly expensive course offered by some American nature photographer, but he can't hear the catgut anymore, and is not sure whether they have stopped playing or whether he is just too far from the window. What if the kid doesn't live in Kaka Nagar but is just visiting a school friend, never to be seen on this court again? He checks his impulse to say out aloud, You squandered your chance at being a great badminton player, now at least don't stand in someone else's way.

Sitara has not even acknowledged his offer by looking up. Of course, how ridiculous of him to think that his daughter would suddenly want to spend any time with him, or do him even the smallest favour! He counts to three in his head, then turns to walk out of the room.

Wait!

He does. Behind him, he hears wooden chair legs scraping against the cement floor and then Sitara's voice again.

I'll come. But I won't play against you.

Should he be proud or ashamed that his daughter is a textbook Reluctant Bribee, down to the final face-saver?

Fine, he says. But hurry up. Offer expires if we're not on court in thirty seconds.

Hi, hello! Can we join your game?

Vicky is so relieved to see that the boy is one of the three children clustered centre court, he doesn't mind that they are ignoring him.

The tall girl is waving a lipstick in the short girl's face, they are both arguing until Vicky's boy raises his voice above theirs and says, We'll spare her this time. I just wanted to teach her a lesson about hubris!

Vicky repeats his greeting and the children finally turn. The boy is more handsome than Vicky imagined but he wears specs, which he'll have to replace with contact lenses. Still, he feels the pinch of disappointment: at 16 or 17 the boy can learn to suppress but is too old to truly overcome his faults to make it to an international level by the time he peaks in his early twenties, though there is definite potential for state or possibly even national championhood with the degree of refinement that Vicky just overheard. But the sense of unmet expectation lingers, and he nods unnecessarily sternly at the taller girl as she puts away the lipstick. These girls are too young for make-up anyway.

I'm Vicky Uncle. This is my daughter Sitara. We just moved into number 10.

Vicky points up at their flat with one index finger and prods Sitara in the back with the other to nudge her onto the court.

Hi, Sitara. Welcome, Uncle. I'm Faraz. I'm in 22. And that's Geeta. She's your immediate neighbour.

Vicky engraves the boy's name and address into an imaginary trophy that he exhibits prominently in his brain's curiosity cabinet. He notes that Faraz's opponent, a solid player if somewhat unserious judging from the audio performance, is a little girl with a racket so worn that playing with it should be listed as child abuse.

Sitara watched your game from upstairs, Faraz, and she's dying to play with you.

No, I didn't! I'm not!

Vicky notes that the tall girl with the lipstick tries to mask the fact that she has a crush on Faraz by laughing at Sitara. He sends another stern look in her direction.

I'd love to, Uncle, but I have to go home now.

Vicky decides that someone as good-looking as Faraz will not be able to resist bundled female attention, so he pins his eyes on the boy as he says, Come on, Sitara darling. I'm sure we can convince Faraz to play one little game with you.

Papa! Sitara hisses at her shoes. He wants to go home!

I really can't, Uncle. My father is waiting for me. But something tells me Geeta here is ready for a fresh start.

Faraz ushers the little girl onto the court, who chirps, Ya, Uncle, I'll play with Sitara!

Contrary to his expectations, Sitara shuffles onto the court like a dinosaur into the doomed future. Then again: the Reluctant Bribee usually wants to earn the bribe rather than just absorb it. Vicky quickly retreats to intercept Faraz, who is getting on a bicycle.

You play here every evening?

Ya, mostly.

Will you be back here tomorrow?

I think so.

Vicky is inclined to return upstairs, but he is unable to resist the hope fermenting at the bottom of his heart that maybe Sitara will change her mind and let him coach her all the way to championhood. Faraz, too, seems to hesitate, and Vicky is aware of both of their gazes turning back to Sitara to observe his daughter's still impeccable serve. The rally unfolds—

And that's when it hits Vicky. His ears cheated him. Not cheated exactly, but they misallocated what his eyes now show him to be the blatant, startling truth. How did it not occur to him to look out the window earlier! So what if they had seen a naked man leaning out in pure astonishment?

It's the girl.

Not Faraz, not Sitara, not himself. As he observes the innate grace that Vicky knows is necessary in any player for them to nurture that screaming precision, the wild determination, the perfect deception, and which only the pros display so openly, a cloud drifts out of the sun's ambit, causing the light to change against her face, which Vicky's somersaulting mind readily associates with a halo.

As his brain reattributes the sounds of the match he overheard upstairs to make her and not Faraz the prodigious player, he notes so many formidable facts he has trouble keeping still, leaving behind Faraz frozen on his bicycle and rushing to the court's sideline: the girl in front of him, whose name didn't even register, who is nothing much to look at with her small eyes, thick eyebrows and thin lips, is younger than he could have hoped for, and she played a superb match with a garbage racket and too-small shoes, which means that with her supply of talent she is going to be what his father never was, what he could not become, what Sitara rejected: simply and inevitably, a star.

With his help, of course.

Vicky can no longer contain his excitement, and short of running to the girl and kissing her forehead can find no other way to channel it than to hurl brash directives at Sitara.

You can't play with a bloody comic book lodged in your buttocks! Vicky shouts as the girl prepares to serve, which makes her giggle and him smile at her.

For the hundredth time, it's not a comic book, it's a MANGA! Sitara shoots back.

The two girls start slapping the shuttlecock back and forth. They are well-matched, Sitara dominating somewhat due to superior equipment and the remnants of their coaching days.

Vicky barely registers that Faraz has come up beside him pushing his bicycle and saying something.

Looks like Miss Mango is doing a fine job giving Geeta another lesson in hubris.

So that's the girl's name. The trophy is instantly re-inscribed: GEETA.

Another burst of exhilaration charges through his veins and he shouts, You're not dancing ballet, Sitara! Legs shoulder-width apart!

Now Geeta is going higher and higher with each shot, boldly trying to drive Sitara to the edge of her court, which would tire her out and clear the way for a deadly smash. They are chasing each other, Geeta managing to restrict the play to her own front court with her high shots.

From the corner of his eye, Vicky notes that Faraz checks his watch and quickly swings himself onto the saddle of his bicycle. Then he's gone.

That very moment the point would have gone to Sitara but she drops her racket and says, Don't feel like playing anymore, striding past Vicky. Keeps walking.

Sitara! Vicky shouts. Come back and finish your match, or the deal's off!

Sitara doesn't come back, and Vicky realises that he doesn't want her to.

Geeta, he says and in his mind his voice resonates into the future, where years from now he will still be saying her name, on foreign courts and into television cameras as her coach and manager.

He picks up Sitara's racket from the floor and offers it to Geeta. Her eyes travel from the handle to the shaft to the stringing before lifting it from his hands like Excalibur. He says nothing, and neither does she. This is all the proof Vicky needs to know that she, too, recognises the sacred importance of this moment.

Later that evening, Vicky sits at the dinner table, food being piled onto his plate by Anjana. She is still wearing her office clothes, which she seems to choose based on only one criterion: hideousness of colour scheme. This one was dried blood with camel hair.

Sitara, he has been told, has already eaten and is finishing homework in her room, a welcome release from having to talk to her about her disappearance from the court earlier. The question instead occupying his mind is how exactly to go about informing Geeta Das Rahman, resident of D II/11 Kaka Nagar, that he would be coaching her starting right now. He wants full commitment, regular hours, the emotional, mental and physical hold that comes with universal coaching rights. Telling her the whole truth—her looming stardom contingent on her complete surrender to him—might excite but also alarm her (anyone would balk at the amount of hard work he will need her to put in); with the same but probably even more severe effect if he spoke directly to the girl's father. But without any revelation it will be difficult to get her to sign up for his project and provide a satisfactory explanation to the father for why a grown man should be so keen to play with another man's young daughter on a daily basis.

Vicky!

Yes?

Are you deaf?

Vicky stops eating, sighs audibly. What is it, Anjana?

Sitara said you humiliated her.

I did no such thing.

Then why would she say it?

Because our daughter has a penchant for melodrama.

You have to start taking her concerns seriously, Vicky, if you ever want her to trust you again.

Although he is determined not to be drawn into an argument with Anjana today of all days—which he is sure he will look back on later in life as The Turning Point—his wife's words burn like acid in his stomach, and he has to take a deep, abdominal breath to stop from saying that if he is honest he blames Anjana and not himself for turning his daughter against him by twisting his love for badminton into an 'unhealthy obsession' and distorting his methods as 'manipulative'. He is not immune to the idea that Anjana is too resentful of him to allow for such a lifelong player–coach bond to form between him and their daughter, though of course she claims to have acted only in Sitara's best interests.

With some delay, Vicky simply shrugs and says, It is what it is.

Anjana reverts to wordless frowning. Yet Vicky now finds the potatoes a little harder to chew, the dal undercooked, the beans too stringy. He was hoping to use dinnertime to mentally script his upcoming recruitment talk with Geeta and her father, but instead he feels a pinch sealing his throat and a stern gaze drilling into the back of his neck.

Vicky's first memory of his father pulling the folds beneath his chin is as a five-year-old, threatening worse if Vicky ever dared to ask him about the All-England ever again. It happened often after that, for being found with badminton gear, for getting caught bunking his tuition to watch a local tournament.

Or when he chose Anjana as his bride. He does not like

it when she reminds him of it during their fights: you only married me to spite your father. He denies it with fervour to make himself forget that the more disgusted Prakash grew with him, the faster Vicky fell for Anjana.

Have some sympathy for her, Vicky. New school, new city. It's hard enough for a teenager these days.

Anjana has lowered her voice as she speaks.

Vicky does not reciprocate.

Children today are coddled and spoilt, that's their problem.

They have other challenges to face.

Whether to buy this or that brand of ice cream?

Now you're just being cynical.

He would show Anjana the meaning of cynical if she thought that's what he was.

Sitara has no passion, no ambition! Everything is just empty resistance. That's why she's such an unhappy child.

Keep your voice down!

In spite of himself, that very first moment containing Vicky's entire love for Anjana comes floating back to him, everything that followed only a proxy of that one instant, like light thrown back from a withdrawing source.

Now blow.

Those were the words Anjana had said to him that day in 1963, carefully placing the live cigarette between his lips hanging slightly ajar. It was Vicky who had asked her to teach him how to smoke. She had come to stay with them in Delhi the summer she turned seventeen. Vicky was eight. She was doing interviews for college, and their parents knew each other from their Lahore days.

Anjana was sprawled on the charpoy on their terrace when Vicky came home from school that day. She didn't notice him at first, and he stood there in the doorframe watching her read Femina as her toe tugged at a loose thread from the stringing. She wasn't beautiful the way he had pictured her but she had something else. English has a word for it: charisma. But Vicky only learned this much later. By then she had been married and divorced and they met again and nurtured these ideas about love against all odds. Prakash was not happy about it—why should his IAS son marry a divorcee almost a decade his senior? As revenge for making me that, Vicky told him, which Anjana overheard but didn't tell him then.

Disgusting, was all his father said in response, missing the wedding and speaking to his son again only once Sitara was born a year later.

Vicky now rarely conjures the image of her long, heavy lips, drooping slightly under the excess weight, the upper lip protruding and covering the lower. The moment Anjana spotted eight-year-old Vicky standing there in the door, she smiled and her mouth transformed into a hammock that carried her entire face. It still does sometimes when she is relaxed, which almost never happens these days, at least not when Vicky is around.

Mashing a piece of potato between his fingers, Vicky decides that if he could, he would go back and make it so that they had only met that one time on the terrace.

At least I'm encouraging Sitara to develop some kind of interest. Did she tell you that I'm signing her up for that expensive photography course?

Yes.

Vicky waits a moment, then flings the potato pulp onto his plate. The role he is supposed to be merely representing is now alive inside him. That's it? Yes? No Thank you, Vicky? How thoughtful of you, Vicky? How generous?

Well, did you ask for something in return?

Don't talk to me like a schoolteacher, Anjana. And don't ask questions to which you already know the answer.

Then don't lie about your motivations!

How would you know about my motivations? You're never around, and when you are, you stand between my daughter and I!

That's outrageous!

The words now flow through Vicky's lips like lubricant. They have said versions of them to each other for years now.

When their voices are exhausted and Anjana stands, slamming the door behind her as she exits the room, a sense of serenity spreads through the flat, like ashes dancing in the wind after a fire. Vicky leans back in his chair. For all her show of detachment, Anjana still needs him, she needs him to feel she is a good mother, a caring wife, the better human being. If only by contrast. Vicky is comforted by the fact that the next step will be reconciliation before they will let themselves grow apart again and then, like mangoes in summer, there will be another magnificent fight.

Morning has begun to encroach when Vicky finds himself on the terrace of their building, sleep shed like a cumbersome cloak. He is barefoot and dressed in his pajamas and robe, gazing across into the garden of D II / 11. Vicky sighs with the conviction that if the world were to function according to his rules alone, it would be a simpler, happier, more efficient place. He watches a vision of himself scuttling down the stairs, ringing the bell, getting Geeta out of bed to the court and putting a racket in her hand. They would start playing—their first session with him as her coach—and there would be no turning back. He wants to move the world, not talk about it. Words are what make life complicated, irrational.

And it was in response to his father's words—that never-ending string of abuses, reprimands and laments—that Vicky gave in and sat for the IAS exam, taking up this hateful job that he turned out to be so successful at and that he could bear only because he decided to treat it like a game with rules he made up himself.

Vicky stands on the terrace, chilly February breeze making the hairs growing out of his nostrils twitch like the legs of a cockroach.

It has been eight years since his father died, but Vicky still blames him for not having fostered his younger self's talents on the court. He could have been someone in badminton, someone big, but his father's strict embargo on the sport, for which Vicky incurred numerous throat pinchings throughout his childhood and teenage years, is, according to Vicky, what ultimately kept him from making the leap from keen amateur to early professional. And all because Prakash made it to the finals at the so-called world championship, the

All-England Open Badminton Championships, in 1947—and then lost.

Vicky understands the corrosive shame of losing, but can muster no sympathy for a man who couldn't pull himself up after sampling its caustic taste. This was his Lesson # 1: A player has to be able to face his own loss in order to win again. And as Vicky grew into his twenties, his sweeping resentment of Prakash became distilled into scorn for this babyish man who gave up on himself because he lost a game, boo hoo hoo, and then tried to salvage his self-respect by destroying his son's chances at a more successful career in the same field.

His Lesson # 2: A father's support is essential for a champion. If Vicky never made it to the state championships for this lack, he would do everything in his power to make sure that Sitara did. Now for the first time he recognises that there is an important sub-clause to Lesson # 2: Father and champion need not be biologically related. In fact, it is better if they are not.

Leaning on the edge of the terrace, Vicky clutches the unlabelled plastic folder that he hides deep inside a drawer of his desk along with the fact he would have no qualms about emptying the family's bank account to see each of its transparent sleeves stuffed.

Instead, only the first three sleeves contain any paper, black-and-white photocopies enlarged to fill the A4 format. The first is a newspaper clipping entitled 'A Hearty Welcome to our Players from Lahore.' There is a single image of a man in whites leaping into the air. The caption below reads: 'Prakash Bhabra's deadly signature shot.'

As Vicky opens the folder and his eyes scan the words he knows by heart, he feels his father's gaze alive on his skin.

So you really think you would have done better than me?

Vicky closes his eyes, blows air out of his nose.

Yes, Papa, I would have, but you never gave me the chance to prove it.

Vicky is now standing in their living room in the flat in Lajpat Nagar where he grew up, his father seated before him on the beige velvet sofa set.

Chances in life are not gifts from heaven, Vicky. They have to be earned and deserved. You snuck around all these years wanting to be a badminton star like Papa, but you never even had the guts to tell me that this is what you really wanted from life.

There's no point arguing with you.

You took the job I told you to take but you make a mockery of it every day with your bribery and favouritism. And you tell yourself that unlike your babyish father, this is mature behaviour.

I have nothing more to say to you.

Don't pretend like you don't care. You do, or you wouldn't have gone all the way to the British Library in London to get this one meagre clipping.

I'm interested in badminton history.

You think history is about collecting facts? You know nothing of what really happened at the world championships. The blood and the sweat. You know nothing about what it felt like.

I know more than you think.

You've read some details that are dead and meaningless:

Prakash Bhabra and Devender Mohan from Lahore were invited to London to compete at the All England in 1947.

You were the first non-whites to be invited! And it was March '47, just before Partition. You can deny it, Papa, but I know it must have felt like you were competing against the whole world, even though until then, as far as badminton was concerned, the 'world' consisted of Denmark, Sweden, Scotland, England and Ireland. You must have felt immensely proud. And intimidated.

Even a child can deduce that much.

Vicky turns the page with force. Another enlarged copy shows a clipping of match results, with one highlighted in fluorescent marker.

All you have is fragments: Prakash Bhabra lost the finals with a score of 15–7, 15–11.

Vicky flips back to the first page with the image of his father set amidst the only longer article he has on the tournament.

Yes, I only have fragments because you withheld everything from me! You never told me you were a two-time national champion by the time this picture was taken! You never told me that your very first match at the All England was against the defending world champion, Tage Madsen from Denmark. And though the last All England had happened in 1939 and Madsen's title was eight years old, he was still the undefeated national champion of Denmark for five consecutive years until 1946, and rumour had it that the Danish were the best players in the world back then. Not as worn out by the war as the English. You had to have known all that and yet it never occurred to you that maybe I'd like to know! You must have known that the odds were against you—

Just because I never participated in a world championship before doesn't mean I wasn't world champion material. I won that match and the next round, too.

I know, Papa! Not because you told me, but because I read it in the papers decades later! I read all about the first round and the second round and even about the draw for the quarterfinals.

Sabotage. The Brits wanted to cut our chances in half.

Vicky pulls the photocopied sheet out of its sleeve to inhale its paper smell and read from the article: The draw had decided that Prakash Bhabra would have to play against his own countryman, Devender Mohan, in the quarterfinals. The two Indians complained but to no avail, as the Badminton Association of England clarified that players compete as individuals in the All England, not as countries.

That tells you nothing, Vicky.

I know it can't have been an easy decision not to play the match.

It was a full house that day. Twenty-five thousand people watching. Can you imagine what it sounds like, twenty five thousand mouths booing you down?

Well, you should have played. Then you would have heard fifty-thousand hands clapping for you.

The coin toss was our only reasonable option.

You felt slighted by the draw. And it was smart, too: that way you didn't wear the winner out for the next round. It says here that they banned the use of the heating system for the tournament because of an acute coal shortage in England that spring.

Prakash laughed from his throat, a deep, vibrating sound that always reminded Vicky of a lawnmower cutting down grass. Don't fool yourself, Vicky. All you have are insignificant details: next you're going to tell me you researched it and that winter was the coldest and longest in a century.

It was. Heaps of snow.

Go back to your files, Vicky, you will never know what that means.

Then tell me, what was it like to play with snow trickling down on you?

You're the one with the facts, aren't you? With the designated folder, even though most of it is empty.

As if to disperse his father's words, Vicky turns the page the way he imagines he would for Geeta in the near future—deliberately, between thumb and forefinger.

Fine, don't tell me. There's nothing you can tell me that I don't already know. Maybe there had been a blizzard the night before the tournament was to begin, and it drove snow through the ventilators and into the arena.

He imagines Geeta's wonder as her eyes fall for the first time on the black-and-white photocopied image of a gigantic hall with a huge cube hanging from the ceiling above multiple badminton courts. Each side of the cube has the face of an electric clock.

Harringay Arena. That's where the tournament took place. Amazing story behind it. Yes, Papa, I researched that, too. You can laugh at me for it, but at least I know all about Sir Alfred Critchley and his passion to bring sports to the masses. There would have been no twenty-five thousand people to applaud you without him. I bet you didn't notice, but there is something striking about the architecture of the arena.

Illuminate me.

No internal columns to support the roof! The audience has an unimpeded view of all the courts. Even today we rarely build stadiums like that in India. And I'll tell you something else: Your refusal to share anything with me just makes me think that maybe you have nothing to say. You're delusional.

You're talking to a dead man, but I am delusional.

I know more than you think, Papa. Because there really was a blizzard the night before, and the tournament almost could not start the next day, because by the morning, the lower layers of snow had frozen due to their proximity to the ice hockey rink on which the wooden badminton courts—seven of them—had been laid and specially sanded for the tournament. Even the application of hot water—which just added another frozen layer within seconds—could not restore the floor. Two courts could finally be cleared with the help of resin but the players kept slipping and getting injured, so the tournament was called off until the following day. That meant more matches per day, and you were not used to playing in such cold. That's why you went for the coin toss! Which you won! And then you faced the Swede Conny Jepsen in the finals. On March 9, 1947. That's when you lost! You lost, Papa! I have the score right here, black on white: 15–7, 15–11. No third game! You lost badly, Papa! You failed yourself and your country and you decided to punish me for your failure!

My son, the orator.

Laugh at me all you want, but stop pretending like there's more to it than that! Plain, unremarkable failure.

So if it had been you, Vicky?

I would have won! And if I had lost, I would have come back the next year and every year until I had that damn title to my name. Vicky Bhabra, world champion!

Is that so?

Yes. I would not have given up so easily.

But you did, didn't you? You gave up, all because Papa did not encourage you. So now you've found your next offering to the badminton altar, all to compensate for your own failings. First Sitara, and now little Geeta Rahman.

I'm not listening to you! Vicky hisses the words out aloud and shuts the folder with an angry slap as if to contain his father's voice within.

In his mind he tears up the conversation with Geeta that he has been scripting at the back of his mind: he is not going to tell her about Prakash. Let his father's memory die! If Prakash never wanted to be a true champion, then so be it. His father always tried to keep him down, the only thing he fostered was Vicky's inner coward. But he was done thinking in small terms. Geeta would prove him right. He would shape her into something that he could never have imagined even for himself. His father had his turn to be a teacher, and he flopped. Now it was Vicky's turn, and he would not squander it.

No, he would not waste another minute.

Naniji is peeling the plastic skin from a Cadbury éclair and popping it in her mouth when I join her in the kitchen. She returns to cutting an onion before she notices me. Abba has gone for his evening walk.

Naniji does not like to share her éclairs with anyone. Abba says Naniji is addicted, which means being enthusiastically devoted to a particular thing, and because I understand how that feels, I have never asked Naniji for an éclair again and have only taken one in secret a few times.

You do the garlic, Naniji says with éclair juice spraying from her lips onto the pile of onions.

Naniji has been living with us for as long as I can remember, though I know that it happened only after Nanaji died, when I was two. Mummy was an only child, like me, and sometimes Naniji tells me stories about her from when she was my age. From her I know that Mummy liked the following things: helping her mother in the kitchen, being kind to elders, going to bed on time and rising early, tying her shoelaces properly and keeping her school uniform clean. She also liked watering the plants, which happens to be one of my favourite things, too.

Abba says Naniji never understood her daughter, but, what to do, it was a different generation and she did not know how to live alone after Nanaji's expiration, so they had to take her in.

I lost against Faraz today, Naniji.

How many times are you going to tell me that, beta?

Winning is vulgar!

A grinning Abba has appeared in the door with a bulging cloth bag, which means he stopped at the Safal shop on his evening walk.

But I'm the better player if you consider that he's much older!

Sports is for boys, Geeta, don't become one. Your calves should remain soft like a ripe tomato.

Naniji is holding a ball-shaped red calf up to prove her point.

How could I, Naniji! See how long my ponytail has become? I turn my back to her and shake my head.

Remind me to put oil in it after dinner.

Abba empties the bag into the sink and mutters in English: You don't want to become old-fashioned like her either.

I'm new-fashioned, Abba.

Yes. And very silly. To Naniji he says, Hai, how hungry I am, Mummyji! Feed me something, won't you?

Naniji slices a cheek off the baingan he has handed her.

A worm, Abba, look!

Oh, no.

Naniji slices the other cheek. More worms.

I'll make potato, Naniji states.

Again potato?

Hé bhag.

No problem. Potato.

Abba turns to go, then stops and comes back.

Before I forget. I met Mrs Bhabra, you know, the new family from number 10, at the shop, and we're going over there for chai next week, as soon they're settled in. I want you to make friends with the daughter.

Why, Abba?

I picture Sitara's unfriendly face from earlier, leaning on a racket—not just any racket but the red and silver Yonex ISOMETRIC from Vijay's glass cabinet—and wearing pink shoes with the glow of foreign about them. I thought it would be quite satisfactory to defeat the new girl in front of the Greek Chorus, especially since they just witnessed me lose. But Sitara's shots came not from Sitara but from a badminton machine inside her. This was the opposite of badminton. It was greatminton. Even Faraz couldn't keep up with it.

No reason. Just be on your best behaviour.

I decide not to tell Abba that I have already met Vicky and that he is a Friendly Uncle, because then I will have to tell him about the racket he gifted me and Abba will think that I like it better than his book presents.

When Abba is gone, Naniji scrapes her lower lip with a loud smack and says, Doing one's best is still never good enough with him.

I finish peeling the garlic and grate the piece of ginger Naniji hands me.

Ouch!

Now there will be a piece of Geeta in our dinner. I suck my finger and wait for Naniji's temporary withdrawal of approval, which doesn't materialise.

Geeta!

I pull out my finger with a pop and follow Abba's voice. He is standing in the front room, holding my new racket.

What's this?

Oh, that, I say, still tasting blood.

I hid it behind the shoe cabinet and did not foresee that he would spot its handle poking out just a little bit from behind it.

Isn't that the racket from the shop? What's it doing here?

I met Mr Bhabra and his daughter on the court, and she had the same racket and after the match they gave it to me.

They gave it to you? Just like that?

Yes.

You must have asked them for it.

No, Abba, really, I didn't. Swear!

I pull on the skin of my throat, which makes me cough.

And you didn't just steal it from them either?

NO, Abba!

Then why did you hide it?

Because! Because?

YES?!

The dictionary has all the words. I don't.

This is really shameful behaviour, Geeta. Especially after I just told you that we're going there on Sunday, you didn't think you should mention to me that we're already under their obligation? You go up there right now, say sorry and return the racket.

But, Abba—

No but! Go now before I bloody lose it!

A moment later I am again standing at the edge of the staircase, which is pitch dark now. I take another step. Who could say what foul creatures live here, ready to grab someone's ankles and drag her into the bushes to Humayun's ghost? I count to twenty. Just because the parent cadre didn't believe me doesn't negatively impact the fact that Vicky really did gift it to me.

Thirty.

So wasn't it unfair to return the racket before playing even a single match with it?

Forty.

Although he didn't say so, Abba clearly has an agenda for Monday or he would not be so angry about the racket.

Fifty.

I drag myself up the stairs. Half-way I start hearing the voices that are attacking each other like the gods and demons on Naniji's television shows. Words are flying past my ears so fast I can barely catch them: LIAR BRATTY FORGOTTEN NOBODY LISTENS RESPECT DREAMS DIED NO PERMISSION SLOGGING DAY AND NIGHT GET OUT! And then a door bangs shut.

I race back down, afraid that Vicky might come out of the flat and find me eavesdropping.

Nobody opened, Abba!

He leans out of the door to glance up at the Bhabra's flat but I know he can't see it very well from there because of the creeper growing all around our door.

Promise me that you will return it before we go there. And that you'll apologise for taking it.

Promise, Abba.

After dinner I start reading *My Experiments with Truth.* Abba says Gandhiji is the most tragic of the Indian freedom fighters, because we all take his name but have forgotten his lessons, and that the country cannot rise until she relearns them, especially not in these Troubled Times, by which he means the collapse of the secular Indian soul. Abba says a man can no longer choose to live a principled life nowadays, because there is too much hypocrisy, corruption and false ideology. Much will have to change, he says, because Troubled Times call for severe measures, and nobody is willing to go that extra mile. The Troubled Times began almost two years ago, when Abba woke me up, because he had had that dream again about how I was kidnapped, and then it turned out that Rajiv Gandhi had been assassinated that night. Mummy, who was home from the hospital, told him not to be sad, that her and Rajiv Gandhi's soul would mingle soon, but that just made him even more sad. He said many innocent people also died and that we mustn't forget the poor Tamils who were being killed and tortured in Sri Lanka because of dishonest politics, but that blowing up the Prime Minister would only destabilise everything further.

Eventually, all three of us fell asleep in one bed, like matchsticks in a box.

I circle Gandhiji's words I don't know in pencil and then look them up, like Abba taught me, in the Concise Oxford English Dictionary, which I got for my last birthday. The first word I looked up in it was 'concise'. It means being small and clever.

Abba? I say to the parent cadre huddled over his own book at his desk. There is no response, so I count till five and then I say, So after I've turned the key in the ignition, which pedal do I push down first? Left or right?

I count till three. Abba-a-a?

Mmh?

Please refer to above-mentioned query.

What?

Finally, Abba is looking up at me. Please advise, na.

Speak plainly, Geeta.

I wrap my lips around each word to avoid any misconstruction, After I've turned the key, which pedal do I push down first?

Abba blinks at me multiply. I observe his eyes slowly letting go of his reading and focusing on my question. But all he says is: Geeta.

I ignore his interjection and guide him through the ongoing inquiry. Which pedal, Abba?

Abba sighs and turns towards me in full, which is a sign that he is now willing to cooperate.

It's called the clutch, but I'm not teaching you how to drive, Geeta. And promise me that you will not try until then.

He slips his fingers under his reading glasses and rubs his eyes.

Clearly, it was a mistake to tell you my secret.

I won't try, Abba, I promise. But can't you at least tell me how you drive now so that I am fully ready when I turn 18?

You still have plenty of time for that. For now all you need to know about driving is that it's dangerous. Do we have an understanding?

I nod. Although Abba has not granted me permission to become an expert in locomotion and although nobody else can teach me how to drive in Abba's exact way so that I can talk to Mummy, he has said nothing about learning through expert observations. In the meantime, I spell C-L-U-T-C-H into the palm of my hand with my dictionary finger.

Although from now on I will be diligently watching Abba drive in great detail and although I can pretend that the driver's seat is Mummy's lap and we are steering the whole world in the right direction together, I know that she is not coming back home, no matter how many kilometres I will drive one day. Because: Geeta lost her mother when she was ten. That's what Abba says when people who don't know us ask about our family, though it's not quite true, because I didn't lose Mummy. I didn't misplace her like Papa does his keys all the time. It's also not true that I lost her when I was ten, because then how come I still keep finding her everywhere?

It has been six days since I received the Yonex from Vicky and strict orders from Abba to return it, which I did but also not.

A rebel through and through is a person who is disobedient to some higher authority, and so maybe a bit of yoobriss is imperative, even though Faraz cooked up such a complicated plan to teach me a lesson about it. When Shipwreck pulled the cap off the lipstick's mouth with a click and screwed its blood-red tongue into view, waving it around under my nose and licking her lips while saying, So I'll do the honours?, I decided that Geeta would never use lipstick, because lipstick is for girls who are secretly aunties with no life plan. The other decision I made was that the moment the lipstick would touch my skin, I would be attacked by a severe headache like Abba has sometimes, and collapse to the floor. Then Faraz and the Greek Chorus would have to explain to Abba and all the other parents in Kaka Nagar what fraudulent practice they were about to perform on me. But that's when we all turned because behind us there was Vicky's voice.

So right now, Abba still thinks I'm playing at being a champion. That it's an excuse for not doing my homework. To prove him wrong it is of utmost importance to win against him, and I'm going to do it playing his own game. Therefore, before I go to the court with my racket, I will practice the flick of my wrist on my dutiful pencil. From the pocket in my jeans I pull out a folded paper, which I have been carrying with me for a few weeks now, reading it when I do my morning business or on the school bus:

3.6. Nota bene: It is to be brought to the notice of the Ministry of Personnel, Public Grievances & Pensions that in case of appointment on deputation/foreign service/transfer from Central Govt. to Public Sector Undertaking and in those cases where the pay scale and DA in the parent cadre post and ex-cadre post are dissimilar, no appointment on deputation/

foreign service/transfer shall be made if by raising the grade pay by one increment plus dearness allowance(s) including interim relief, if any, permissible to a person in parent cadre post-exceeds the emoluments in toto comprising pay plus dearness allowance(s) including interim relief, if any at the maximum of the ex-cadre post.

I have memorised all the words I circled last time and this time there are no more words to circle, because I am understanding it all perfectly.

Today is Sunday and Abba—and all the other parent cadres in Kaka Nagar—have the day off from their Ministries, so maybe one little feeling shall be permissible after all: interim relief.

Whenever it's Sunday and morning it is Abba's routine to take out his tape recorder from the almirah, drop in a cassette and lie in bed listening to Mohammed Rafi's voice until lunchtime. I think the music is Abba's driver's seat to Mummy, because it always puts him in that mood where he doesn't seem to give two hoots about whether I am circling words in pencil and looking them up or not. In fact, he seems not to notice me at all.

So I, too, have my Sunday morning routine. I ride the middle branch of the champa tree in our garden, which grew specially so that it is easy for me to climb it. In the jamun tree at the corner a bird is calling. It sounds like my heart beating: Ca-doo! Ca-doo! Ca-doo! There are almost no cars on the main road and the colony, too, feels empty. Winter is almost over, and very soon the crisscross of sunlight on my naked arms will begin to burn. But up here I can forget that the parent cadre has forgotten me and can almost escape his sad songs, even though I can still hear the tune through the open window of Abba's bedroom: Yeh mera prem patra padh kar, ke tum naraz na hona...

Interrupting Abba's music is a different melody coming from farther off. Saleem Uncle is practicing his harmonium, which in turn is his Sunday morning routine. I can hear the spin and swirl of the notes that sound like a kite dancing in the wind.

I lean into the branch of the champa and rest my right cheek against the soft bark—part 2 of my routine. Soon a tiny lake forms between my and the tree's skin. It is a strange state of affairs that sometimes, when you are feeling sad, hearing a hint of something happy only makes you more abundantly sad. My left eye cries freely onto my dangling knee. I wipe my cheek and then a streak of dust from the long leaf that's tickling my hand. Its light-green, thick veins make it look like the skeleton of a fish. On the ground around the stem there are crumpled brown versions of it that will crunch under my soles when I jump down from my branch. Does each leaf feel completely alone up here, even though together they make such a beautiful tree? And when one leaf falls to the ground, do the other leaves feel sad or is the tree secretly happy that she has space for new leaves?

I look across our garden, beyond our gate and at the Club House on the other side. Why can't the world be made not of thousands of feelings but only of feathers and strings? And what is the word for something that is always there but still cannot ever be found again?

All this is why I need to be good at badminton. The best,

in fact. Because on court I can be a real champion. And how does the dictionary define champion? Someone who never loses anything.

Later that afternoon, a shooting star crashes at my feet.

Ooout! Game Geeta!

I perform my victory dance—balle balle balle balle balle—before scooping up the shuttle and trading sides with Faraz. I am playing barefoot to avoid squeezage from too-small shoes and combined with the racket this is proving to be My Day.

Good one, Smalls. But next game you're getting crushed. Even your fancy new racket won't save you.

Just admit that I'm better than you.

You'll be begging me for mercy in a few minutes.

I think I've never won a game against Faraz by such a clear margin: 15–10!

I give him a high serve. We're rallying back and forth when from the corner of my eye I notice something moving on the roof of the building, which is the terrace of number 10. I lose the serve to Faraz but when I look up nobody's there.

It's four-all when Faraz's wristwatch begins to beep.

Shit, yaar!

It's not even five o'clock yet! And it's Sunday, so your father's home anyway!

We're going for a wedding in Faridabad, and I still have to get ready.

Can't we just finish the game, Faraz? Pleeease!

No, ya, Smalls. I have to go. We'll finish it tomorrow.

Just one more point, okay? Winner wins all.

You're still going for that after last time?

Come on, Faraz, please, just one little point!

Someone should inform him that I'll have to return my magic racket when we go for chai at the Bhabras tomorrow evening, or I will be turned into pumpkin pulp.

I'll play you for that point.

We turn and there is Sitara, wearing the pleated white miniskirt of her school uniform, even though it's Sunday, paired with a matching t-shirt cut off at the waist, which does make her look like a full pro. She's carrying a different racket this time, and I'm afraid she will see mine, which is actually hers, and demand it back, but currently her eyes are pinned on Faraz.

Miss Mango! You're back.

Because if anyone gets to squeeze one more point out of Faraz it should be me, I say, Unfortunately, Faraz has to go now.

Sitara says to Faraz, Because you're scared to lose to a girl?

That's when I see something I have never seen before: A Faraz who does not know what to say back. He is just looking at Sitara, then he blinks and says, Sure, okay, why not? I'll play you for a point.

But you're going to be late!

Faraz grins at me.

I think this is going to be quick and ruthless, Smalls.

I want to tell Faraz that I, too, am quick and ruthless but

then I realise that I am the only witness to what is going to be a very juicy state of affairs.

So instead I say, And if you win?

If I win, Miss Mango has to play a full match against me tomorrow with two comic books crammed into each one of her back pockets.

They're called *mangas*.

You don't say.

This makes me giggle. Sitara is not really smiling but just testing the elastic of her lips

Done. And if I win, every day for the next one week you'll write on your forehead in permanent marker: 'Sitara is the best.' Sitara pulls the pen from her pocket for public display and then puts it back.

Someone has been secretly paying attention, Faraz says.

Sitara just shrugs. I hand over my side of the court to her by moving to the sidelines and picture the moment I tell the Greek Chorus about this. Faraz rang my doorbell early today, because of Faridabad probably, so none of the others are on court yet and they're all going to burst into flames of envy for having missed out.

The coin toss goes in Faraz's favour. I think I see his hand shake when he holds up the shuttlecock, sending it flashing high above the net before Sitara returns it.

It is common knowledge that the shuttlecock is the key ingredient in badminton, but with Sitara's shots it's as if she's trying to make each feather sparkle to boot. The sound her racket makes when she hits it is as crisp as when you bite into the Kashmiri apples that Saleem Uncle sends over to our house on Independence Day. Though I think Sitara bears definite potential to be named a Public Grievance very soon, I can't help but watch her play more closely than Faraz.

They have been going back and forth, back and forth when Faraz swings his racket all the way towards his shoes and returns a very high shot so that Sitara has to run to the edge of her court, and I'm picturing her playing with comic books weighing down her shorts.

Instead, I get to see another thing I have never seen before: Sitara faces her own back boundary line as she returns the shuttle. I think that it will never go where it's supposed to, but not only does it reach Faraz's side of the court, he has to leap from the side he's on to the other in order to lift it high over the net. As Sitara raised herself up on her toes, all the pleats of her skirt are swinging back and the white t-shirt flies up as she smashes the shuttlecock into Faraz's stomach.

Still out of breath, Sitara calls to Faraz.

Quick-and-Ruthless, you should go, you're running late.

I minutely observe Faraz, who is breathing even harder and trying to smile at the same time.

I ask Sitara, What about his punishment?

My story will only be half as compelling if she forgets to do it.

I'm going to spare him today, because I just wanted to teach him a lesson about yoobriss.

I change my mind: from personal experience I know that sparing someone their punishment is far superior to a compelling story. So I issue a full approval to Sitara and say: Winning is vulgar.

In response Sitara somehow grins and frowns at me at

the same time, and Faraz chuckles and opines: Says Geeta Rahman at championship point.

I spell V-U-L-G-A-R into the palm of my hand.

Faraz is re-directing his grin in Sitara's direction now.

Got it. Don't judge a manga by its cover. But instead of getting his bicycle, Faraz jogs over to the net, pulls it down and hangs his neck across like a fully faulty bidder.

What are you doing, Faraz? Your father will be angry!

My punishment.

But she's sparing you!

That's very generous of her. But I insist. Just today.

Sitara looks annoyed but also not. You really want to attend a wedding with writing on your forehead?

Faraz thinks about this for a moment, then rolls up his sleeve all the way to his shoulder and offers her the skin of his arm.

All right, she says. A valiant warrior. She hands him the permanent marker.

Faraz looks up at her. You have to write it.

Don't be silly. You can do it yourself.

No, you write it.

Faraz really is being substantially silly, because good authority has informed me that he is a class topper and very good at spelling but maybe he does not want to risk making a fool of himself again in front of Sitara by getting her name wrong. Sitara is chewing her lip, which forms the tiniest of smiles, then she pops open the pen and starts moving the tip over his skin. A moment later, he turns to me.

What do you think, Smalls?

In big letters it says: SITARA IS THE BEST. I think that another, shorter name would have looked better there.

What if your father sees it?

For the first time since I have known Faraz, his eyes don't shift like a shuttlecock in the wind at the mention of his father.

He's a cop, no. He knows that you must not shirk from due punishment.

Although I am one hundred per cent sure that Faraz will try his utmost best to hide the writing from his father under his festive clothes, instead of disputing his claim I remind him, You owe me one point.

Sorry, Smalls, have to run now. Tomorrow, hn?

Faraz takes his bicycle leaning against the wall of the Club House building and waves to us as he pushes down on the pedal. Sitara is already walking home. I watch them go, then wait for patchwork-Faraz to reappear through the gaps in the Ashoka hedge. I see him slow down as he goes on the narrow section of road along the mud room before disappearing from my view.

I hug my new racket to my chest. If only the parent cadre could have seen me earlier! My deadly smash and the way I tossed the shuttle over the net like Faraz's lucky coin. Then he would definitely allow me to keep the racket.

Again I see something move above me on the terrace. Again nobody. How did Sitara get up there so fast?

I try to play by myself, I hit the shuttle to invisible Faraz, then change sides and return it to invisible Geeta. The longer I do this, the more silent the wind becomes. The sun is low now and the court in the shade—this is badminton optimum.

Hi, Geeta.

Suddenly Vicky is standing behind me with his arms folded over his chest, hands tucked into his armpits. His racket is leaning against his thigh, as if he had selected this specific pose before saying hello.

Shall we finish the game you started with Sitara the other day? The score was 4–2, I believe. Your serve.

Was it really Vicky watching me play from the terrace? At least someone saw it!

Yes, Uncle!

He is leaning forward so I serve to his back corner, he returns in kind, I race backwards and drop the shuttle over the net but he's already there and shoots it into the back court again. He drops it over the net, I do the selfsame and we repeat this until my shot gets caught in the net.

Well played, Geeta. You have excellent deception but you need to work on your precision.

Vicky scores a point with a smash.

Uncle, how do you spell that? D-I-S—

Vicky laughs. You don't need to know how to spell it. All you need to know is that it's your strength.

I pretend to smash but at the last second just drop the shuttle over the net and win the serve back.

See? That was deception. You make your opponent think you're going to play a certain shot but you play an entirely different one instead, so that he or she moves in the wrong direction and can't reach the shuttle in time.

I didn't know different shots have different names, Uncle. I just play whatever feels right in that moment.

Anyone can learn the names, Geeta. It's the technique that counts. I've been watching you play, you know. You have a couple of bad habits but you're very good.

Thanks, Uncle.

I want to ask Vicky what my bad habits are but I'm afraid that he has already spoken to Abba and will say: Not returning rackets that you promised you would.

I swear I don't normally forget to water the plants on a daily basis, only now—

Not those kinds of bad habits, Geeta. I'm talking about the court.

Vicky lowers his racket. You know, when Sitara was your age—how old are you again?

Twelve.

So when Sitara was a couple of years younger than you I started training her professionally. She's like you. A natural. Graceful but relentless. She could be competing internationally by now but she got fed up and threw it all away. Now she won't even play badminton for fun, as you already know. Only to teach people a lesson.

So he was watching!

Why, Uncle?

God knows.

Vicky's serve is unlike anything I've ever seen: it turns the shuttlecock into Ram's arrow that's going straight for my neck. It's very difficult to return.

Her mother says that it's all my fault, that I poisoned the well for her but I think in the end she just didn't have it in her.

You mean badminton?

Vicky is running into the net. Missing the shuttle and breathing hard he says, To be a real champion.

Even before he can catch his breath, he continues

speaking, which sounds funny, like when a cartoon snake talks on the television. It sounds like: Geeta, I want to make you a once-in-a-lifetime—

GEETA!

Naniji's voice booms like that of an angry genie.

The pile of unshelled peas is duly remembered by yours truly. As are the unwatered plants and the unscrubbed brass utensils that Naniji and I clean with soaked imli every Sunday.

Uncle, I'm off, see you, bye-bye!

As I run homewards a minute component of Geeta wonders if this would have been the most pertinent moment to return the racket to Vicky before tomorrow's appointment, but now I am already past our gate guided by Naniji's flaming eyes, and I am sure there will still be ample opportunity to rectify the current arrangement pertaining to restoration of said racket.

The door opens and there's Mrs Bhabra with her short hair and big bindi and black salwar kameez with white bandhini bubbles that make her look like a bottle of Pepsi.

Hello, Aunty! I hand over the box of pedas and say what I am supposed to say as per prior instructions by the parent cadre: Homemade especially for you by my Naniji!

Pepsi Aunty pinches my cheek as I slip out of my chappals and squeeze past. I couldn't see the ten plus years in her face—her hair is as black as mine and the only wrinkles on her cheek are around her lips and eyes from smiling too much.

The living room is so full of furniture that I almost miss the centrepiece, a fountain that sputters water over a pink rock with a bulb inside it. The room still smells of whitewash. Only the view from the living room window has not retired with the Old Khuranas: the roadside half of the badminton court.

I like going inside other peoples' houses, because it makes me wonder who I would be if this were my house. In the Bhabra's D-II/10 I would be half princess, half poodle.

Hello, Mr Rahman. Hi, beta.

Vicky shakes Abba's hand and pats me on the shoulder, which is far superior to cheek-pinching.

Hello, Mr Bhabra. How nice the flat looks!

I know that Abba is lying, because only the highest degree of simplicity in all matters pertaining to Life-in-General meets his approval, and a pink bulb-filled plastic fountain negatively impacts the latter, so again I feel there must be a good reason for why he wanted to go meet the Bhabras after coming home from work, because Abba has already labelled them typical Punjabis, which the Concise Abba Dictionary defines as unrefined, crafty loudmouths who engage in periodic buffoonery. The only other thing I know that is unrefined is the expensive jaggery Naniji insists on buying, and Abba disapproves of that, too.

Sitara, darling! Geeta is here!

Pepsi Aunty cranes her neck into the flat.

And sorry, han, about the misunderstanding with the racket. I scolded Geeta for not having returned it to you before this morning.

Geeta is made of ice. All that I am able to move is my begging eyes up to Vicky, who meets them and laughs.

Oh, that. Vicky makes a waving gesture. Not to worry, Mr Rahman. In fact, I told her to keep it. I insisted.

That's very generous of you. So why did you not take it, Geeta?

I, um—

What the parent cadre does not know is that wrapped in newspaper behind the almirah is the new hiding place of my red and silver YONEX racket.

No problem, she can pick it up tomorrow, Vicky says, which the PC seems to accept as an answer, because he refrains from further investigations.

I breathe a sigh of interim relief as we sit down on the sofas, which look like coffins of dark, carved wood and are excessively uncomfortable. Luckily, Pepsi Aunty turns to me and says, Come, I'll take you to Sitara.

She directs me out of the living room and then through a white door, which closes behind me. I would have preferred to stay with the grown-ups, but I have orders from the parent cadre to make a new friend.

Sitara's Sitaraless room is the same as mine in our flat but hers overlooks the backside of the Club House. There's a big bed in the middle, at least twice the size of mine, and right now it's serving as office for the white teddy bear sitting at its end. To my left is a cabinet with glass sliding doors, behind which I can make out trophies and medals. I picture myself returning the shuttlecock facing my back boundary line as I reach out to open it—

Hi, Geeta.

The voice came from the corner. I go around the desk that has a bookshelf attached to its outer edge, behind which I find Sitara bent over a sheet of paper. She is surrounded by piles of comics—what did she call them, mangoes?—so that I can't see what she is doing. The writing on the cover of the topmost comic looks like the menu at the Chinese Room in CP, except that you can't read any of it.

I told Mummy I'm not quite finished with my work yet, so why don't you sit there until I'm done. She points at the teddy bear on the bed. You can play with Gabbar.

I want to tell her that I'm not a baby to play with teddy bears but I remember the parent cadre's directive. Instead I say, I already finished my homework.

This isn't homework.

What is it, then?

It would have been preferable to ask her what kind of a failyourownlife spends her free time at her desk when she could be on the court with me. I sneak up behind her and make my neck as a long as a turtle's. Now I can see that she is drawing a figure of a girl under an umbrella, which she is colouring red. Next I notice that from the sky it's not raining drops of water but hundreds of tiny shuttlecocks. I take a step back before she sees me spying, though I haven't yet read the words inside the bubble coming from the girl's mouth.

A story, Sitara says after a pause.

About what?

She sighs, puts the non-writing end of her pen into her mouth and turns to look me up and down. Don't mind me saying, but you wouldn't understand.

I just turned twelve!

Only someone too young to understand would think it has anything to do with age.

Sorry to say, but that makes zero point zero sense.

Sitara, however, has already returned to her paper and is scribbling as if each line means an emolument. I think about informing Sitara that I can also tell her a story, and it's called How To Be A Failyourownlife and it's all about her only. Instead, the door opens and the maid brings a tray of Horlicks and Good Day biscuits and puts it on the bed where I'm sitting. I drink mine and, because Sitara is not paying attention, eat more than my share of the biscuits.

I realise that as of right now Sitara is not willing to show me her story, so I will have to find a way to either quickly impress or distract her.

I'm really good at finding words in my dictionary, actually. You can just ask me if you need any help with that.

Sitara turns and smiles at me for the first time. You're cute. I suppose you want to play or something?

Baddy?! I try not to sound too enthu when I say, Your bed can be the net! Gabbar can be umpire! And you can write on my forehead if you win!

The last part is a fully empty promise, because she will not dare to do it with the parents around.

I'm not that into badminton. Sorry.

But you beat Faraz, and Vicky Uncle says you were almost a champion.

Right. Emphasis on almost.

No, like, really close to being a maximum top champion!

Look, it's sweet how you're such a badminton nut but take it as a friendly warning: don't let my father fool you.

He's obsessive and he's manipulative and he doesn't take no for an answer. In short, he's the worst coach in the whole world.

Although I was hoping for a moment that Sitara and I could be bona fide friends if she would just stop pretending that she doesn't care about badminton, she is now showing off a bit too much about how her father will do everything for badminton and mine clearly won't, so I say, Oh, I already have a fully professional coach.

Is that so?

I don't like Sitara's raised eyebrow and her half-smile, so I quickly add, Ya, my Abba is training me. We're starting tomorrow.

Sitara turns back to her paper. She starts scribbling again and says, Well, good luck to you, then.

I wait for more conversation but it's not coming.

The net of boredom around me grows fast, so I slip out of the room without Sitara noticing. Or caring.

Your Geeta's got real talent, Mr Rahman.

Abba: Hehehe.

Why is he so nervous? I wonder, standing outside Sitara's door and listening to the grown-ups' voices from the living room.

Right now for her tho everything is badminton-this, badminton-that. But in my heart I know that if she were to go to a top school like DPS or, say, SPV, she would definitely set her mind more on academics. She's exceptionally bright.

No doubt, Mr Rahman, but you should encourage her sports. My late father, Prakash Bhabra—

Not that story again! Pepsi Aunty interrupts. I've heard it at least once for every star in the sky.

But he hasn't, na! My father was a famous badminton player.

How interesting.

No, what's interesting, Mr Rahman, is how my husband went about turning our daughter into one.

Now that story I've heard too often, Anjana.

Sitara was just a baby, but as soon as I turned my back, the milk bottle would be gone and there was a shuttlecock in her tiny hands. Poor thing trying to suck on the cork and almost blinding herself in the process.

What rubbish.

I understood too late that he insisted on naming her Sitara, because he was so sure she would be a badminton star when she grows up.

Twinkle, twinkle, little Sitara, Abba says, which makes me giggle.

She hates badminton now.

She hates me, not badminton.

What are you saying, Mr Bhabra. Hehehe.

Be that as it may, as a mother I fully agree with you, Mr Rahman, you must send Geeta to the best school possible. Badminton she'll grow out of, and then what?

Exactly. The thing is, getting her admission has become so difficult, and, in all honesty, Geeta's marks are average. I feel so sad seeing my little girl growing up without a mother, you can imagine, Mrs Bhabra—

Poor bachcha!

Listening to Abba trying so hard to make friends with Vicky and Pepsi Aunty for an unidentified reason is substantially confusing. Abba never makes pertinent attempts to win new friends, and is generally not a fan of people per se, so he must have a very important reason for seeking the Bhabras' approval. I feel significantly guilty for not having helped him in terms of befriending Sitara, but this undertaking is as far away as possible from hitting a shuttlecock under water. Maybe I should steal Sitara's ongoing painting and finish it for her in the most commendable manner and thus win her friendship based on merit? Or I could convince Abba that at least there was a welcome narrowing down of differences and that Geeta should hence be released from all further friend-making duties.

Circulating these thoughts, I have been reorganising the marble chess figures on the shelf so that they form a very orderly queue unlike anyone in Kaka Nagar has ever seen. They are queuing to watch Geeta beat Faraz by the largest margin ever. It needs to be ensured that everyone in attendance has a front-row seat. The crowd enters the Club House, which requires rearrangement of figures along the outer edge of the chessboard, all of them looking in, with one very tall and one very small figure facing each other on the empty middle. I am looking for a stick of some kind to designate the net when I hear shuffling behind me and position myself in front of the chessboard to avoid red-handed catching.

Did Madam eject you from her room? Vicky is standing before me but before I can answer he is pointing at my creation and saying, You know, I always say badminton is chess for the body. Tennis and cricket you play with your arm, but badminton you play with your mind.

He beckons me with his finger.

Come, I want to show you something.

Trusting Vicky to take full blame for the messed-up chessboard if and when the need arises, I abandon my position and follow him into the room on the right, next to Sitara's, away from the living room. It's Vicky's and Pepsi Aunty's bedroom, even though there is only one small bed in it. On the wall above the desk hangs his badminton racket on a gleaming metal nail. He pulls out a plastic folder from a drawer but does not open it.

So you got a scolding at home for the racket?

I nod very slightly at the hole in my trainers.

But you decided to keep it anyway because badminton is more important to you than a father's vimms?

Though it can't be that another grown-up wants me to say that something is more important to me than anything to do with Abba, I know that Vicky loves badminton, too.

My father's main vimm is that I should develop an interlicked, which I haven't found in the dictionary yet so all I know is that I don't seem to have any of it.

Vicky chuckles, and because the cracking of accidental jokes about Abba would definitely qualify as a Public Grievance, I make my eyes very big and steer them at the folder, so that Vicky stops questioning me and shows me whatever he wants me to see.

Trust an old crook like me: you don't need interlicked in life. You need stamina.

What's stamina, Uncle?

It's shouting back at this foolish world. It's not being afraid to get laughed at and leaving no stone unturned for your passions.

Like a typical Punjabi?

Vicky laughs. Your father's words?

I want to quickly deny the allegation but, luckily, he changes the topic.

Say, Geeta, have you ever asked yourself whether it's normal for a twelve-year-old girl to beat a seventeen-year-old boy at badminton?

Finally an easy question!

I know Faraz's game too well, Uncle.

Has anyone ever told you that you could play badminton professionally?

You mean for money?

Can I ask Vicky that if someone plays badminton for money instead of for fun it makes them less of a failyourownlife?

Not just for money. To play professionally means to live and breathe badminton.

Abba says I already do that.

I could make you a real champion, Geeta. I've been waiting for four long days to tell you that one day the whole country will know your name.

Geeta Rahman?

Geeta Rahman! But we'd have to start training right away.

The more I try not to, the harder it seems I am pulling my upper lip towards my chin.

What's the matter?

Sitara says—

Oh, don't listen to Sitara. My darling daughter is turning into a bit of a bore, frankly, and she's a bad loser to boot.

I glance at the door to make sure that nobody is eavesdropping before I whisper to Vicky that, secondly, Training is expensive. What I don't say is that if Abba doesn't have enough financial outflow to make donations to a better school for Geeta, he definitely doesn't have it for badminton training.

Without prior notice, Vicky takes my hand and holds it a bit too tight. The black hairs on his fingers look like burnt grass.

I'll train you for free. No strings attached.

No strings?

Vicky nods so enthusiastically that I don't ask how we're supposed to use our rackets without the stringing.

But there is one condition.

Geeta?

Vicky's hand leaves a warm trail on mine just as Abba appears in the door behind us followed by Anjana Aunty.

There you are.

Abba's eyes dance between Vicky and myself. Time to go, he says in his cautious voice. Nani must be waiting with dinner.

And that's how badminton was invented! Vicky says, patting his folder and ushering me out of the room.

Although I find Vicky pervasively confusing in general, bottomline is: he is a natural fan of my expertise in badminton, and that constitutes an utterly and comprehensively unprecedented affair.

Rehearsal of my speech has been ongoing since our visit to the Bhabras yesterday. It's less of a speech and more of a memorandum, actually, which is a message used in diplomacy, which is the art of dealing with people sensitively and effectively.

Abba-a-a?

Jaani?

When Abba calls me Jaani he is in a gentle mood, so my diplomacy is already working. I sit down on the second cane chair next to Abba's in the garden, where he is reading the newspaper and sipping his tea. The air is cool and moist, fitting for a chilly morning in February. Abba is wearing his brown shawl over his pyjamas and no socks in his blue rubber chappals. He always turns the chairs so that they face the garden and not our gate with the Club House and badminton court behind it. I always thought that the second chair is there for Naniji or me to use but now that I have diverted time from getting ready for school to join him here I think that maybe it's for Mummy. I pull my foot from my chappal and run it over the tips of the grass. The dew is making my sock wet.

Abba, I—

Yet another maha aarti in Bombay. Hasn't the Shiv Sena had enough? The kar sevaks danced on the broken dome, and then the killing started. Stabbing, arson, mob violence. Hundreds are dead already, Geeta. *Hundreds*. Muslims, Hindus, police. Pavan says every day there are articles in the local newspaper calling for more violence on both sides.

Why, Abba?

Abba shakes his head at the newspaper. With Babri

Masjid they created a monster that nobody will be able to tame in the end. You mark my words, Geeta. India is in flames. Even when they put out the last police station set on fire, the country will still be burning. And this time it's going to be people like you and me who will suffer the most, not just those poor people getting butchered in the slums. Split loyalties, they'll say. Go back to Pakistan! they'll scream.

Who will, Abba?

The orange hordes. The far right.

I want to ask him of what, but I am afraid that this will only negatively impact Abba's mood towards me, so I stay silent.

It's all a bloody joke. That's why I keep telling you that you will always have to excel at whatever you do. Be better than everyone else. This may sound obvious but only success triumphs failure. There's no middle ground for someone like you. You especially will never belong to just one side.

Why?

Because you're a threat to everything they believe in. You represent a certain kind of future that makes them feel small. They want to live in some golden age past, which doesn't exist, it never has! It's a myth they're desperate for, and they'll kill whatever and whoever stands in their way.

I clutch Ram's arrow around my neck. They're going to kill me, Abba?

Abba drops the newspaper to his lap and pulls me towards him. He holds my hands in his and waits for me to look him in the eye.

Nobody is going to kill you, Geeta. Understand?

I nod. And then I tell Abba that I saw them from the

school bus the other day: the orange hordes. They stopped the traffic and swarmed on either side of our bus carrying pointy trishuls. One of them was waving around a sword. At one point, a group of them started banging on the door, shouting to be let in because the children should hear what they had to say. Somehow the teachers managed to convince them to move on. I slipped down from my seat and hid on the floor until I heard the bus's engine rumble on and felt movement. I got home an hour later than usual that day.

Abba lifts my chin and I look him in the eye once again.

You should have told me, Geeta.

I didn't want to think about it again, Abba.

He rubs his neck with the palm of his hand—a sign that he is thinking about something.

Nobody wants to kill you. They want to kill the idea of you, if that makes sense. You're Gandhiji's dream. And that's your strength, don't ever forget that—or they win.

I chew the inside of my lip. If Abba wants me never to forget in order to keep them from winning, this means that Abba wants me to win instead. This contradicts his prior statement and means that sometimes winning is not vulgar but commendable, which I thoroughly and fully agree with, because I think winning is the opposite of lacking good taste: it tastes better than anything else.

Now go and get ready for school.

Although I know that Abba and I have different definitions of success, which even my dictionary cannot sort out, I still take Abba's new broody mood as an auspicious sign, because he is thinking about my future, as am I.

Abba, I wanted to ask you something.

It was Sitara who gave me the idea, though Abba and I haven't spoken much about our visit to the Bhabras yesterday. Abba only said afterwards, No manners, talking badly about each other in front of us. And he doesn't really want you to have that racket, or he would have given it to you there and then. Why wait and say you can pick it up tomorrow?

But when I go to the Club House after school today, I will tell Abba that their maid brought the racket downstairs and insisted that I take it, and then I won't have to hide it anymore.

Abba promotes his eyebrows to a higher rank and looks at me. I clear my throat.

I want to bring to your notice, Abba, a proposal for an appointment on deputation in the public sector. There is no emolument but as your daughter I promise to give you the maximum most dearness allowances in return. The dear*est* allowances, in toto. Will you be my professional badminton coach, Abba? As you are seeing, I am having equal dedication to my studies, where I am making such big increments and—

When Abba drops the newspaper into his lap with force I first think that he is very angry. But before I dare to look at his face I hear his gurgle of a laugh.

Have YOU been taking pages from my files?

I shake my head at my lap. Then nod a little.

Oh god, no. And I blamed Four-by-Four!

Abba sighs into his fingertips. Although her real name is Pushpa, Abba refers to his PA as Four-By-Four at home just like Mummy used to because of her geometric shape.

All last week I insinuated that she had lost them. Now I'll have to apologise to her. And you'll return the pages to me before you go to school.

I nod again. Since Abba was laughing and not angry—I thought if Abba ever found out about the pages there would be a minimum of two slaps—he must have been a little impressed with my words. Before the newspaper rises to his face again, I say, So will you train me, Abba? To increment my badminton?

In the short pause before Abba speaks I'm wondering if I should tell him that Vicky also wants to be my coach, but that I would give the job to Abba instead if he really wants it.

What exactly do you mean by 'increment my badminton', Geeta? I've told you many times that you should not use big words falsely. Leave that to the likes of our corrupt new neighbours.

The laughter has suddenly disappeared from Abba's voice. He mutters: It's just my karma that I have to lick the boots of people like that. This is what India does to you.

Abba sighs forcefully and brings his face closer to mine. I hold my breath and wish I could issue a temporary withdrawal of my words.

What were you thinking, stealing pages from my files? You could have put me in jail! And what is this never-ending nonsense about badminton?

I just thought we could play together in the evenings, and you could see how good I am and teach me—

Sportspeople are glorified gladiators, Geeta. Is that really all you want from life?

This time I stay silent. If Mummy were here she would recruit the most pertinent words to seek Abba's approval. She always did. But the last days have been completely and utmost disappointing in terms of learning to drive from

Abba through observation, because he has not taken me anywhere in the car, so my intercom line to Mummy is still not connected.

You have a brain! And you live in a time and place where you're allowed to use it. My own mother—she had the highest IQ in my whole family but she was married off at 14 and from that point on her main job was to listen to my father spouting idiocies all day long. Don't you see how lucky you are?

I just thought, Abba—

A sob shakes all of me. Mummy will not be transferred back to us, even if one day I learn to drive and hear her voice deep inside my heart.

Abba ignores me, so I quickly wipe my nose.

For God's sake, beta, you're not a baby anymore, however harsh it may seem to you now, you have to learn to be realistic. In India there's not even a livelihood in sports. How will you eat? I've never stopped you from playing for fun in the evenings, have I? You're always free to do as you please in this house. But if you're going to start speaking of professional coaching then it's my duty as your father to make sure you don't fall into some pipe dream.

I rub my cheeks on my sleeve and nod.

Come here.

Abba pulls me on his lap. Have I ever told you the story of the little boy growing up in Lucknow?

I shake my head even though the answer to Abba's question is yes.

His parents were not educated but he understood at a very young age that he wanted more from life than what they could offer him. So he studied hard and learned about philosophy and science and English, he won many scholarships and he began to travel. What he did not tell anyone was that he was deeply in love. Not with the girl who would become the Mummy of his future daughter, because he hadn't met her yet, but with something very powerful: poetry. He thought he was doing all this studying and learning and travelling so that he would grow up to be a poet. He filled many notebooks with his writing and when he met the girl he would marry he filled her heart with it, too. And for two years he lived as a poet, while she got a job to support them. He made a small name for himself. But then he began to understand that to be a poet and to live as one were two different things. To make a living as a poet in India you had to know the right people to get awards and grants and you had to flatter them, even if you thought their work was nonsense. You had to start writing like them. And you had to choose: either you were a Hindi poet or an Urdu one. To be both at the same time was suspect and unwanted. So the boy, who was by then married and expecting their first child, a beautiful little daughter, just like he and Mummy always wanted, decided to stay a true poet in his heart rather than become a false one out in the world, and he took a job like everyone else.

I am waiting for Abba to keep going but all I can hear now is the soft whistle from his nostrils as he breathes.

Sports in India is the same, Geeta. Completely corrupt. They'll break your spirit and on top of it you won't make a living off it. You have better chances to become the next Prime Minister than to succeed in sports. Better just enjoy playing right here with Faraz and the other children in Kaka

Nagar and focusing on your studies. It will all make sense to you when you're older, I promise.

Maybe I should not get older but stay twelve?

He buries his nose in my neck and hair and whispers, Believe me, if I knew how I would have stopped time long ago.

Then he strokes the hair from my face and tucks it behind my ears. However irritating this stubbornness of yours is, you remind me so much of Mummy when you have an idea and just can't let it go.

I huddle close to Abba and make sure he hears my chuckle.

Good girl, no reason to cry. What did I tell you from the day Mummy got ill? This is not a Greek tragedy, madam, it's a fully desi chutkulla. Got it?

I lean my whole weight against Abba.

Got it.

As soon as the white Ambassador pulls up in front of our building that afternoon I shout Time Out! to Faraz and race to the Club House gate. A suit-and-tie-Vicky is climbing out of the car, which faces the wrong way because of the detour it had to take to avoid falling into the mud room, where work has stopped completely because of a union strike. This has been a big Public Grievance for all the car-driving grown-ups in Kaka Nagar, and a Happy Coincidence for the Greek Chorus, which has trampled the mud stairs into mere bumps. One of them is planning to have her birthday party down there, with shovels for everyone.

After my morning with Abba, I used logics to make a decision: Abba said he doesn't want me to be a real professional badminton champion, but he also said that when I am stubborn I remind him of Mummy. Mummy is obviously more important to him than badminton. So the very fact of my being stubborn is more important to him than what I am being stubborn about. This means that what I am about to do may seem like I'm disobeying Abba, but in reality I am doing the exact opposite.

Vicky Uncle!

Hello, Geeta.

You said, no, that you can train me? I look around and whisper, For free! And you said there was one condition? I also have one condition!

Vicky's face is turning from a frown to a smile to a grin.

Come upstairs in exactly ten minutes. Sitara and her mother are still out. As you know, they don't approve of my methods, and I want to talk to you in peace about this before they come home.

I nod before I run back to Faraz.

What was that about, Smalls?

Nothing!

You're grinning like you just won the lottery.

Maybe I did!

Faraz is launching his sideways laugh at me. That's not how it works, Smalls. Never forget that we're born to lose. Match point!

Can I tell you my condition first?

Vicky's arm around my shoulders leads me to the coffin sofa, on which we sit side by side.

Sure.

I notice the maid standing in the door with a tray. She offers the cup of tea to Vicky.

Shall I bring Horlicks? She nods at me with her head.

I say, No, thank you, I just had my milk. This is a lie but I am too excited to have anything other than words in my mouth right now.

When she is gone I turn to Vicky and say, First of all, professional sports in India is completely corrupt. True or false?

What is this, a job interview?

I return Vicky's grin. Then nod.

True.

Are you sure?

Yes.

All right. Next question. Is it easier to become the Prime Minister than to succeed in sports?

Definitely true.

Really?

Vicky nods his enthu nod.

Really, Uncle?

Vicky shrugs and nods.

Okay, last question. Please think carefully before you give your answer. You cannot make a living in sports in India. True or false?

I almost want to plug my ears out of fear that he will agree again. Instead, my fingers find Ram's bow and arrow around my neck and hold it tightly in my fist.

Well.

False?

Falsish.

Thank God!

Well, let's put it this way. It's true that there's little money in it but that's beginning to change.

That still counts as false!

Just last week a friend in the Badminton Authority told me that Prakash Padukone is setting up the first ever badminton academy here in India to train young talent. This means sports sponsorships. It's all finally happening for your generation.

Who's Prakash Padu—?

Oh dear, we'll have to do badminton history lessons as part of your training. He's one of the greatest Indian badminton players that ever lived, though personally I think Syed Modi, may his poor soul rest in peace, had more style.

I take a deep breath.

So Uncle, this is my condition: I will only let you train me if you promise that you will make me excel. Because I have automatic split loyalty, so I need to be better than everyone else and you have to promise me that you will make me the best player there is.

I have been staring at my hands but when I look up, Vicky's face is so close to mine I can see myself in his eyes. I move back, afraid that for some reason I am going to make him cry. Maybe I should not insist on such strict rules.

It takes a lot of courage to follow your passion against everyone's will, and Sitara never understood that about me.

Vicky leans into me and cups my face in his warm hands.

Geeta, you'll laugh when you hear my condition.

I reverse out of his grip and say, What is it?

You have to promise me that you will put badminton before everything else.

Of course! I promise. A thought bangs against my words. But, Uncle.

Yes?

My Abba is not a natural fan of badminton.

He will adjust. Once he hears a packed auditorium chant your name, he will adjust. That's my promise back to you.

What if before that he wants me to stop playing?

Don't let that worry you. I've already taken care of it.

Although I cannot imagine any situation in which Abba would experience a sudden upward revision of badminton, I want to believe Vicky so badly that I decide not to make further inquiries.

Come, I want to show you something else.

Vicky steers me into Sitara's room and in front of the glass cabinet. You see these trophies?

I nod.

They're worthless. Cheap metal, you can unscrew the cup from the base. Even the kabadiwalla will not give you anything for it.

But, Uncle—

Exactly! You said it, Geeta: BUT! But for a real champion, their value is priceless. One day you will have a cabinet full of trophies, and you will remember in the tiniest details how each one of them was won, how much sweat and blood went into every single one of them, and nothing can match the motivation that will give you.

I want to ask Vicky how long it will take me to collect a full glass cabinet of trophies but the phone rings in the living room and Vicky excuses himself. I start counting: four trophies and five medals. I want to try one around my neck but the glass door of the cabinet is locked. I stroll over to Sitara's desk to investigate if the key is where Abba keeps his valuable objects.

The top of her desk is completely empty. Sitara has too many pens of all colours and styles in the drawers. When I open the last one I find a pile of pages drawn by Sitara. Topmost is the cover of her story showing an upside down shuttlecock, in which the cork grows into the body of a girl like a mermaid, and all around it are the words of the title: The Smashing Confessions of Sitara B.

I take out the whole pile and turn the first page. A baby with very large eyes is using a badminton racket as a bridge to crawl from her crib to a table piled high with food. In a box at the top she has written: ATTACK NO. 1!

I turn another page. The baby is having its first birthday party, and all the babies are wearing shuttlecocks on their heads instead of pointy hats. Then I notice that all the babies are sitting on the stringing of a huge badminton racket, which is tilting upwards so that they are about to tumble off. There are no words in this picture.

I flip ahead to the last page and find what Sitara was drawing the other day. Only now there is a second figure next to the girl with the umbrella. A boy. The shuttlecock rain is happening only over the girl. But the shuttlecocks have been painted over to make hearts. The boy is standing in a burst of sunlight. Inside the bubble extending from the girl's mouth it says: Falling in love is like the feeling of monsoon but without the wetness of rain, don't you think? And the boy's bubble answers—

Geeta?

I quickly stuff the pages back into the drawer, feeling disgusted with Sitara for thinking about boys and love and wishing for Vicky's sake that she would be more interested in badminton instead, though if she were, Vicky would be her and not my coach now. I step through Sitara's door and bump into Vicky.

Remember, Geeta, if we stick together, no one can stop us.

He presses me against his belly, arms around my shoulders, sticking us together.

I look at my feet to avoid the source of the talcum-powder-cum-perspiration-smell that's flooding my nose. I push against his belly with my hands and he loosens his grip.

Sorry. Didn't mean to startle you. I'm just so happy right now.

Before I can stop myself, I am giggling. Vicky is giggling back but I avoid his glance, because what's funny to me is that such a grownup man wants to be my friend so badly, and I wish I could share this joke with Abba but something deep inside tells me that this will only make the parent cadre think of Vicky as an even greater Public Grievance.

As if Vicky is reading my thoughts, he says, I'm going to take care of everything tomorrow, Geeta, and we'll start training the day after. Tomorrow evening I'll come over and speak to your father, and I guarantee you that he'll agree.

Today is Thursday, February 11, 1993, eleven days post-birthday, and a historic event is imminent: Vicky and I are about to begin our first official training session for a bona fide and professional badminton tournament, with Abba's unexpected yet fully legitimate approval.

How this happened I am not in possession of knowledge about, but yesterday, while I was playing with Faraz, Vicky showed up even though it was still his office time, and told me that there is a U-13 junior championship organised by the Badminton Association of India in Delhi in early April. He said he wants me to compete in it, because the first step towards becoming badminton history is to have tournament experience outside of Kaka Nagar. He thinks that I might even win something. My response: Abba will never allow it. That's when Vicky grinned at me and said, He just gave me permission to register you.

I asked Vicky how this was possible, because it wasn't even evening yet and Vicky has not come over to speak to Abba officially, but all Vicky said before disappearing again was that fate was on our side and that we would start training tomorrow.

At night I couldn't sleep and decided to double-check with Abba to avoid later misconstructions—and Vicky was right! I told Abba that Vicky Uncle wants to play badminton with me in the evenings, for free, careful not to use the word 'train', and informed him of his approval to be a part of a tournament. Abba just patted me on the shoulder and said Good Girl but something in my eyes must have stated utter confusion, because Abba then sighed and said right now I must make a gargantuan effort to please Vicky, because the

Bhabras have connections to SPV, which is the best school in all of Delhi. In the Concise Abba English Dictionary, gargantuan means an excessively large amount of anything positive, which is in effect the only nice thing he has said with reference to Vicky so far.

And therefore today, Thursday, February 11, 1993, eleven days post-birthday, a historic event is imminent: Vicky and I are about to begin our first official training session for a fully authorised badminton tournament.

When I arrive on court at 5:30 p.m. sharp, Vicky is already there dressed all in white, and a plastic pin on his shirt reads COACH. He is beckoning me over.

I have something for you.

From a plastic bag he retrieves a shoebox, which he opens to reveal crisp new yellow and black trainers that have the glow of foreign about them.

For me?

Vicky nods.

Badminton shoes. Soon, soon there'll be shops right here in Delhi for all these kinds of things and more, but these I still had to arrange to be brought for you all the way from Malaysia. Try them on.

I take off my old ones and slip into these. When I stand up, I feel as if I am walking on a cloud.

Thank you, Uncle, I say, guilty for not having read the dictionary more carefully so that I could have a specialised word for this utterly butterly delicious feeling, so all I can think of is correcting myself: Thank you, Coach Sir.

This makes Vicky's eyes smile, though he says, Come, let's not waste another minute. We have a lot of work to do.

We walk towards the shadow side of the court together.

Here's the plan: Warm-up comes first, followed by practice. We'll train Monday through Friday, and on the sixth and final training day of every week you'll only play matches against Faraz while I coach you from the sideline. That's when you'll be applying all that I have taught you so far.

I am understanding that my training will leave me little to no time anymore to read Abba's files or watch him drive or to visit Aunty's Bird Clinic, which I feel substantially guilty about, but now that I have Abba's approval I have decided to put all my shuttlecocks in the badminton basket, because I would rather serve professionally on the court than off it.

After what feels like an abundance of drills, Vicky says, We're going to move on to your backhand clear now—the first step towards perfecting the reverse slice drop shot, which was my father's signature shot, by the way. You have good overall deception, but we need to strengthen your fundamentals.

Vicky shows me the steps and sends me to the other side of the court.

Racket face towards me, Geeta, not the tree!

I adjust the angle of my wrist.

That's the biggest problem we're facing. You have some bad habits that you need to work very hard on eliminating from your game before it's too late.

I release the position and jump on the spot. Then I take position again, realigning my body.

Good. Now show me the steps. One: Set!

I arrange my arms, feet stable.

Left arm out, Geeta! You want to show your opponent that you're ready. Always a tiger, never a mouse!

I push my chest out and stretch my left arm further.

That's it! Two: Back!

I fold the racket towards my left shoulder.

Yes! Remember you have to go back to go forward!

I nod at Vicky. For a moment I cannot imagine that there was ever a court without Vicky on it, whom I'm only calling Coach Sir now. Though he laughs every time I say it, I get the feeling that he secretly likes it.

And now—thack! Forward! Again: One, two, THREE! Slow, slow, FAST! Now with the shuttle.

I make contact with a sharp clap.

Yeees! That's it! God gave you a wrist, so use it!

A cough from the sideline makes us both turn.

Bhabra Sahab, God gave us wrists, too, and we'd like to use them now.

Saleem Uncle steps on the court as he speaks. Next to him is Angad's father. Both are dressed in white shorts and polo shirts. They play here every evening, but usually never before seven. Then I notice that the floodlights are on, and that it must be past seven already.

Just five more minutes, Saleem Sahab. She's almost got it now.

Sure, Bhabra Sahab. We've already heard so much about your great aspirations for our Geeta.

So the Greek Chorus has already spread the news of Geeta's imminent championhood.

Faraz's father remains standing on the court. Vicky looks at him for a moment, clearly expecting him to step back but when he doesn't, Vicky plays the shuttlecock to me.

One—two—thack! Again.

Now that I am aware of Faraz's father watching me I can't concentrate on set—back—hold. Mr Saleem carries in his voice a hand that's ready to slap. Faraz hears it, too, which is why he always leaves the court on time. Though Vicky is playing the same shot to me again and again, I keep making mistakes now until Vicky gives up.

Thanks for your patience, Vicky says to the waiting fathers as we leave the court.

Didn't you just mention bad habits that need to be eliminated before it's too late? To me, this seems to be such a case.

Mr Saleem is smiling at Vicky.

Before Vicky can answer, Angad's father adds, without smiling, The court is for all the residents, Bhabraji. Please avoid hogging it.

Mr Saleem, Mr Ahluwalia, sorry to make you wait today. But one day you'll read this girl's name on the front page of your newspaper and then you'll be happy you gave her the chance to get proper training.

Be that as it may. Angad's father scratches his armpit with the base of his handle's racket. This is a residential colony and not a gym.

Faraz's father clicks his tongue. No need to turn a mole hill into a mountain, Gurinderji. Mr Bhabra is new here, after all. I'm sure from now on he will comply. Sharmaji!

Sharmaji steps out of the shadows. Give him a copy of our Resident Association's Rulebook.

While we wait, Vicky meets my eyes. I like that there is some annoyance but also a largish quota of curiosity in his eyes. Abba's eyes would be wide with anxiety by now, but I cannot imagine a situation in which he would voluntarily enter into a discussion with the two Most Scariest Uncles of Kaka Nagar.

I say Khuda Hafiz to Mr Saleem, because he is looking at me with expectation as we leave.

It's Khuda HAfiz, Geeta, not Khuda fizz. The Almighty is not a carbonated drink for you to consume.

Khuda HAAfiz, I repeat, a little too loudly, preparing to make my escape before he can say anything else when Vicky addresses Saleem Uncle again.

I understand why you're feeling so tense, Mr Saleem. It must be a tough time to be a cop and you must be thanking your stars that you're not posted in Bombay right now.

I follow my duty, Mr Bhabra, not my stars. And tense can be defined as either strained or taut. I prefer the latter.

Vicky nods. I admire that. It's people like you who will save this country.

Vicky turns suddenly, and I follow. A moment later, we are standing in front of my gate and his staircase together.

Always a?

Tiger!

Never a?

Mouse!

That's right. He leans into me and whispers, They can stop us this one time, but we'll just start earlier from now on.

What about your office, Uncle?

Let me worry about that.

Uncle, look!

I take two deliberate steps back, then run and jump as far as I can.

Vicky turns and walks towards me again with a grin.

That's right, you first have to go back in order to go forward.

We are about to turn towards our respective home cadres when he stops and says, Speaking of which. If we can't do our practice today, let's at least have a history lesson instead.

That's when I suggest that we go home, because then Abba can finally be friends with Vicky officially. But it's Naniji who opens the door and tells us that Abba is not back yet.

Over tea with Naniji, Vicky says that history is not about facts but about people. That's how I learned about the Duke of Beaufort, who named badminton after his house; and about the Prince of Wales, who came to Calcutta in 1875 and played his first game of badminton on the Lieutenant Governor's lawn for the newspapers to write about; and about a Parsi from Sealkot, who invented professional badminton rackets made of wood and sold them (I will have to tell Vijay about him); and about Sir Alfred Critchley, who built Harringay Arena and Stadium in 1927 for greyhound racing (poor man's horseracing, Vicky calls it) and boxing, and also for Vicky's father to become the second-best world champion at the All England in; and about Sir George Thomas, who was even older than Sir Alfred and who held a record 21 All-England titles and was not only a badminton legend but a chess and tennis champion to boot, on top of which he was a model of good manners, because if he beat you in a match he would apologise to you after; and about the Deodhar sisters—Tara, Suman and Sunder—who ruled Indian badminton in the 1940s; and about Lady Leela

Ginwala, an Anglo-Indian heiress hungry for badminton, who raised shuttlecock geese on her estate outside of London after World War Two because of the shuttlecock famine in England; and about Syed Modi, who would have been India's biggest badminton star by now if he hadn't been murdered five years ago, though Vicky would not tell me by whom; and about Prakash Padukone, who is India's biggest badminton star, even though he retired a few years ago. Vicky said it was Prakash Padukone who in 1980 finally won the title that his father, the original Prakash, had failed to win that day in 1947: champion of the All England. But, Vicky says, he won it for a different, cropped India.

My favourite lesson, though, comes last. It's the one about Geeta Das Rahman, who Vicky says will one day be a major part of Indian badminton history.

Akbar Rahman turns to Four-By-Four, who is wearing the strained look of someone failing to draw attention to herself.

Does Geeta not like the present? Four-By-Four asks.

We both prefer the past, Akbar replies, surprised to be asked an imaginative question by his secretary. Only then does it occur to him.

You mean the *birthday* present. Did I not tell you?

Four-By-Four shakes her head ever so slightly, and a teeming sense of shame suffuses his body for not having thanked her for the gift earlier. His eyes graze the table calendar on which the day's date sits enshrined in a red plastic frame: Wednesday, February 10, 1993.

I'm sorry, Pushpa, I thought I had already told you. Geeta likes it immensely.

Four-by-Four looks unconvinced. If she doesn't like it, I can exchange—

She slept in it last night, that's how much she likes it. I had to pry it off her this morning.

Finally, Four-by-Four smiles, but the shame persists on his skin like a film of sweat. She must have waited every day since Geeta's birthday—has it been, what, *ten* days already?—for Akbar to say something. The dress meanwhile, a hideous urine-coloured thing with endless frothy ruffles that looks like it came out of a horse's bladder, lies bundled in the glove compartment, Geeta never having set eyes on it. He'd have to tell her about it now and make sure she'd call Four-By-Four to thank her effusively. Four-By-Four was thoughtful that way, and generous for her means.

His eyes fall on the glossy photograph of six-year-old Geeta devouring a slice of watermelon, which Sakshi slipped under the glass tabletop of his desk on his first day in this office.

The phone rings. He pulls out the handkerchief he keeps in his drawer for the sole purpose of wiping the surface above and around the picture, so that Sakshi's thumbprint embossed across Geeta's emerald sundress becomes clearly visible once again. How thankful he is now that she never listened to him when he told her to hold photographs from their edge.

Sir!

Akbar looks up. The gap between her teeth never fails to irritate him. One day he will do it: push her down into her chair, pop her head back and fill it with a piece of Amul cheese.

Yes, Pushpa?

Akbar wears the practiced look of a hassled man.

DC Handicrafts on the phone. His mother requests a stand at the expo.

Four-By-Four smiles at Akbar and taps the fingertips of her free hand first on today's date on the table calendar and then against her temple. He traces an invisible noose around his neck. The IAS should offer courses in advanced pantomime, Akbar thinks, given how often you need it to settle impossible situations. They both know that all stands are already booked for tomorrow's opening of the earthenware exhibition at the trade fair grounds, but that someone will have to be booted off the list to keep the Development Commissioner's peace at home.

He takes the receiver from Pushpa.

Akbar Rahman speaking.

As he waits for the DC to come on the line, he returns to the problem occupying his mind since lunch, which kept him from hearing Four-By-Four's entreaty in the first place: a suitable translation for *kal*. How could he render in English the nuance of the Hindi that united in a single syllable two contradictory but interwoven worlds: yesterday and tomorrow. He had promised Pavan a translation of his poem for the editor of that American literary magazine who sought Pavan out during her visit to Bombay. Pavan, for whom English was a matter of pragmatism not intuition, trusted Akbar with his work, and he did not want to disappoint him.

Rahman! You know what's to be done, yes?

Akbar affirms and lets the DC speak, interjecting only the expected Yes-yesses or Sure-sures to manifest his presence on the phone. He did not have to listen, because the script was always the same—the DC making his request using phrases such as my hands are tied and family is family, and call me should you ever need anything, anything at all.

Yestermorrow.

Toyester.

English was an ostentatious language. So full of itself. Literally: it had many more words than Hindi but always needed to draw attention to itself. It was like a gush of water that flooded your nostrils and shot out of your ears. Hindi was quieter. It was the dust that coated your hair and stuck in the folds of your skin. Hindi was an edible language—earthy and delicious—while English was simply inevitable.

Four-By-Four takes the receiver Akbar hands her and hangs up.

The question is, was it his or her idea? she asks with a grin.

Definitely his.

Maybe he secretly wants to take up pottery himself?

His cups would have no bottom, so that you can keep shoving the bribes in.

This makes Four-By-Four's lips quiver with giggles and the hairs on her chin stand up. When she first started as his PA, Akbar told Sakshi that Pushpa was the ugliest human being he had ever set eyes on, shaped like a four-foot cube. But in the days after Sakshi's passing, Four-By-Four was the only one who let him cry in peace, tears dripping into his lunch or on his files, neither dissolving from the room, nor trying to comfort him, just making sure he was not disturbed as the air-conditioner rumbled on in the corner.

So let's see the list, then, he says. Which poor bastard is it going to be?

She grins and raises herself from the chair, which shifts and squeaks. I'll make the phone call, sir.

Akbar grins back. What happened in Four-By-Four's

childhood that she enjoyed lying on the phone so much? Maybe he should encourage Geeta to make more prank calls now to inhibit such a habit later in life.

Four-By-Four pulls out a stapled document from a pile of papers—of which only she knows the order—and passes it to Akbar, who pretends to start reading even as the thought of his daughter persists and spreads. Does Geeta like the present? She seems cheerful enough on most days. Her grades dipped in the last eighteen months, but that was to be expected, of course. If that Bhabra fellow would really help with her admission, one major worry of his would be taken care of. So far he has just been encouraging Geeta to get to know the Bhabra daughter, but he heard from other neighbours that she is an oddball. And Bhabra himself has been seen playing badminton with Geeta. Akbar promised Sakshi: he would do whatever lay in his power to not let her death get in the way of their daughter leading a full and happy life, which, Akbar knew from his own miserable childhood, was best achieved through intellectual stimulation. When Sakshi was still alive, she would sometimes take Geeta to the court and they would have what Sakshi later described to him as a lacklustre game of badminton with Faraz, with that same old racket that Geeta had now insisted on replacing. It was only after Sakshi's passing that Geeta's interest in the game turned obsessive, which proves to Akbar that beneath all that chirpiness lies a thick layer of grief. He would call Bhabra in the next couple of days and ask about the progress with the admission. Go meet him in person, Aki. This is what Sakshi would say now, and he would squirm and make excuses until she would relent and go herself.

Before he can stop it from happening, a tear gathers and slides down his lashes, falling onto the sheet of paper in his hand with a soft pop. The drop magnifies a name: RAVINDER KALRA.

Kal. Yestermorrow. Toyester. The two could mix in language, but not in life. Sakshi would never relent to him again.

Ravinder Kalra, Pushpa. He's the one we'll cancel. But I'll do it myself.

Sir, you don't—

No, I insist.

Akbar stands with such determination that his chair rolls backwards and bangs into the wall behind him. He checks his watch.

But I have to take care of some urgent business first, and then I'll go straight home and call Kalra. You go ahead and call the DC and tell him his mother can have stall no.—?

Pushpa leans in, her squat finger quickly finding the blurry name.

Seventy-nine.

Akbar watches as she copies Kalra's name and phone number onto a sheet of paper and places it inside his open attaché.

Thanks, Pushpa.

You're sure, sir? I can make both calls.

No, Pushpa. No more excuses. The man is getting unfairly booted, and the least I can do is show him the respect of telling him myself.

Not the truth, though, sir?

Akbar sighs as he looks into Four-By-Four's eyes

that always appear distended behind her thick, smudgy glasses.

Never the truth.

Akbar realises his mistake as soon as he enters the anteroom of Vicky Bhabra's office. The sofa is already occupied with waiting men, and Bhabra's PA is a tall, skinny man with the deep-set eyes of an owl and a head that swivels on his neck to keep track of the goings-on at the office.

Is Mr Bhabra in? Akbar's voice squeals like an out-of-tune flute, and he clears his throat before repeating the words, louder this time.

The PA finishes the sentence he has been scribbling on a page. Only then does he glance up. May I know your name, sir?

Of course the PA would not tell him whether Bhabra was in until he told him his name but doing so without meeting Bhabra would be the worst-case scenario, casting Akbar in the role of the spurned suppliant and Bhabra in that of the hardworking, merciful king. Yet he did not want to wait in the room with the other men, who all looked like car salesmen in their nylon safari suits in either grey or beige. Sakshi would roll her eyes at him but he would explain to her that he was not being chicken-hearted—one of her oft-used words—he was just maintaining his dignity.

I'll come back another time, Akbar says and turns around before the PA can ask for his name again. In his determination to inject speed and purpose into his gait, he misses the sound of a door flying open behind him.

Mr Rahman! Rahman Sahab!

Akbar freezes, twisting his head back. From the corner of his eye he sees Bhabra approaching. Akbar turns around and reaches for the outstretched hand, feeling the squeeze all the way up in his shoulder.

I thought I saw you from the window, and I was expecting you to come right in, but I realised Gupta doesn't know who you are.

Bhabra holds the door open for Akbar, speaking without break. You know how it is with men in our position. Good I stepped out.

As soon as he enters the office and the door closes behind them, Akbar's sense of triumph dissolves into the sudden sensation of having walked into a trap. Why was Bhabra being so nice? Akbar was the one asking for a favour after all.

Bhabra leads Akbar not to his large glass desk with six chairs arranged around it, as if he were always in conference mode, but onwards to the sofa set and coffee table at the far end of the spacious room.

Was Bhabra making fun of him? Was he luring Akbar to beg him for help, only to turn him down in the end? As Akbar lowers himself into the maroon upholstery of the armchair, he decides that at no cost would he bring up Geeta's admission.

Sorry to barge in on you like that, Akbar begins, immediately regretting that he opened with an apology. I had some work nearby and, you know, there's that urgent business of the ditch to take care of. It's not right, and we are going to launch an official complaint.

Akbar forces himself to stop talking, watching his knuckles turn white as he knots his hands together in his lap.

Yes, of course, the ditch. That's what we're here to talk about. But first things first.

Bhabra does not continue and Akbar eventually raises his eyes to meet his. This man was not one to mince words. He would ask for a bribe, and would charge extra for meeting Akbar during office hours.

What will you have, Rahman Sahab, tea or coffee?

Oh! Tea. Hehehe. Definitely tea. Akbar feels himself sink deeper into the foam. How many bottoms had rubbed against the velvety fabric in this armchair's lifetime?

He should not have come.

Actually, cancel tea. I have to get back to the office, but I just wanted two minutes of your time to tell you about the ditch, so we can move forward as a residential community, united and strong.

Bhabra presses a switch, which Akbar only now notices is connected with wires and screwed onto the leg of Bhabra's armchair so that he can reach down without adjusting his posture. Electric birdsong erupts just beyond the office door, which swings open a few seconds later.

Two teas, Bhabra says to the head poking in barely long enough to hear the words.

All right, just a quick tea then. You see, the ditch poses a danger to all our children. Ditch isn't even the right word. Pit is more suitable, perhaps. Or crater. Either way, it's a cavity. And it's an invitation for mischief, that's what it truly is, and we have to eliminate it as soon as possible.

When he looks up again, Bhabra is staring at him with a face expressing exactly nothing.

Well, you can't really eliminate a cavity, can you? Akbar says in a small voice. But you can fill it up. Seal it.

He glances up and meets more blankness.

Render it invisible and relegate it to realm of memory.

Akbar swallows and vows not to speak another word until the tea arrives.

He breathes out in relief when he hears Bhabra clearing his throat.

I'm not good with words, Rahman Sahab, but I, too, have been thinking constantly about that ditch. Or whatever you prefer to call it. All I can say is that I stand with what's best for our community and especially our children, so go ahead and launch that complaint in my name, too.

Thank you, Bhabra Sahab, that's all I wanted to hear. I'll take my leave then.

Akbar raises himself but Bhabra leans forward so abruptly that Akbar retreats into his chair. Just then the door flies open and the inexorable cup of tea is placed on the glass table before Akbar, like a padlock confining him to the armchair. Bhabra relaxes into his seat as if he, too, knows that Akbar is now safely held captive.

Speaking of our children, Bhabra begins once the peon has left the room and the first sips of tea have been noisily ingested. Akbar watches the quivering zigzag of the light reflected in the milky brown of his cup. A wrinkly skin is beginning to form on the surface.

I've spoken to the principal of SPV, and he's agreed.

The skin is a perfect island in the middle of the round lake of tea. It occurs to him that when people speak of someone having it all, they mean someone like Bhabra: successful at his job, financial security, a wife and a pretty daughter at the right school.

Mr Rahman, Geeta can start at SPV after the summer!

Akbar finally looks up to meet Bhabra's stare. The blankness has been replaced by a look of sheer delight, as if he and not Akbar were Geeta's father. A shiver runs through his shoulders and then relief, as if Sakshi had gripped them from behind to make Bhabra's words real to Akbar.

That's wonderful news, Mr Bhabra. I'm eternally grateful. But is there a donation? I think I mentioned that, financially speaking—

No donation! That's the beauty of it.

But her grades? The principal knows that they slipped recently?

Mr Rahman! Good news is good news! Trust me. He's fully informed, and he wants Geeta to join for the new school year.

You must know the principal very well.

Akbar looks up to see Bhabra's eyes shift.

I've met him a few times. Bhabra clears his throat. There is one condition.

Ah.

The principal wants to start a sports focus at the school, and with Geeta being so exceptionally talented at badminton, he is willing to admit her on his new sports quota, since, as you say, her grades are somewhat lacking for such a top school.

I see.

To secure the spot on the sports quota, she will need to have shown a strong performance in a prominent tournament.

Akbar checks his impulse to sigh and presses his jaws together instead.

Of course. She needs to win Wimbledon before she can get admission.

That's tennis, Rahman Sahab. Very different. Tennis you play with your arm, badminton you play with your mind. It's chess for the body.

How interesting.

Indeed. And we're not talking international—not yet. But there is the annual Under-13 Championship happening in Delhi in early March. If she competes in that, she'll definitely win something and get admission.

That sounds like a bit of a gamble, Mr Bhabra.

Bhabra grins at Akbar, whose jaws clamp together again.

I suspected that you're the sceptical type. Here it is, black on white. Bhabra produces a sheet of paper and hands it to Akbar.

Akbar is familiar with the SPV letterhead from Geeta's last rejection letter. He reads the text once, and then again the one line stating that this is a conditional offer of admission contingent on having achieved distinction in a recent sporting event. He hands the sheet back to Bhabra.

Keep it, Rahman Sahab.

Akbar glances at the typed letter again before folding and tucking it between his thigh and the armrest.

So what if she doesn't win anything at this tournament?

Good question. The thing is: She will win.

What makes you so certain?

Because I'll make sure of it.

The umpire is your friend as well?

Bhabra's laugh erupts so suddenly that the cup in Akbar's hand almost slides off the saucer. Akbar places both items on the glass table, unable to smile at what he did not intend as a joke.

Even if he was, I would not have to avail of his friendship. Because, Rahman Sahab, I've seen your daughter play, and she's a marvel on the court. I can tell from her deception that she has a high IQ, that's how good she is!

I'm not sure the two are linked, but thank you. I hear you have been playing with her.

Like I said, a marvel!

That's very kind. But I'm not sure I understand—

Mr Rahman, I'm offering to officially coach your daughter right up to the tournament, I'll make sure she wins, to guarantee that you'll get your admission.

Mr Bhabra, I think I mentioned that due to my wife's prolonged illness, my finances have been—

I'm not going to charge you for the coaching, Mr Rahman! That would be extortion!

Right.

The wrinkly skin, his perfect island, now hangs limply over the lip of Akbar's empty cup and he resists the urge to remove it from his view.

What exactly does official coaching entail?

Oh, nothing you need to be worried about. We'll use our court, so there's no issue of transportation. We'll train five times a week, from 5 to 7 pm on weekdays, and from 9 am to 12 noon and then again from 5 to 7 pm on Saturdays. Sunday is for resting.

That sounds like a lot for a girl her age.

Mr Bhabra brings his head closer to Akbar.

Don't underestimate your daughter, Mr Rahman. Not to mention that we barely have a month before the tournament.

Bhabra waves an invisible obstacle away and laughs again. What is one month of hardship for such a life-changing opportunity?

No, Bhabra Sahab, I couldn't ask that of you. To take so much trouble, it doesn't seem right.

Arré, no trouble. You know badminton runs in my family, and I would be honoured to coach a young player as talented as your Geeta, who has been through so much at such a tender age.

She has, indeed.

If only he could pause this moment and ask Sakshi for advice! He was not equipped to make such big decisions by himself and without mulling them over for days. Bhabra's offer sounded too good to be true, but what if, just this once, it was simply true? One delicious free lunch thrown in with life's expensive menu of misery.

All right.

Akbar notices Bhabra's eyes narrowing ever so slightly as he smiles. Wonderful! It's a deal. So you just sit back now and let me take care of everything, Mr Rahman. You deserve a break, too.

Bhabra rings the bell again, and the next moment the cups are being cleared. Rahman knows this is the cue for him to leave.

As he stands, a strange thought occurs to Akbar and before he can stop himself he says, You had the letter ready and were waiting for me, Mr Bhabra. It's almost as if you knew I was coming.

We have a spiritual connection, Mr Rahman. Maybe we were brothers in another life.

Akbar pictures Sakshi snickering in the background, which manifests itself on his face as a tentative smile.

Bhabra clearly mistakes it as an affirmation of Rahman's brotherly affection and returns it with no reservation. This makes Akbar's smile expand, further encouraging Bhabra's ruminations.

Maybe I did know you were coming. You have a strong presence, Mr Rahman, and now that I think of it—yes, I could definitely sense your approach.

It bothers Akbar that Bhabra is acting as if he somehow got the better deal, even when it's Akbar whose favour has been granted. As he takes his leave from Bhabra and ambles out of the office, Akbar blows air through his lips, setting them aflutter. Then he tries smiling again, which caused him to feel so utterly relaxed a moment earlier. Maybe if Sakshi were here, she would tell him now that he was being a paranoid bore. That in this life, beauty was so common, all you had to do was see it.

Hours later, at half past midnight, he is still sitting at his desk at home, where he's been since returning from Bhabra's office, with just a short break to eat dinner with Geeta and Mummyji. He observes the smudges of ink on his fingertips, the crumpled pages with different versions of the translation arranged around him like dormant creatures. He has not found an adequate rendering for kal, and he promised Pavan to send him something last week. He would have to put something in the mail for Pavan in the morning if it was to reach in time for the editor to see it before her departure.

That's when Geeta's voice startles him.

Can't sleep, Abba.

He didn't notice her standing there, and wonders how long she has been watching him.

Before he can tell her to return to bed, she is climbing onto his lap, and he has to push his chair back to make room. Although she is almost a teenager, there is still that scent of milk emanating from the top of her scalp. She sinks into his embrace and he decides to rest his chin on her head.

Are you writing a poem?

I'm translating one.

What is it about?

How do you tell a child about that inextinguishable itch to take your own life?

It's about a man stuffing things in a bag and hanging it from a nail.

What things?

Abba sighs. He should ask her to go back to bed soon, or they would be sitting here for hours.

All kinds of things. Dreams, desires, promises. Expectations.

But they won't all fit in one bag.

This makes Abba smile and relax into the backrest again.

Good point, jaani. I'll tell Pavan you said that.

Abba?

Hm?

Vicky Uncle wants to play badminton with me in the evenings, for free.

I know.

And there is also a tournament.

Yes.

Can I participate?

Akbar sighs. Right now you must make a gargantuan effort to please the Bhabras, because they have connections to SPV.

So that means yes?

Unfortunately so. I was going to talk to you about it tomorrow.

With that, he sends her back to bed. Her comments on the poem triggered an idea that he is able to articulate only once he hears the rustling of sheets in the next room. It is a memory that sweeps in, of Sakshi careening down a steep slope on a small wooden sled in Kashmir on their first trip together, the ends of the shawl wrapped around her head tittering in the wind like a dragon's tail. He had declined joining her on this adventure, sinking deeper into the snow at the bottom of the hill as he watched his future wife gather speed. The unmitigated thrill inscribed on her face released a sense of bliss so unbearable that he kissed her right on the mouth as soon as she skidded into his orbit.

The fact that this particular memory, easily one of the most valuable, lay dormant in his mind these past eighteen months, only to be unearthed by Geeta's words in this moment, made him look forward to the future for the first time in years.

He picks up his pen with renewed zest. Three hours later Akbar puts it down again. He slips his fingertips under his reading glasses, rubs his eyes and then yawns. He leans back, unable to contain the smile that inhabits his lips. Then he writes the words *For your personal delectation* on the topmost sheet covered in his writing. He opens a drawer to retrieve a brown paper envelope, stuffs in the papers, seals it with spit and writes Pavan's address on the front.

He did it. He reworked the entire translation. It was perfect. And, with Geeta's unwitting help, the words he was looking for finally found him.

Forgotten days that are yet to come. Kal.

The sight of his hands—princely, Sakshi would call them and if he took the bait and amplified the compliment by adding *regal* and *distinguished* and go so far as *heroic*, she would clarify with a grin like a smear of honey that she had not meant fit for a monarch but unfit for physical labour—these hands now holding his attaché to his chest as he exits the car parked in front of his office building remind him with a bone-chilling jolt of an unmade phone call.

He freezes as his mind computes the fallout: the inevitable argument earlier that morning between the DC's mother and Kalra over who gets to have the stall, culminating in mutual pottery smashing; Kalra threatening to go to the papers; the DC accusing Akbar of sabotage and taking action against him. He would have to degrade himself with extravagant lies and endless promises to make up for it, and the DC would still make his life miserable for years to come. It was not his intention to reach the office so late today, but the line at the post office had been merciless, and riding the wave of exhilaration from the previous night he decided to allow himself this little indiscretion. What a mistake that had been.

I forgot, Pushpa! He blurts as he barges into the office, startling her. I simply forgot! Is it all over?

How could Four-by-Four look so satisfied in the face of such calamity! Whose side was she on?

No, sir, I called Kalra yesterday before I left the office. Just to be sure.

You called him? Akbar lets the meaning of her words unfold. So everything is fine?

Everything is fine, sir. Good morning.

Four-by-Four would have every right to reprimand him or at least point out that she knew he would forget. Instead she holds his gaze and he feels an almost ancestral love for her in that moment before he averts his eyes, as if she were a great-great-great-grandmother whom he would never know but without whom he would never have existed.

Good morning, Pushpa. Akbar drops into his chair. Thank you.

After work Akbar does not go home. The shock of the morning coupled with his acceptance the previous day of what effectively is a two-tiered bribe from Bhabra—to get Geeta into SPV through Bhabra's influence and to get her in a good position in the tournament—has left behind a strain of bitterness and he can't decide which would be more unbearable to face now: Geeta's chirpiness or Mummyji's punishing silence.

On a whim, he decides to stop at the IIC bar, determined to order that Bloody Mary which he always pretended to dislike when it was Sakshi's favourite drink, an act that allowed him to tease and flirt with her. This was their last outing as a couple before she was confined to bed, the Mary required to be virginal due to the heavy medication Sakshi was already on. Akbar felt unable to return until that day, driven by the certainty that he would find her comforting presence there, but as he sits in the cane chair he feels nothing except for the pitying glances of the waiters, whom Sakshi all knew by name. He orders a Virgin Mary, sipping it hurriedly before stepping back out into the scented air wafting over from Lodi Garden and the Coffee Shop's vents.

On the drive back he takes a detour to speak to Sakshi. If she eluded him at the bar, he would not stop driving until he found her here.

Why can't I ever get anything right? Answer me, Sakshi!

What's the matter, Akbar?

I'm such a fool! And with my luck, my translation for Pavan will probably be lost in the mail due to the mayhem in Bombay, because of course I forgot to make a copy.

Things are calming down now. The riots are over. I'm sure your letter will arrive.

And if it doesn't?

Is that really why you're so upset?

Yes and why shouldn't I be? Anyone would be upset if they had to live my life!

You mean the life of a thoughtful father loved and adored by his wonderful daughter?

Don't try to sugarcoat! You're always trying to sugarcoat!

I'm sorry you're feeling overwhelmed. I'm just reminding you of the important things.

What could be more important than having a sense of control and purpose in your life? Like that Bhabra, silly man though he is, he knows what he wants and he gets it.

Your daughter is more important than having the illusion of control.

Stop bringing Geeta into this! Do my own feelings not matter at all?

How are you feeling?

Lost.

Then find yourself again.

What does that even mean, Sakshi?

I think you should go home and tell Geeta how you feel. Talk to her. She'll understand.

She's a child!

She's your daughter. You need someone right now.

I need you.

I'm always there for you.

But you're not, are you? You're not there and never will be.

You're more than what you think you are, Akbar. Always have been.

Akbar turns the car into Kaka Nagar and pulls up in front of their building. He cannot bring himself to respond to Sakshi, whose last words sounded as if she were both proud and ashamed of him.

He knocks his head back and takes a deep breath, reminding himself that Sakshi was always right. He will go inside and share with Geeta the pain he's been through, today and all the days before. She is old enough. If he can make her understand that in this world there is little room for true genius or genuine love, she would recognise in his pain elements of her own unarticulated grief, and together they would find a way to move forward in this desolate, lonely world.

He steps out of the Maruti, accelerating his step until he is at the front door, fiddling with the key and at the same time pressing down hard on the bell.

Seconds pass. He pauses, hears no movement on the inside. He presses down again, fingertip turning white against the plastic switch before he finds the right key and is about to shove it into the hole just as the door is pulled open.

Where's Geeta?

Hé Bhag! First you come home late, and then you ring the bell like the house is on fire.

Where is she?

Taking a bath.

Now? She'll catch a cold!

She came home sweating like a donkey. Did you know that she plays badminton with that nice man from—

Nice man? When did you spend any time with him? And I thought you're against sports.

He dropped her off after practice today.

They already started? I only spoke to him yesterday!

Well, what was I supposed to do, send him away without offering him tea? He's such a smart man. And so spiritual. Maybe Geeta will learn a thing or two from him.

Mummyji skirts around Akbar to close the door behind him, nudging him into the room in the process.

Did he tell you that you two were brother and sister in a previous life?

Maybe we were, who are you to judge?

Akbar slips out of his shoes and picks them up to put them in their usual spot on the top shelf of the shoe rack.

What's this?

The shelf has been cleared of his shoes, stuffed in further down with the others. In their place, exactly in the middle, stands a pair of shiny new trainers with an imported brand embossed on their side.

Oh, he gave her these. They look expensive.

Yes, I can see that. What I want to know is who moved my shoes?

Geeta did, of course. She was so proud of them.

Proud? She was proud? Pride is a sense of satisfaction you derive from your own achievements, not from accepting gifts!

He grabs the shoes by the laces and snatches them off the shelf, taking a beeline for the bathroom door. He pictures the floor cracking under his steps, opening an abyss that he wishes would swallow him whole.

He shoves the door, which jams, and when he pushes again, harder this time, it flies open and hits the tiled wall with a bang. Geeta is pouring the last swirl of water in the bucket over her head. She starts, sitting on her red plastic stool underneath the tap, hair pasted all over her forehead like stamps as she looks up with Sakshi's big eyes. Akbar squeezes the ends of the laces between his thumb and forefinger, the shoes attached to them swaying at his knees like a scolding finger. It was ridiculous to think that he would tell her about his day and she would understand. Even Sakshi did not understand! We are born alone and we die alone.

Tell me, Geeta, do you think we're beggars that we get other people to keep gifting us things?

Geeta stares, then lowers her eyes and mumbles, But I need them.

What?! Speak up if you dare talk back to me!

Akbar is aware of the hole in Geeta's trainers, has been telling himself that soon it would be too hot for closed shoes anyway and that he could get away with not buying her new ones until after the summer. He knows he is being cruel shouting at his naked daughter in the bathroom, but he relishes the rage that turns him into a man of action. He snatches a towel from the hanger and throws it at Geeta. She wraps herself in it but stays on the stool, and Abkar takes this as permission to continue his scolding.

You think I can't buy you new shoes?

Geeta remains silent.

Answer me! Akbar digs his hand into his pocket and removes a handful of change. Here!

He tries to aim at the white tiles next to Geeta's feet but a coin strikes her toe. She doesn't even flinch, which makes Akbar avert his eyes to see a two rupee note beginning to flatten out as it absorbs the leftover water from his daughter's bath.

Why don't you go yourself to buy new shoes, since you always know everything better these days!

Akbar hears a Hé bhag coming from behind him.

At least let the poor girl get dressed before you rip her apart. You only were saying that she'll catch a cold.

Mummyji, you stay out of this!

Yes, yes, Mummyji must always stay out of everything. Mummyji is 'old-fashioned'! Next you'll ask me to stay out of my own life and die. Nonsense life this is anyway. If only Sakshi were here to see you like this!

Akbar turns on his heels, unsure what he is about to do when he feels his fingertip poking his mother-in-law's chest.

Yes, go ahead and hit me in front of your daughter!

Leave Sakshi out of this! I'm dealing with it my way!

Akbar hears a suppressed sniffle coming from behind him, and he is grateful for the chance to turn his back on Mummyji. Let them all cry! Let them share his pain in this way if all other paths are blocked.

You think I don't know that just one of the packets of cash offered to me by every import-export clown for a government contract is enough to get you into any school?

Today Geeta will learn that crying does not solve anything. If it did, Prime Ministers would call him, Akbar Rahman, to settle international disputes.

Just because I'm taking Bhabra's help doesn't mean you have to keep accepting gifts from him! Didn't Mummy and I teach you anything?

Akbar cranes his neck towards Mummyji's room and shouts, I also wish that Sakshi were here to see this!

When he turns back, Akbar feels his voice dancing as it swells.

I don't expect much from you, Geeta, but the least you can do is show me some little ounce of respect for everything I'm having to deal with here all by myself!

He wants to shake Geeta, wants to force her to make

him stop. Why isn't she saying anything, justifying his lack of control with a tantrum of her own? He remains silent, checking the impulse to fall at her feet and ask her forgiveness. He seeks out her eyes but they are fixed on the ground, so he cannot even see if she is still crying. The urge to feel her embrace is so strong that his fear of holding a limp body, no longer willing to return his affection, makes him retreat. Not intending to say it out aloud, he cannot but turn away once he hears himself mutter, I wish I were dead instead of your mother.

He takes refuge at his desk, praying that she didn't catch his words as he stares down at a page from the book he opens at random. Then he hears Geeta making her escape from the bathroom. Of course she would want to be as far away as possible from him. If he could he would do the same.

Abba never wants to see me again, so I run from the bathroom to my bed, where I slip on my pajamas, and then proceed straight to where Abba's car keys are hanging from the hook. I steal them quickly and let myself out of the front door in the most silent manner possible.

A moment later I am sitting inside our Maruti parked outside our gate. There must be a lamentable word in the Concise Abba Dictionary for transgressing beyond our gate dressed in pyjamas, but because Abba is already immensely angry with me, I am having no fear of getting caught. I lock my door so that even if I am discovered I cannot be easily accessed.

I wish I were dead instead of you! I shout. Then shout it again. I stop and listen. No response from Mummy. If I were dead like you, Mummy, I wouldn't have to deal with everything here all by myself!

Only silence. Maybe I should ask Mummy a question to cause stimulation for a reply. Why can't Abba not be so angry with me all the time? I continue to sit in the car and stretch my neck to make sure that he is not coming. The door to our flat is still. Abba must be substantially relieved that he doesn't have to see me.

Mummy? Are you there?

I listen to the deepest place in my heart as per Abba's directive, but still I can't hear her. I put the key in the ignition like I've observed Abba do many times. Maybe it only works when the car is moving. If I drive the car and finally hear Mummy's voice, she will definitely share her expertise with me in the department of steering the whole world in the right direction at all times. I turn the key. The car makes a giggling sound like it's laughing at me but does not start like it's supposed to. I try again, quicker this time. The car rumbles and shrieks. Even though Abba refused to give me driving lessons, he did tell me to C-L-U-T-C-H, which means the act of tightly grasping something, so I let go of the key and squeeze the steering wheel as hard as I can, tighter than the grip of my racket. Maybe that's how she did it.

Mummy?

As soon as I learn to drive I'm going to ask her specifically whether she agrees with Abba that I am a fully deficient daughter and whether Abba will stop being angry with me once I get admission to SPV. I try to move the gear but can't with just one hand, so I use the muscles of both of my arms to push the stick to the left and then up, making sure to swerve it with the base of my palms just like Mummy.

Mummy, waiting for you only!

I try once again to start the car but the motor just mutters something and then falls silent as soon as I let go of the key. I'll have to observe Abba more closely if I want to talk to Mummy. It is at that moment that I realise that Mummy can never ingest Abba's elaichi-and-aftershave-aroma again, which makes my eyes suddenly blurry with tears and before

Geeta can say subject to revision without notice, I am sliding out of the car and running home, turning back half-way only to remove the key and lock the car doors.

A moment later I am peeping through the doorframe of Abba's room. Abba has his face in his hands, and when he looks up I see that his eyes are red, same like mine.

Abba, it's all my fault!

No, it's my fault! What have I done?

Abba presses me against him and breathes loudly into my hair.

I'm sorry, beta. I'm sorry!

I'm sorry, Abba! I shouldn't have taken the shoes!

My voice sounds like Abba's tape recorder when the batteries are finishing. I intervene to sob and take another breath.

I shouldn't have just handed you over to that man, all for your stupid admission.

All Vicky Uncle wants is to make me a real champion, Abba. I want that, too, because then I can play for money and buy my own foreign shoes. I don't want to make you angry, Abba, I just want to be—

Shhh, beta. Abba is wiping his eyes and stroking my back and I try to breathe regularly like a law-abiding citizen.

Abba picks me up and carries me to the bed, which automatically makes the tears stop. He cradles me in his lap like a substantially augmented baby.

What else has Vicky Uncle promised you?

That one day the whole country will know my name!

Abba swallows as if in slow motion, which I have identified as a sign for him wanting to say something and not knowing how. Maybe now he will finally believe that badminton is my way of steering the whole world in the right direction.

And when he talks to you, or when he trains you, does he touch your hand the way he did when we went to their house and I came into the bedroom?

No, Abba! The tears start again, because Abba is misconstructing what I am trying to tell him.

Enough crying now, beta. Come.

Abba lifts my chin and smiles into my eyes. But the hairy bulge between his eyebrows is still there.

Vicky Uncle will definitely get me admission at SPV, I say, knowing that this is what Abba wants to hear.

Yes but at what price?

He promised me that it's all for free!

Abba shakes his head slightly, then says, So when he's training you, does he sometimes come over to your side of the court to show you, you know, how to hold the racket properly?

I know how to hold the racket properly, Abba! This particular misconstruction makes me giggle.

Abba takes a deep breath and examines his hands. My poor child, he says. If only your mother were here. She would know exactly what to do.

About the shoes?

When Abba looks at me his eyes are black and shiny like a fresh stamp pad. He has the saddest lips that ever smiled.

You really like being on the court, no?

It's my number one favourite.

And you're sure he has not misbehaved?

It is advisable at this point not to tell Abba about Vicky's provocation of Saleem Uncle.

Because if he has I don't care two hoots about SPV or anything else, I'll never let him so much as talk to you again! I'm sorry I said to you earlier that you must do what he says and do it well. Of course you don't.

I'm afraid that the parent cadre is about to end my training sessions, just like that, so I say, No, Abba, he's gargantuanly well-behaved.

This somehow seems to worry Abba, though the next second he sits up straight, which almost ejects me from his lap. I pull myself up by his sleeve.

I've an idea. From now on, whenever you go for training with Vicky Uncle, I'll come watch.

Really, Abba? You'll come watch me play?!

I think that when I am finally a real champion this will be the moment I will remember for when Abba turned pro-badminton.

Just promise me you won't meet him without me. Not once.

Double promise!

Maybe Abba can even learn from Vicky how to train me so that later Abba can be my Coach Sir.

But do I have to return the shoes?

Keep them. I'll not give him the pleasure of causing a scene. But he'll know that I'm watching him.

Thank you, Abba! Thank you thank you thank you!

Although I never knew that fights with Abba could lead to so many good things in one go, there is something in Abba's voice that sounds like a warning.

Abba?

Yes, jaani?

I don't want you to be dead like Mummy.

Fully against all my intents and purposes, this suddenly renews Abba's flow of tears. He presses me against him so hard that I can barely breathe. His sob is making my body shake, and I hug him as tight as I can. After a while we are both just breathing like regular bidders.

Abba whispers in my ear: I miss her so much. I want to do everything right by you but I just can't the way she used to. I'm full of mistakes, Geeta, and I hate that you have to witness that every single day. Your mother was—she was like my personal alphabet that gave meaning and direction to the whole language of my existence. I'm lost without her. I'm confused all the time. I'm weak.

Abba's tears stop suddenly, as if his words turned off the tap. Then he continues, his voice no longer shaky. But I would not trade my life for anyone else's. I'm grateful for everything I have.

I don't want Abba to start crying again, so I say, I'm also full of mistakes, Abba.

No, you're not, Geeta. You're everything your mother and I wanted in a daughter. The fact that you say that shows I've failed you. But I'm going to do better from now on, I promise.

Me, too, Abba. Me, too.

My eyes are glued to Abba's foot pressing down on the clutch as he turns the key in the ignition. His feet do a quick dance as he moves the gear and suddenly his foot is off the clutch and his other one is pushing on the pedal to the right.

Won't you just show me how to start the car, Abba?

The parent cadre just shoots me a look.

You're still not letting go?

I try to secretly watch Abba's hands and feet but it is impossible to keep track and to boot Abba is now watching me, so I lean back in my seat and look out the window until Abba parks the car in front of Sonodyne. We have reverted to Khan Market to buy a cake for Naniji, because Abba, very Abbalike, feels substantially guilty about his apoplepsic attack yesterday and she very Nanijilike is substantially sulking about it. Abba's words. He made me look up apoplepsy in the dictionary right after, and I was so relieved that we were back to looking up words that I didn't have the heart to tell him that I couldn't locate it.

As we go up the stairwell to Pat-a-Cake, each step suitably modifies the foul smell from the lane into that of fresh bread. The shop itself is small, with a glass and aluminium counter display of biscuits, cakes, tarts and patties on the right. The bread is arranged in a pyramid on top of the counter, the plastic sheaths crisp and a little foggy from the warmth of the loaves. After the counter you may kindly proceed to the left into a white-tiled seating area with small Formica tables and chairs. Each table has a red-and-white chequered tablecloth of tissue paper and a water glass at its centre with a money plant in it.

I press my finger against the glass. That one!

Not the pineapple cream? She liked it for her birthday.

I shake my head firmly and Abba delivers instructions for retrieval and furnishment of chocolate cake with the words

I'm Sorry Dearest Mummyji

We Love You

Uncle, can you initiate action for two hearts next to 'Mummyji' and three exclamation points after 'You'?

I glance at Abba. Rather than stealing pages from his files, I copied three sentences from the one lying in his office bag into my notebook this morning. His eyes are narrow but there is no other sign of admiration for my language augmentation. The man is still staring at me, then looks at the parent cadre and asks, Sir, you are authorising this action?

He's smiling. Abba half nods, half shrugs, and then tells me to stay exactly where I am while he goes to buy cheese and idli mix, which the ration shop in Bapa Nagar doesn't sell. While Abba is speaking I hear a familiar laugh from the seating area around the corner from the counter, so I wait until he is gone and then inch my way to that section without the cakeman noticing.

What I see calls for instant freezage: sitting at the very last table over two half-eaten patties are Faraz and Sitara. Sitara is examining Faraz's open palm in her hands, which he is finding very funny. I go up to them. Faraz jumps a little when he sees me and their hands slip under the table.

Smalls!

Are you two exchanging dearness allowances?!

I think of Sitara's drawing and wonder if the boy in it was Faraz. Now that I am thinking about it he did look a lot like him.

What? No, ya, Smalls. Hey, is your Dad here, too? Faraz is squeezing himself against the back wall as if he wants to push it away.

Ya but he's downstairs buying cheese.

Oh good. Interim relief spreads on Faraz's face. Cheese toh is the best.

Sitara was searching for something deep inside her bag but now she looks up and says, Oh hi, Geeta. We're just waiting for some friends from school.

But you go to different schools.

Faraz and Sitara look at me like two faulty bidders, then Faraz states, You're right.

It's very uncivil not to tell the truth.

Uncivil! Oho, Smalls. I was afraid that all this backhand clearing, reverse slicing and deep smashing is going to properly fry your brain, but I didn't think it would happen so quickly. Faraz lets his lips hang.

I'm in the process of developing an interlicked.

Renewed giggling from Sitara at her bag.

The real truth is, Smalls, Sitara is helping me with my homework.

But you're the class topper!

That's the thing, if she doesn't help me, I won't be. I think my own interlicked is not nearly as developed as it used to be.

Sitara blinks and nods.

So where are your textbooks?

Faraz leans into me, as if Sitara is not to hear what he's saying: Sitara won't do it for free and my cash flow is limited, so I'm paying her in chicken patties. He whispers, She's on number seven!

Sitara shoves Faraz and now it's my turn to giggle. Too bad Sitara is not as generous as her father with her teaching fees, though I'm not sure whether or not to fully believe him.

Smalls, do me a favour, ya? Go and make sure your Dad doesn't come here and don't tell him you met us, okay? And definitely don't tell your Coach Sir either. Actually, best not to tell anyone at all.

Okay but why?

Because I'll get in trouble, na, for not being class topper anymore!

Khuda HAAfiz pops into my head and I quickly nod. Ya okay, promise.

I wave goodbye before Abba comes looking for me. When the parent cadre returns I say, Abba, can I have chicken patty?

Abba's eyebrows agglomerate. Cake AND patty?

On our way home, picking patty crumbs from my clothes, I think about the first time I saw Faraz. We had just moved to Kaka Nagar, and Mummy and I would drive around the colony together before dinner to, as she put it, find our bearings. One day we discovered a shortcut which took us through a narrow unpaved path that cut through the colony. There, on a pile of discarded bricks, sat a boy, same age as Geeta now, his head in his hands. Mummy stopped the car and went to talk to him. I watched from inside. I couldn't hear what they were saying but eventually I got out of the car to remind Mummy of my postponed presence. Mummy must have been saying something funny, because just then the boy smiled, and it was fully sideways like I'd never seen before.

After that day, the three of us started meeting in the afternoons at the Club House for a game of baddy.

Whenever I think of this memory I have to remind myself that the boy was Faraz, because I never saw him cry after that and later it was usually me who was crying, because once Mummy fell ill, Faraz would come ring our doorbell every single day and with his silly jokes and his teasing would convince me to come to the court to play badminton with him, even when I didn't feel like it because Mummy was back in the hospital and I didn't know when I could go visit her next.

All this makes me want to inform Sitara that I am Faraz's senior-most friend in all of Kaka Nagar, and that teasing Yours Truly always has been and always will be his topmost priority, because it comes before, during and after our joint badminton, no matter how much Sitara distracts him from his studies first so she can study extra hard with him later.

The chair is eagerly awaiting the parent cadre's presence. It's almost six and I can see Vicky pacing the court as we cross our gate. Even though we are so late, I am substantially excited that Abba is coming to court with me for the first time. He will get to see me serve and observe my deception and my improving footwork. Of course, it would have been preferable if he hadn't made me cancel practice on Friday post-Khan Market and then again on Saturday, because he had a severe headache, even though he didn't mind sitting at his desk all day instead, reading a new book of poems.

You're late, Vicky chides me, and I nod because I was never late for practice on my own. I want to tell Vicky that I had to wait for the parent cadre, who was in urgent need of feeding after returning from office. My request for permission to go solo was denied.

Oh, don't be so hard on her, Mr Bhabra, Abba tells Vicky. She's only a child.

You're right, Mr Rahman, she is a child. The only problem is that there are other children, lesser badminton players than your daughter, who will defeat her at the U-13s because they came on time every day.

I can tell that Vicky's opinion of Abba is undergoing a downward revision not just with every instance of lateness but with every statement from Abba's mouth.

We begin our warm-up routine. Abba is standing too close for me to stretch properly, so I secretly move away a little.

Don't overstretch, Geeta.

She's doing fine, Mr Rahman.

Abba shoots air out his nostrils.

People don't know that you can get slipped disc from meditating wrong.

I can promise you that she's not going to get a slipped disc, at least not while she's on court with me.

A promise is a promise is a promise, Abba says, smiling but also not.

The truth is, I really like having Abba here. He is talking substantially more than he is supposed to, but all this is a small price for the fact that he is about to see me deliver some absolutely unmissable drives and smashes.

After the warm-up, Vicky makes an announcement. Today, Geeta, we are stepping up our game. Today we begin our new agenda: the reverse slice drop shot, which follows a cross-court trajectory and requires perfect control over your racket. My father was famous for this shot, and given your special talent for deception, I have a feeling that this might become your signature shot, too.

I glance at Abba to see if he heard the compliment, but he is looking at Vicky like he's a rioter at the protest march.

Because with it you can deceive your opponent in the most special way: by finding exactly the right balance between a gentle stroke and sufficient power.

I am not sure what Abba means when he says, Sounds sadistic.

Vicky blinks at Abba, then calls me to the net. He has pulled something out of his bag and is walking up to me. It's a photocopied picture of a man leaping into the air.

Geeta, you need to understand one thing: in badminton, power is subtle. Greed for power is punished. Why? Because you have to set up a winning shot. No shortcuts. You need to really work a rally, you have to wait for the right moment and learn to recognise it when it's there. Do you understand?

I nod.

You, my dear, display an eagerness on court that borders on restlessness. I've told you so from the beginning. You have to streamline and pace yourself. You have to iron out those folds before they become mountains and turn to stone.

You're quite the poet, Mr Bhabra.

Vicky ignores Abba, smiles and points at the image. I am suspecting that Vicky is speaking louder now to make sure the parent cadre keeps hearing what he's saying: This was my father's strength and I want you to have his picture so that you can look at it and remember what I just told you: Patience and hard work is everything.

Thank you, Coach Sir. I take the picture and put it in my pocket. From the sideline, I hear Abba muttering, Stating the obvious.

So let's get to work!

As soon as Vicky comes over to my side of the court, Abba jumps up and stands behind me.

Mr Rahman, could you please step to the side or you'll get hit.

Sure, sure, Abba says and moves a few inches.

Vicky continues, Let's do the shot breakdown.

He takes up the stance and I imitate him.

One, you're in a sideways position. Two, both arms are up in the air. Three, shoulders are also sideways, racket grip is at eye level. Your weight is on your racket foot.

Vicky turns back to me and twists my shoulder further. Abba comes closer again. Vicky lifts my arms by pulling up my wrists. Abba clears his throat slowly and loudly.

There. That's your standby position. Now listen carefully: the key is to hit the shuttle at its highest point. Watch. Vicky takes up position again and swings the racket in slow motion.

See: rotate shoulders forward, elbow up, wrist locked! Then slice the invisible shuttle inwards with your racket face angled outwards! Then follow through the shot so that your racket's end point is your non-racket foot. Geeta, you're not looking!

I am!

You racket face angles—?

Inwards?

Vicky sighs.

Outwards!

Vicky starts repeating the instructions, and I'm really trying to listen and get it right, so that there is no need for Vicky to lift my wrist again, because I think next time Abba will do or say something to stop him. I kneel on the floor and re-tie my shoelaces, making sure that I tie up all my thoughts in the process. I don't need them up here. I tie a double knot. And add another.

One: Stand by! Two: Reverse slice! Three: Follow through!

My trick works. When I stand up again, my mind is empty. As we go through the swing motion again and again, Abba gradually retreats to the sideline.

I realise that even when the Greek Chorus makes up my audience, I never feel watched the way I do now with the parent cadre, but I think that must be because I am so happy he's there and want to make sure I only play my best game for him. I'm sure soon I'll be able to bring the sum total of my mind to focus on what Vicky is saying.

We are doing drills now, with Vicky hitting the shuttlecock so that I can slice it.

In two out of three shots, the shuttlecock spins well beyond the sideline.

That doesn't look out to me, sir! Abba says to Vicky, which I wish he wouldn't.

It's out, Abba.

The parent cadre smirks. With Mummy's lisp he says, Spoilsport! Then adds, What happened to your special talent for deception?

I still have to practice to get it right!

Not that kind of deception, Mr Rahman. You're confusing her.

Vicky is right. All this conversation with Abba is making my brain wobbly like Naniji's fruit custard. I blow air from my mouth and close my eyes for a moment. Why is it not working, Vicky Uncle? Coach Sir?

What did I tell you earlier, Geeta, hm? Have you not been listening to me at all today?

Patience and hard work, I mumble.

Louder, please.

Patience and hard work!

Thank you. Today all I want is for you to get a hang of the motions involved.

We continue with the drills. Every time my racket makes contact, the parent cadre applauds but also not.

Your hand is too high, Geeta! Your other hand! Again!

I think she's doing it very well!

She's learning, Mr Rahman.

We're taking a break from the drills when Abba brings me my water bottle and promulgates, Chalo, I think it's enough for today, no? Don't want my daughter to drop shots till she drops. Hehehe.

The parent cadre's index finger nudges me to the sideline. I deposit a big mouthful in my stomach with painfully rushed swallowing, resulting in water sprayage on Abba's arms prior to mouth wipeage on sleeve.

But we haven't even started the practice match!

Though I really like having Abba there to witness my staggering growth rate as a badminton champion-in-progress, I think that maybe it would make it even more special if he didn't come to the court with me every single time I practice, but only once in a while.

You can do it tomorrow. I'm sure Mr Bhabra has better things to do than to play with you all evening. We have already imposed on his free time too much.

To my utmost surprise, Vicky does not raise a single objection. He simply nods and says, You're absolutely right, Mr Rahman.

Vicky starts packing his rackets, towel and shuttlecocks into his bag.

Say 'thank you,' beta.

I shout Thank you to Vicky but he's already turned away from us and is waving goodbye as if this is exactly how proceedings are supposed to go, as if he has only been waiting for an excuse to suspend training. I decide against seeking clarification slash help from Vicky at this juncture, because I don't want there to be a fight between Coach Sir and parent cadre.

Abba puts his arm around me as we walk back towards our gate.

Shall we read a book together? Your pick.

I shake my head and wanting to but still trying not to sound angry, I say, Too tired.

Good thing we finished training early today, then.

I say nothing, though I substantially disagree.

Did I tell you my translation of Pavan's poem is getting published in America? Everyone loved it! And you know what else? Today was the first day with no news of communal violence on the front pages. First time since December! I think things really are calming down, finally.

As Abba keeps talking, I think of my champa tree, of how the badminton court looks like a cement lifeboat from up there, and of all the new words that I have been most diligently copying from Abba's files to Geeta's notebook via my dictionary, and then I dutifully acknowledge that my feeling about this arrangement is now subject to fair adjustment: though I really like having Abba there for my training, I would like it even better if he never came to the court with me again.

The day after curtailment of practice was Tuesday: match day with Faraz. It is the only day Abba grants me permission to go to the court alone, because like all Uncles and Aunties in Kaka Nagar, he assigns older brother-like qualities to Faraz, because of his Gandhiji specs and soft voice.

Faraz and I waited for fifteen minutes, played knocks and warmed up, but Vicky did not make his appearance. So I went upstairs to summon him, my stomach heavy as if I had just swallowed a brick. It was the maid who opened and told me that the sahab log had all gone out. Faraz and I played anyway, but it was not the equivalent without Vicky there to tell me what I was doing right or wrong, which is the key to my championhood.

Now it is Wednesday afternoon, and I am not sure whether Vicky's absence yesterday signifies that we will no longer train together.

Abba has taken sick leave due to a cold and is taking a

nap, ditto Naniji. I, too, am lying on my bed and observing the ceiling fan, trying to make my eyes trace the isometric path of a single blade, even though it's still too chilly for ventilation but I don't want to fall asleep again, because my dream just now was that someone was making me hammer a nail into a wall of sand, and I kept failing for obvious reasons, and in the dream this meant I had to die.

It is the middle of February but still I am wrapped in my razai, wondering why God made it so that it's much cosier to lie under a blanket with a running fan than with no fan and no blanket. If Mummy were in attendance, she would be lying awake with me and together we would be accelerating time.

I get up and visit Naniji on her cot in the living room. There is a slim gap between her eyelids, as if she doesn't fully trust the world to let her sleep in peace. I can observe segments of the blue rings around her black eyes that Abba informed me come with age. Every time Naniji breathes out, her cheeks become two small balloons and she produces a sound like fffffff, as if the plain act of sleeping demands at least a show of effort. A bubble has formed in one corner of her mouth, where it sits shivering and dreaming of escape. I burst it with my pinkie and move on to the parent cadre in the bedroom, who appears to have collapsed battling the white bed sheet that is wrapped around his left ankle, squashed under his right leg and heaped into a pile on his exposed belly button. One arm is flung over his eyes, while the other is blocking the empty half of the mattress. It's been a long time since I remembered that this is the same bed that Mummy slept in with him, and I am having an excess of badminton-non-impacted love for Abba for not having exchanged it for a smaller one.

On the table next to it lies the content of the parent cadre's pocket: a few scrunched-up notes, a pen, an almost-empty packet of Goldflake, his car keys.

I could take the car keys. I could go for a quick solo chakkar of the park and ask Mummy what to do about my badminton practice. I have duly observed Abba start the engine many times now, and today would be a suitable day to feel like an independent young woman.

I decide against it. If I hurt myself or injure the car, Abba will hang me upside down and never talk to me again.

The indigo curtains turn the afternoon light blue. Up near the rod, the two sides of cloth begin to separate in the shape of a triangle, which a ray of sun is using to escape from the heat outside. In celebration, it is making all the tiny bits of dust in the room dance.

Abba is sleeping so noiselessly that I have to focus on the rise and fall of his chest to see if he is still alive. A thought flies into my head: If it had been up to me, would I have chosen Abba or Mummy to stay back with me in life?

On the one hand, Mummy was perfect in every way. On the other, the parent cadre has a tendency to display faulty behaviour. So I think I would have chosen Mummy if it had been up to me, especially because independent young women should be allowed to go to the badminton court on their own, and she would have known that.

Without any prior warning, Abba's noiseless breathing explodes into a snore so loud it makes me jump involuntarily. I feel my heart thumping inside me and take a deep breath.

Why does Abba always have to give me such bad surprises? Now his breathing is a mixture of noiseless and explosive. Why can't he just choose one behaviour instead of being silent one moment and loud the next?

I lean over Abba and place a thumb each over his nostrils, like lids over two tiny pots. With his next inhalation my thumb-dhakkans are pulled shut, and a slight shiver passes through Abba like when water begins to boil. His mouth opens with a funny pop and now he is snoring loudly without taking a break only. I pinch his nose between thumb and forefinger and cup my other hand over his mouth. I see myself hammering a nail into a wall of sand again as I increase the pressure until, with a sudden jolt, Abba jerks his head to the side and smacks his lips.

A new thought arrives: If Mummy was in such a hurry to get away from life, which includes me, she was not perfect after all. And I'm sure Abba didn't mean to stop my practice and cancel my chances of playing and winning at the U-13. Not least because he still wants me to get into SPV. And I'm sure Vicky will keep training me. He promised to get me admission. I carefully untangle the chadar from the parent cadre and cover him with it.

At least Abba doesn't die easily.

I take the car keys and a moment later I am sitting inside our Maruti, which the afternoon sun has turned into a hot case like the one in the school cafeteria.

Hi, Mummy.

No reply.

I put the key in the ignition but don't turn it yet. Instead, I push down on the clutch like I've watched Abba do. I try to remember how exactly Mummy used to hold the steering wheel and experiment with different versions: with just the left hand or just the right, with my two index fingers, with both hands at the top, side or bottom of the steering wheel. Pressing down on the clutch tickles the muscles in my thigh. I let go. Instead of my foot pushing down, the pedal shoves back my foot. I try again. This time I count to ten. The tickling intensifies but I make it to the end. Maybe this can be good practice for badminton also, since Vicky has said that I need to improve my overall fitness. I do it again and again, until I no longer have the strength to push the pedal down even just halfway.

Mummy? Can't you please make it so that Abba lets me go to practice alone again?

I listen more carefully to the silence this time to determine whether this is a Mummy silence or non-Mummy one. Not a word, no sharp inhalation. Not even eyelids blinking. Clearly, Mummy cannot hear me when the car is switched off. I turn the key in the ignition. The engine comes on.

Mummy! I shout. Mummy!

Since she cannot be having more important business to attend to than talking to me, it must be concluded that she cannot hear me unless the car is moving.

I could press down on the clutch one more time and change the gear by shoving it with the base of my hand like I've seen Abba do, and then somehow make the car drive me around, but I decide not to try this time, because I promised Abba that I wouldn't, and a promise should not be exchangeable like a wrong size or a broken antenna. Feeling commendable for doing exactly as Abba asked me to, I am now sure that it was all a big misconstruction with Vicky, and that he'll be happy to hear when I see him on Monday that due to abundant clutch pressings I am now excessively overall fitter.

It's been exactly one week now since we stopped training. Vicky failed to make an appearance on Wednesday also, and on Thursday afternoon Pepsi Aunty announced to Abba at our doorstep that we were to come for interview at SPV at the end of March but that Vicky was too busy at work to continue training me. Abba was so happy about this double news that he took me and Naniji to Nirula's right away, but even two scoops of 21 Love, which adds up to 42 Love, tasted as bland as cork.

On Friday I thought about visiting Aunty's Bird Clinic, but Abba said that the brigadier, who is also her husband, told him at the Safal Shop that Bird Aunty, whom Abba always refers to by her full name, Benita Philips, is sick with a stomach upset. So I sat down at the bottom of the mud room to be alone with Geeta. Even though the grown-ups are in a perpetually non-compliant mood about the ongoing ditch situation, I personally deem the mud room a most agreeable extension to the Club House, especially now that I have been officially abandoned by my Coach Sir.

Only when I heard Vicky's office car approaching from the other side did I race up to street level.

Why can't we keep training, Uncle?

I'm too busy, Geeta,

But you weren't busy before.

Yah, well, that was before your father started breathing down my neck.

Abba's explosive snore echoed in my ears and I stay silent.

I really don't know what to do, Geeta, but I can't train you with him around, distracting you and questioning me constantly. I thought he was just a regular reluctant, but he's a cynic to the core. Those are the impossible ones. I failed you, Geeta. I failed us.

Although I would have needed my dictionary to fully clutch Vicky's meaning, I nodded with utter comprehension, and said, But what about the tournament?

Vicky sighed, looked at me and said, The neighbours are also gossiping about my 'motives.' Even that cop came to talk to me again. Sorry, but it's over, Geeta. The cat's out of the bag.

Can't we put it back in?

Have you ever tried putting a cat inside a bag, Geeta?

In protest of the parent cadre's misbehaviour and Vicky's giving up, I have rejected playage of badminton ever since, even though I am now once again permitted to go to the Club House alone. It is substantially harder than I thought to be noticed as a rebel through and through.

Now it's Monday again, one comprehensive week after we stopped training, and I have just come home from school to find a Bombay Dyeing plastic bag hanging from the latch of our front door. I pull out its contents. BADMINTON GAZETTE, it says on the cover of the magazine, and below it, THE OFFICIAL ORGAN OF THE BADMINTON ASSOCIATION OF ENGLAND. Vicky showed me a picture of his father in it last time, though this cover has a different image. It smells so strongly of naphthalene balls that I keep it at arm's length and breathe to the side. There is a yellow sticker on it stating HANDLE WITH CARE! in big letters. Vicky told me that he had found old badminton magazines at a flea market in London and the handwriting does look very Vickylike—grown-up but also not. I check the date on the top right of the cover: November 1946. I cannot help releasing a loud sigh. It appears that 'Geeta the Future Badminton Champion' is now ancient history. Vicky must have put the magazine here for me to find so that I can continue my badminton education on paper at least, even though it's my off paper education that I am missing most dearly.

After lunch I take the magazine to my bed. On page one there is an ad in the corner entitled A Boon to Women Badminton Players. I read on: Bervic Patent Corset Garters promises to all women who prefer to discard Stockings on suitable occasions a full and modern sporting experience.

I consider tearing out the ad and showing it to Abba ahead of my next birthday but then I remember the yellow sticker.

I start reading the first article, entitled *The Great Resumption*:

For the whole of the past seven long years hundreds of thousands of Badminton players in our country have been eagerly awaiting the time when it would be possible to forget many of the things which worried us in our time of stress and once again be able to spend as many hours as we desired in coaxing a piece of cork, decorated with lovely white feathers, over an equally harmless piece of netting.

I re-read the passage. Could it really be that the writer is having full awareness of Geeta's badminton impediment? It provides interim relief to know that I am not the only badminton player in the world with curtailment of court time.

The war in Europe ended eighteen months ago, and yet a vast number of halls are still cluttered up with various official and unofficial belongings, which had been dumped in them by various governmental authorities. This is deplorable in the extreme.

Maybe I should copy these sections for Abba and slip them into one of his files for leisurely reading? Then he might begin to sincerely regret interfering in my badminton game through his official body. My eyes move on to the next line:

It is time that our governmental authorities gave a little attention to our game, which is able to do so much to provide the very essential athletic exercise so necessary to the retention of that physical fitness without which Britain cannot keep her place foremost amongst the nations of the world.

If I replace Britain with Geeta and nations with class toppers, Abba is bound to at least attempt to reconsider his view. Perhaps I should replace *keep* with *achieve* for more accuracy and precision, however. I am going through the rest of the magazine, trying to think of how to get Abba to read these lines without using my handwriting or tearing the magazine. I could cut out letters from old newspapers. Or get my teacher to write it in adult handwriting, though this will generate unwelcome commentary.

I turn the next page and there is a picture of a piano. It is part of an article called *In Pursuit of a Limber Wrist* and below the picture it is stated: *I learnt to play the piano as a child, and my teacher used to prescribe me a course of badminton every now and then to improve my staccato du poignet. I figure the benefits of this exercise go both ways.*

I consult my dictionary to find out the concise meaning of certain words and then take note of the fact that since I am not allowed to continue my training, I could at least attempt to use this time pursuing my limber wrist.

In the evening we all are gathered at the Club House, and I keep thinking I have forgotten to put on my shoes or wear clothes even, until I realise that it's the first time I am here without my racket.

I am sitting among the Greek Chorus, something I only do in accompaniment of Faraz. The topic of conversation: Chole Bhature at Sweets Corner in Sundar Nagar vs. at Nathu's in Bengali Market.

Theirs is too spicy, Shipwreck opines.

Yum, but, Faraz controverts.

A short distance away from our circle sits Sitara under the jamun tree with a comic book. Although she's pretending that she isn't, everyone is in possession of the knowledge that she is listening to our dialogues. In a moment of silence, I notice all of us following Faraz's gaze to my former Coach Sir's daughter.

Shipra states: Buddha got enlightenment under an apple tree, so maybe some people think jamuns work, too.

No, stupid, Faraz counter-states. That was Newton. Buddha was figs.

Figs toh I love!

I think you're confusing fruit salad with enlightenment, Shipwreck.

I watch Sitara suppressing a smile via intense blinking at the open page in her lap.

Stop being mean to me, Faraz! Shipwreck shoves Faraz and pouts at him.

Faraz is laughing now. Not my fault! You make it too damn easy, yah!

Having awaited this natural break in conversation, I widen my nostrils and breathe in sharply like I'm Mummy about to say something important and ask, Does anyone here have a piano I can borrow?

Faraz interrupts his laughter to divert his eyes towards me, then begins again. You're not alone, Shipwreck! Clearly, I'm surrounded by geniuses.

I ignore Faraz, whose main life plan is always to tease me, and repeat my question.

Angad asks what I want a piano for, and because I know they won't understand and use it only to create an opportunity to laugh at me, I say, To improve my staccato.

This makes everyone giggle.

Smalls, yah! All you have to do to improve your stinkato is to take a bath!

Now everyone is laughing out loud. Even Sitara is looking straight at us and smiling with unnecessary broadness. Maybe Faraz is not my Sugreeva but my Bali. In any case he behaves like a first-class monkey. I should ask Naniji why Ram would rely on either of them for help. Suddenly, with the image of Naniji, an idea shoots into my head like Ram's arrow. I jump up and before Faraz can finish shouting, Hey, Smalls! Joke, yah, come back! I am running homewards and into Naniji's room.

Anu leans out of the window. Moments before: a cough. Definitely feverish. Perhaps tuberculoid.

Someone is sick, or what? Anu thinks she is thinking, embarrassed the next instant to hear her voice speaking the thought out aloud.

She glances up through the creeper growing rampant on the outer wall to see if the source of the menace is located at the neighbour's above. And that's when she fails to notice her granddaughter dashing past. Anu closes the window—no need to invite the germs in—therefore missing the sound of quick footsteps approaching. The next second she is startled by Geeta bursting into her room like a balloon under pressure.

She keeps the volume of the television set low precisely so she can keep track of the comings and goings around the house, even though the odd film song or jingle would probably help to lift her spirits. But the cough messed everything up. Now she is unprepared for whatever misdeeds her granddaughter is about to involve her in.

Naniji! Teach me harmonium, no! I'm free now and I'm informed that you're also free. Shall we start?

Before she can reply, Anu reaches for the packet of Cadbury éclairs on her cot that doubles as a sofa during the day, untwists a wrapper and pops the candy into her mouth. She bites down on the chewy shell, forcing out the chocolate paste. Soon it blends into a thick, chunky pulp in her mouth. Now she feels calmer. Maybe she closed the window just in time to keep the stranger's cough from settling down in her throat.

She sits on the cot and only now do Geeta's words register in Anu's mind. She makes her jaws work extra hard to eliminate all lumps before ingesting the liquid.

Since when are you interested in learning harmonium?

The girl's breath is still accelerated when she replies, Since always! It's just that my time has only now freed up. So can we start?

They say in old age you revert to childhood, but Anu finds no trace of her granddaughter's capriciousness in herself.

Nobody in the history of music ever learned to play an instrument in a hurry.

I'm just so eager to learn!

Anu points at the god on the television screen with a stern finger. The jungle of plastic plants around him gives the setting the look of a puppet show. She must write to the channel to tell them to use real plants, and this time she mustn't forget.

Playing music is a divine activity, Geeta, it's a gift to the gods. So we must always show our respect to the instrument. Through patience and devotion.

I'm ready to be fully patient and excessively devotional, Naniji. Just please teach me now, na!

Anu scrapes the spit, now coloured brown, from her lower lip with the nail of her thumb, which she smears first onto her index finger and then on the seam of her sari. Though she has no desire to find out what preposterous chain of events prompted this sudden interest, the idea that her granddaughter should finally and explicitly want to learn something from her is not unappealing. There are many important lessons the girl needs to imbibe, and fast.

All right.

Thank you! Thank you! Shall I get the harmonium?

Geeta slips off the bed and peeks under it before Anu can stop her. There is a system to how the objects beneath are arranged, starting with the metal trunk that went with her to the groom's house on her wedding day, and she does not want Geeta messing around down there.

What harmonium? Anu says loudly to lure her granddaughter out from under the bed.

Geeta's head reappears. *Your* harmonium!

I don't have a harmonium.

But you're always talking about how it's gathering dust!

It is! My harmonium was gathering dust in Kanpur and is almost certainly doing the same now in Delhi.

So where is it?

I told your parents it was as stupid idea. I was finding it hard enough to play it with just one good eye, so what are those poor children going to do with it, you tell me.

What children, Naniji?

Though she tells herself that she does not do it on purpose, Anu likes to see the confused looks on people's faces when she talks. Young people these days think they know everything, but the truth is they understand nothing. She is just providing a public service in humility. Not that anyone ever wants to listen to her anyway.

It was donated to the Blind School when I moved to this house.

Geeta's face sinks fast, like a big ship.

Then how will you teach me if we don't have a harmonium?

I thought you would have arranged for one, since you're so eager to learn.

She tries to veil her disappointment with a cutting tone, quickly plucks another éclair from the packet in her lap and savours the calm spreading in her gut as the flavoured paste oozes into her cheeks.

Geeta stands, says, Okay, Naniji, let me see what I can do.

Then she disappears again.

Anu hears Geeta in the next room dial a number on the squat black phone that Anu has not used since Sakshi's passing. She has nobody to call now, and the sound, which mimics her son-in-law's snoring that she hears through the walls when she lies awake at night, makes her lips twitch with displeasure.

Hhhnnngg kkrrr

Hng kr

Hhngg kkrr

And then Geeta's voice, Hi Pushpa Aunty, can I please talk to Abba?

From the moment she met him, Anu felt that Akbar was too serious for Sakshi, too focused on his own thoughts. She even told her daughter so, but of course Sakshi pinned any criticism of Akbar on Anu not wanting her daughter to marry a Muslim. Young people and their overconfidence. When he was finally cured of his poetry affliction and took up a respectable profession, she was surprised to hear that it was not just any job, but a secure position with one of the world's most powerful institutions, the Government of India, though meanwhile she has given up all hope that one day he will start acting the part.

Abba, can you ask Saleem Uncle whether we can borrow his harmonium?

Anu finds it interesting that her granddaughter always speaks to her father in Hindi when she wants something from him. Which is often.

Please, Abba, please ask him, na. He can take it back whenever he wants to play it himself and we can have it while he goes to office.

Another, shorter pause.

To play it! Geeta exclaims. Anu's lips commit to a smile while Akbar seems to have something longer to say before Geeta gets a word in again: But it's not an 'antic'! It's a divine activity, and fully beneficial for your wrist to boot—

Geeta's tone turns plaintive. Can you at least ask for ours back from the Blind School?

Before she hangs up Geeta grumbles an English goodbye into the phone.

Anu expects her granddaughter to show up in her room again, but the flat is completely silent—a suspicious sign—and Anu slips off the bed to make sure her granddaughter is not getting up to her usual mischief.

Anu walks unheard towards Geeta's room and peeks

around the corner. The girl is lying on her bed, her head hidden behind a magazine. Considering the fact that this family is always short of money, it amazes Anu that more things always show up in Geeta's hands.

Anu retreats. Back in her room, she breathes with caution, but the air does not feel more contaminated than usual. Or does it?

She puts another éclair into her mouth, careful as usual not to touch the candy with her fingers. Menace lurks everywhere in the city and it forces its citizens to behave unnaturally. In the city, we become a danger to ourselves. It is what made her daughter sick. Anu is sure of this. Not genetics, not bad luck, no matter what Sakshi and the doctors said. It was Sakshi's own blood that turned against her. Now only Geeta can restore the old order, can learn to cook, start behaving, marry one of her own, whoever that might be for a girl as internally confused as Geeta. All this reading is only confusing her more. And this running around outdoors is exposing her to unnecessary hazards on a daily basis. How Sakshi and Akbar could not see this is a frightening mystery to Anu. And the most frightening part is that the more she fights for her granddaughter, the more Geeta and Akbar treat her like a nut case, dismissing and humouring her, giggling at her comments.

But Anu was used to this from Sakshi. Her own daughter never saw the blood and the sweat that Anu poured into raising her. Anu had been a strict mother, too strict on occasion, perhaps, but since when was discipline bad for children? And God knows Sakshi was not an easy child to raise, always questioning her authority and getting into trouble at school. Besides, Sakshi's father had been lenient to the point of negligence, so of course Anu had to step in, but even that was held against her, with Sakshi always preferring her father to her. The two of them would sit close, talking in low voices for hours like criminals. Sure, there had been the hot coal incident, but it had only been that one time and Sakshi probably did not even remember she was so small, the scar almost invisible by the time Sakshi started school. And she had not once denied Sakshi food, the way the other mothers routinely did when their children misbehaved. Even when Anu locked Sakshi in the storeroom she always made sure there was a packet of biscuits on the shelf. And still Anu never once complained about the nightly sewing work she took up when Sakshi needed a new school uniform or when her husband was put on the expensive medicine, because he could only work part-time since his accident. She never once complained about her spectacles that would have needed adjusting or the extra roti she denied herself. Still, despite all that, for most of her daughter's adult life, Anu had to just call her daughter on the phone for Sakshi to take immediate offence. So what if she would call the office several times—were they saving lives in that office? Definitely not. And she never called without reason, like that time when the newspaper had explicitly said to avoid eating the yellow of eggs, Sakshi's favourite food, so of course she would want to let her daughter know as soon as possible. But somehow Anu was always the villain in the tale playing out in her daughter's mind.

The chime of the doorbell ruptures Anu's thoughts. The way she has to unstick her tongue from the roof of her mouth makes her wonder whether she dosed off in between. Bad luck again. If she had left the windows open, the noise from outside would have kept her awake and alerted her to the person approaching. Another ring. Something about its thrust, curt and forceful, lets Anu know that it's not her son-in-law. All the more surprised she is to see Geeta's distorted face through the peephole. If sneaking out like this does not warrant one tight slap, she doesn't know what does.

When she opens the door she sees the man standing next to Geeta, and Anu's palm stays in place. The man is tall and his heavily hooded eyes and freshly shaved cheeks give him the look of a meticulous fox.

Where's the girl's father?

What are you doing with my granddaughter?

I'd like to speak to the girl's father.

Anu finds the man's calm, polite manner instantly dubious.

Who's asking?

The man takes his time clearing his throat and adjusting his posture.

Inspector General Salman Saleem is asking.

Geeta's eyes supply no answer. Her granddaughter is staring at her feet.

What has she done now, Inspector Sahab?

I would prefer to speak to her father.

He's not home. So you can talk to me.

When is he coming back?

God knows. He's a poet, so time is a metaphor for him.

Anu looks up to find a hint of a smile on the Inspector's face.

Maybe you are the right person to talk to after all.

She considers asking him in, but decides against it. He seems decent enough, but he is still a stranger, a policeman and a Muslim on top of it. Wasn't Akbar always going on about how these were dangerous times? She steps out under the awning and closes the front door behind her. The Inspector takes one step back to accommodate her.

I found her spying on my windowsill. Flat 22.

Please don't arrest me, Uncle!

Geeta! Did you sneak out of the house to spy on this man?

Geeta's lips tremble as she nods.

Why on earth would you do that?

No reply.

You see, Madamji, in my line of work I hear good lies all the time, but hers is a first.

Did you steal money from him, Geeta?

Geeta looks up, her eyes bursting with indignation and tears.

She claims she wanted to learn the harmonium by observing me play.

And at once Geeta is eight-year old Sakshi, her cheek glowing red as a consequence of Anu finding a coin missing from her purse. When the milkman returned the money the next day, having discovered his accounting error, Anu called Sakshi to the kitchen to give her a sweetened roti by way of an apology, but Sakshi entered displaying fingernails painted a garish red, which earned her daughter a slap, and so Sakshi never got the explanation or the roti.

She's telling the truth, Inspector.

Right. Because blood is thicker than water.

Anu wants to tell him that her granddaughter's blood is so diluted it might as well be water, but this cop might take offense, so she merely sniffs and repeats her assertion before she explains, She came to me today asking for lessons, but I told her I no longer have a harmonium, so the girl, fool that she is, must have thought this was a reasonable alternative.

You play the harmonium?

Since the age of ten.

Rahman, fool that he is, never mentioned.

This time it is Anu who finds herself smiling at the policeman.

He turns to Geeta. So you really want to learn?

Geeta nods.

And if you had a harmonium you'd take daily lessons from your Naniji starting today?

Anu observes Geeta's wretched look adjust to the sudden change of her fortune before the girl nods again, eagerly this time.

My son has one that he hasn't used in months. Sometimes laziness can be confused with lack of talent. Or is it the other way around? I forget. Anyway, I'll have someone bring it over. And no more spying! Next time I'll have you arrested.

With that, the Inspector nods at Anu, who watches him walk out their gate before she ushers Geeta into the house.

An hour later, Anu leans forward and unlocks her lips for a smile as she runs her fingertips over the cool and velvety white of the keys.

It's not as nice as mine but it will do, she says.

It's not badminton, but it will do! Geeta responds. Her

fingers squeeze in between Anu's hands like an obstinate spider.

No! First we touch it like this and then to our heart. I told you, playing music is a godly activity, and we must show our respect to the instrument that gives us this gift.

Anu watches Geeta mimic her gesture.

Now. We play the harmonium using the first four fingers of our right hand. With our left hand we operate the bellows at the back.

What's a bellows?

It's like a bag of air that grows and shrinks as we move it. It's what makes the sound audible.

Like a microphone?

Anu shakes her head. More like shaking leaves that make us hear the wind.

Anu plays a couple of tones to demonstrate but she fails to resist, and her fingers continue to move across the keyboard. The tune that emerges is one of the first she learned, easy to master for a child but surprisingly intricate for the listener with its winding melody that soars up to the ceiling like Anu's eyes and then spins back down, precise yet somehow unpredictable.

When Anu opens her eyes again after the last note has died down, Geeta is looking at her with a shyness she has never seen exposed on her granddaughter's face. Anu quickly sucks in the substantial amount of spit that has gathered in the corners of her mouth, should that be the source of Geeta's embarrassment. Anu decides that if Geeta makes fun of her now, she will not let her hit a single key on the harmonium.

But Geeta continues to sit still, awaiting instructions, and an exquisite feeling unfolds like gauze in Anu's gut that maybe her granddaughter enjoyed the short performance.

So, Anu says. Sa Re Ga Ma Pa Dha Ni. The musical scale. She demonstrates the keys one after another. Now you!

Anu feels the weight of Geeta's body pressing against hers. The last time this was the case, Geeta had been a baby.

There is no sound!

What did I tell you about the bellows?

Geeta adjusts her posture so that she can operate the bellows at the back.

There! Naniji, my first Sa!

Baba, you can't play the harmonium perched on your knees like that.

Re! Ga!

Sit properly!

Ma! Pa! Dhaa!

Geeta! Stop it!

Geeta lets go and wiggles free of Anu's grip.

Sorry, Naniji.

Now you go sit on the other side of the harmonium and your lesson today is just to learn how to listen.

No, please, I really want to play!

This is not a game! It's—

A divine activity!

Yes, correct. And today you will just listen to God's music.

Anu wants to see that look on Geeta again, as if she is seeing her grandmother for the very first time. Let her feel properly embarrassed that until that moment she always took her grandmother to be no more than a useless element of her life, like the dirty dregs in a cup of tea.

But won't I be even closer to God if I play the music myself?

Arré, you barely produced three sounds while squatting like a beggar and you think that's music?

But—

No but! If I'm to be your teacher you will do as I say! End of discussion!

With that, Geeta crawls around the harmonium and cowers down there like one of the street dogs after the boys have pelted it with jamun seeds outside the temple gates.

Anu chooses the most challenging piece she knows, the one she was still improvising on when they gave away her instrument. Harmonium was like Punjabi—not in itself difficult to learn. You could pick it up overnight and tell yourself that you were proficient in it. But to know all the idioms in Punjabi, to use it for the word play that made the language distinctive, you have to wrap yourself in it and wear it down for years, like a favourite shawl. Harmonium, too, relies on the player constantly adapting the instrument to their personality and mood, making it their own and breaking the rules wherever necessary.

As her fingers begin to glide over the keys, Anu keeps her eyes open. But this time Geeta's look remains unfocused, shifting from Anu's hands to her own toes and back, chin sinking further into the palm propping it up. Anu picks up the pace but Geeta continues to be unimpressed. She boosts the volume but her granddaughter is not shaken from her reverie. Maybe Anu imagined Geeta's earlier enthrallment.

Maybe this was just another ploy to remind Anu of her role in this house and her place in the world.

The next afternoon Anu skips the nap before her visit to the temple. Akbar sometimes half-heartedly offers to drive her if he's back early from the office, but she prefers to walk from Kaka Nagar to the Sri Ram Mandir off Lodhi Road. On those walks, she feels as if she herself is an éclair that someone released from its dark, constrictive wrapper. If they think they are trapped with her, they would do well to remember that she, too, is trapped with them. It is on those walks that she feeds the roadside cows the banana peels she has gathered and kept in the fridge over the past days, and from the savings stored away in her metal trunk buys just enough packets of éclairs as will remain unnoticeable in her cloth bag. Of course, Geeta and Akbar have long noticed her growing fondness for the candy, and periodically they bring back a packet for her from their shopping, but they never have the same effect as the ones she buys from her own resources, so she keeps those separate and untouched in her trunk.

A brisk pace takes her to the temple in under twenty minutes, but she manages to drag each way out for up to an hour. Although Geeta and Akbar believe her to be spending most of her time away at the temple, she is usually there for no more than fifteen minutes, taking one round of the grounds to make sure everyone is doing their job from the pandit down to the sweepers, correcting the posture of the teenage devotees and taking a nibble of the prasad to check that it's not stale. She likes to think of herself as the department of income tax conducting an audit, and she does not appreciate the growing number of lads in saffron headbands coming in to shout slogans and disrupt everyone's peace of mind with their leaflets ever since she saw Babur's mosque crumble like an old biscuit on the television screen. At least in this one respect she has to tacitly agree with Akbar—something is different now. Lord Ram knows, of course, that he can rely on her like on no other accountant, state or private, which is why she does not need to spend hours there in confused prayer or fierce crusade like all the others.

That day, as she edges past Kaka Nagar's public nuisance, the municipality's own Grand Canyon, and turns onto the main road, she sees a familiar figure gazing up into the silver oak at the corner, her short grey hair fraying out all around her head like a nest. Anu adjusts her path to intersect with hers.

Still room for more birds?

The woman does not turn or even respond right away. Anu can't remember her name, but it is something Christian like fork or fish finger. All Anu knows is that Sakshi used to go to her house on the other side of Kaka Nagar with a bag full of crumbs, which Anu found out only by chance, when this woman approached her on her walk to the temple to offer her condolences shortly after Sakshi passed. Apparently she keeps all kinds of sick birds in her house to cure. Occasionally, they cross paths, and Anu is always surprised that she dares to step outside of her house looking so unkempt.

I'm waiting for the vulture mother to return to her nest.

There was something about the way the woman had looked at her when she uttered her condolences that had made Anu acutely uncomfortable. As if she knew something about Anu, even though to Anu she was a perfect stranger. Whenever she sees her, Anu seeks her out in the hope that this time her misgivings will be disproven but the feeling just flares up again like a dormant rash. It occurs to Anu in that moment that the woman has not looked her in the eye since that first encounter.

Is that what my daughter said about me?

Anu expects the woman to laugh at her joke and refute it, of course, vehemently so, but the woman stands absolutely still, does not even bat an eyelid, as if she anticipated Anu's response. She cannot help her voice from swelling when she adds, Did Sakshi really call me a vulture mother?

The woman now throws a glance at her like crumbs tossed at a hungry bird, and says, Does that nest look stable to you? It doesn't to me. Sorry, what were you saying?

Anu starts walking without looking back. Clearly, this woman's obsession with birds has made her more than a little cuckoo. No wonder Sakshi felt drawn to her.

Anu arrives at the temple in fifteen minutes that day, rings the bell and has to ring it again because she forgot to check the resonance, and then sits down on the marble steps for the first time in months. She lets her glance touch on all the key elements—swept floor, orderly queue, prasad, arti—and leans her back against the pillar.

If Sakshi spoke about her in this way to strangers on the street, what did she have to say about her to everyone else? No wonder Geeta never shows her any respect. Sakshi had obviously given her full permission to mock her grandmother and Anu cannot help but wonder that morning what exactly had gone wrong that her daughter lacked all grace. Without wanting to and yet unable to thwart it, Anu steps into a memory that she usually keeps locked away.

After the bone marrow biopsy, which confirmed the diagnosis and the severity of the cancer, Sakshi would still go for her appointments at the hospital like she was on a campaign trail and just had to convince enough voters in her favour to win this particular battle. She would return from the chemo with her sleeves rolled up and describe in great detail the bleeding patients, fly-magnets, really, waiting to be treated in the hallways—the things people are made to bear in this country! She would claim to have eaten a big meal on the way home. Akbar, on temporary leave, would pretend to be extremely tired and retreat to bed, even though it was usually only late morning and Geeta was at school. Anu would do the same, so that Sakshi could vomit in peace while they pretended to sleep, and Sakshi could then crawl into bed next to Akbar and fall into what she would later often describe as an edgeless, murky slumber.

This went on for weeks. Geeta at first didn't seem to notice her mother's hair loss, and later apparently believed Sakshi's explanation that there were demons residing in her mane that she wanted to exorcise by shaving it off.

Then came the day that Sakshi, who insisted on going to work for a few hours every week, collapsed on the office floor one afternoon, and was hospitalised. The cancer was responding aggressively. Sakshi agreed to get radiation.

Still, she would make Geeta giggle uncontrollably when she would tell Akbar in a stern tone that she had heard the rumours, and just because she was sequestered at AIIMS this did not mean that Akbar was now free to start a new family with Four-by-Four. Anu suspected that the voice Sakshi used then was meant to mimic her own. Sakshi would produce a permanent marker and ask Geeta to write her secret messages on the tubes connecting her to the machines, for her to read at night. Anu was always in the room, but Sakshi never asked her to write anything. She was wanted there, apparently, yet somehow unneeded.

Until those days began when, not too long after, Sakshi would be in too much anguish to see her husband and daughter. She would ring up in the morning and say, Tell Akbar to go see *Sanam Bewafa* with Geeta in the afternoon, so they can tell me about it tomorrow. And then she would ask Anu to come alone that day. Anu understood. Only a mother can bear to see the desert unfurling behind her child's pupils and still be determined to continue the fight. Sakshi knew that Akbar would break if he saw it. He would simply stop functioning, like a screw stripped of its thread, and fall. Anu understood that her daughter needed to retain the egg of hope taped to the family's heels. And so Anu saw most of her daughter when she was too sick to smile, too angry to eat. When she realised that Sakshi's cheerfulness in front of Akbar and Geeta was now just an act, she knew with certainty that her daughter was dying.

That same day Anu took Sakshi's wiry hand in hers and begged her daughter to tell Geeta the truth.

It was in the name of hope, of course, that Akbar and Sakshi had lied to their daughter about the nature of the disease. Sakshi might be fully cured, so why put Geeta through the trauma of expecting her mother's loss, when perhaps her mother would survive? Anu realised that Sakshi knew she was dying long before any of them did, and Anu, orphaned at sixteen and married off barely a month later, could not but fight for Geeta to be given some reasonable amount of time to accept her fate.

Although Sakshi had pretended not to hear Anu's words, barking instead that she was going to freeze to death in this horrid room before any cancer could get her, a week later Akbar took Anu aside before their drive to the hospital and informed her that they had decided to tell Geeta, and that Sakshi had specifically asked for Anu to be present.

Anu could not take her eyes off Geeta all through the drive and the walk to Sakshi's room, knowing that whatever rosiness resided in Geeta's eyes until then would disappear forever with this conversation.

Come, sit, Sakshi had said. Abba and I want to talk to you.

Oh-oh, Geeta responded. Is this about—?

No, it isn't. The waves in Akbar's voice made Anu want to put a hand on his shoulder, but she didn't.

Geeta fell silent with such gravitas that Akbar and Sakshi, too, said nothing for a moment. Then Geeta spoke, in a voice so small it would have fit into a single one of the colourful capsules that were Sakshi's constant companions now:

But you said you were getting better.

Geeta, with her close to ten years on this planet, had seen the invisible words.

She knew. She collapsed into the arms of her mother, whose loud sobs Anu had not heard since her daughter's childhood, and then Anu's view was blocked by Akbar's shaking shoulders enclosing them. Anu remembers wondering if this time her own tears would flow but of course they didn't. They didn't when her parents died, they didn't on her wedding night, did not throughout Sakshi's illness and would not when Sakshi passed. What use were tears anyway? The task of finding lasting happiness in life was as impossible as isolating a drop of water at the bottom of an ocean. People could be resilient at best, but not happy, and the only chance of achieving resilience was to walk through life along the winding path of acceptance. Tears were merely cobblestones hindering the wheels of time.

After what seemed like an eternity, the cocoon opened and Geeta sat shivering at its centre. Throughout Sakshi's explanations that followed—blood cancer, irreversible, one year tops—Geeta sat silently on the edge of her mother's bed.

After that, things changed. Anu was no longer asked to come alone, and Sakshi no longer barked at Anu. Sakshi's humour returned, albeit in such a deep black shade that Anu told her off repeatedly, especially if Geeta was around. Sakshi improved. It was as if the lie itself had grown cancerous and with its elimination some semblance of tranquillity returned to the family. For a few months they all thought that maybe life would go on like this forever—Sakshi even returned home for stints.

And then, just as they had got used to their routine, her blood turned on her with a vengeance.

Anu sat on the edge of her daughter's hospital bed, the small slices cut from a Cadbury's chocolate éclair in the palm of her hand. She slipped one between Sakshi's lips hanging open.

Sakshi's jaw shifted as she sucked on the candy. Then she said, If I had known that I was going to die so soon I would have eaten more of them as a child.

Instead you never had to see the inside of a dentist's office.

Sakshi chuckled at what Anu had not intended as a joke, and then continued to observe Anu with a steady gaze. I know you always did the best you could, Ma, in your circumstances and position.

I don't know what you mean by 'in my circumstances and position' but I did do my best, and I think that was pretty good. Better than most, if we're honest.

Sakshi did not reply, of course, and then changed her mind and did reply. She said, Maybe one day you'll understand.

Anu remembers thinking that it was here that Geeta's arrogance started, though where Sakshi got it from eluded Anu. She wanted to blame Akbar but the truth is it was there long before she met him. Anu said nothing, she simply slipped another slice of the éclair onto Sakshi's tongue as if to sedate her, before her daughter's insinuations flourished into accusations. After the third slice, Sakshi fell asleep.

Anu, on a whim, put the remaining ones in her own mouth, guided by an urge to understand what Sakshi as a child had found so appealing about these brown beads wrapped in plastic. Her tongue wrapped itself around the little bits like a blanket warming a child, and the resulting sweetness felt like a reward. The soothing sensation in her gut was instant. She touched Sakshi's hand lightly with her fingertips as she pictured Sakshi at Geeta's age, caught red-handed with the forbidden candy in her mouth right before dinner, and for just a flicker of a moment the scene ended not with a slap but with a kiss on her daughter's bulging cheek. Anu squashed the vision between her clenching eyebrows. Children, including Geeta, only stood to benefit from a few well-intentioned slaps—after all, Sakshi eventually lost her taste for the candy and maintained her perfect set of teeth until the end—but in this household nobody was going to listen to her.

When Sakshi did not awake from her sleep, Anu looked at her daughter throughout her final coma period with imploring eyes, willing her to awaken just once more. When she didn't, Anu could not help think that it was typical of her daughter that her last words to her mother should be soaked in reproach.

Anu returns home from the temple that day with a firm decision in her fists. She would be the best harmonium teacher for Geeta, no matter whether the girl respected her for it or not. Her granddaughter's perception of her would not change all of a sudden, but it was Anu's duty to share her musical skills with patience and devotion if she was asked to do so. It was Lord Ram who explained this to her, all with one look into the deity's eyes when she stepped into the inner sanctum to take his blessings on this difficult day.

Anu takes it as a good omen that Geeta, back from school in the meantime, is hunched over the harmonium when she enters her room. With a sharp breath Anu dismisses the twin thoughts of whether her granddaughter has also been rummaging around in her things and whether she took the instrument's blessings before touching it.

I see you're ready for your lesson.

When Geeta does not respond Anu wonders whether the girl has fallen asleep on top of the instrument, which would demand at least a small verbal rebuke, if only out of principle.

Geeta?

Anu is startled first by the suddenness with which Geeta sits up and by the loud sob that seizes her the next moment. It's all my fault, Naniji!

Anu silently thanks Lord Ram. She saw it in his eyes today, the impending intervention.

It's all right, Geeta, you're only a child, you can't know everything. From now on you'll change. And I'm here to guide you, all the way to your marriage.

Geeta looks up. Abba didn't tell you what happened?

Anu feels her eyes narrow before she shakes her head.

Faraz got caught! Yesterday, when Saleem Uncle went in his room to get the harmonium for me.

For us.

It's all my fault! If I hadn't spied on him, then Saleem Uncle wouldn't have escorted me home and then Faraz wouldn't have thought that his father had gone out but instead he came right into his room when Faraz least expected him to!

All right, but what about our lesson?

Faraz is not allowed to leave the house anymore! And he's barred from seeing Sitara! She's not my topmost friend, Naniji, but Faraz is maximum sad now. And it's all my fault!

Anu wants to tell Geeta that if she is so concerned for some neighbour's sadness, perhaps she might once in a while be moved by the pitiful position of her own grandmother. Instead, she says, Do you want to learn to play the harmonium or not?

Geeta's chest heaves with a heavy breath.

Yah, she says, nodding and wiping her cheeks with the base of her palms. Yah, okay.

They go through Sa Re Ga Ma Pa Dha Ni Sa again, and then again and again, until Geeta manages to play it as a sequence with Anu assisting her on the bellows. By the end Geeta is so focused on moving her fingers along the keys in the right rhythm that Anu is certain she has forgotten all about her friend's woes. Thus is the nature of time: For those who have something to do, time is like a crammed storeroom in which you never dwell too long on what you're looking for. For Anu, time is a mansion with bare walls and covered furniture, a mansion to get lost in and still know that you will never be able to fill the empty space.

Over the next four days, Geeta does not miss a single lesson and even practices on her own. She has freshly mastered the musical scale, when Geeta pauses to bite her nail at the end of their lesson.

Naniji?

Yes?

I have a brilliant idea.

Hm.

You know why I was able to learn to play the harmonium so fast?

Anu does nothing to stifle the sharp laugh that explodes from her lips along with a drizzle of spit. It took you almost a week to learn how to play just the musical scale!

Maybe, but as a badminton player, I have an excessively limber wrist. And now that I am playing the notes and bellowing them at the same time, I know for sure that you can improve your mastery of harmonium by playing a round of badminton with me.

No, thank you.

No, I want to thank YOU, so you have to play badminton with me!

Hé Bhag, if that's the only way you can think of thanking me, I am clearly out of place in this household.

Please, Naniji! It's really good for your wrist, I promise! And you will feel comprehensively thanked to boot!

Prancing around with a stick in my hand for all the neighbours to see sounds more like punishment.

It's called a racket! And it's really the complete opposite of punishment! Just try it, Naniji, and I promise you'll like it.

No.

But I have no one else to play with!

Go ask your father.

Don't waste your time, comes Akbar's voice from behind them. He is standing in the doorframe with his office bag, grinning. Anu did not hear him enter over the music, and she remains silent: for once she is in full agreement with her son-in law. It's as if Geeta decided after her mother's passing that only badminton would provide the necessary distraction.

And besides, you always say, no, that all the heaviness goes away when you feel God's grace? That's how it is when I'm playing badminton, so it must be a divine activity. Or at least my divine activity. And I want to share it with you, because you of all people will understand.

Are you saying I don't understand? Akbar asks, hurt.

Anu cannot remember her granddaughter ever mentioning a positive quality in her that her father lacked, at least not in front of both of them, and before she can give it a second thought, she blurts, All right. Fine.

Geeta's hands fly into the air as she performs some kind of a victory dance.

But not in the Club House. In our garden. And let's wait another half hour till the sun has set some more.

Great idea, Mummyji, you can call it blind man's badminton.

To her surprise, it is Geeta who comes to her defense before Anu can say anything.

Now that Naniji has agreed you're the only person left in all of Kaka Nagar who has never played badminton!

If that's my only distinction I'll gladly accept it.

What's a distinction, Abba?

Go look it up.

Okay, later I will, promise. Come, Naniji, we should go warm up! You can use my old racket. Abba, you can't miss this!

But thankfully Akbar waves around a thin brown paper envelope and says to his daughter, Sorry, I have other historic events to attend to. Pavan finally sent me his new poems.

As we step outside, Geeta whispers to Anu, The only reason I didn't allot time to argue with Abba just now is because outside it's getting dark and frankly inside I'm getting a little hungry. And, with all due respect, Abba tends to starve badminton sessions rather than feed them, so maybe it's for the best if he is not in attendance this time.

Anu nods. Her granddaughter has never whispered anything to her in confidence, so this must finally be Lord Ram's promised intervention, two weeks behind schedule.

In the garden, Anu feels as if she is wearing not her usual sari but nothing at all. The racket in her hand drags behind her like a limp broom. Why on earth did she agree to this! The neighbours were probably already focusing their binoculars, ready to savour this spectacle in all its juicy details. She produces the emergency éclair from inside her sari blouse and almost swallows it whole before her teeth get hold of it. Anu does not resist when Geeta, with unprecedented tenderness, adjusts her arms and feet to make her stand in position. She says, Grip your racket like you're holding a little bird in your hand. Firm enough so it doesn't escape, but not so tight as to crush it.

Loudly, for the neighbours, Anu says, I would never even think of crushing a bird in my hand!

You're not supposed to crush it, Naniji. But don't let it escape also!

Geeta runs backwards and shoots the featherball to Anu, who somehow manages to return it.

Good shot, Naniji!

Her granddaughter's praise throws her off even more, and Anu misses the featherball, but she picks it up and is able to send it back to Geeta with the help of her racket. Anu is grateful that Geeta is playing gently, not trying to trick or outrun her in order to highlight Anu's obvious deficiencies and age.

After the first truncated strokes, Anu manages to outrun her expected failure to bring racket and featherball together, and return the shot once again. This is followed by another and then another exchange before the featherball lands at Anu's feet. Anu picks it up.

As their rackets go up and down between them like moons directing the rising and falling tide, for a fraction of a moment Anu becomes the featherball floating through the evening sky, and with the slap of her racket as it makes contact her entire consciousness is lobbed over her head to sail into her granddaughter's reach. She feels suddenly light, perplexingly grateful that this should be all that will remain of her when she joins Sakshi in the cycle of rebirth. Her dancing, falling soap bubble of a consciousness, to vanish forever at her granddaughter's touch.

Naniji, I just had an interesting thought.

In spite of the stitches piercing her insides, Anu feels serenity suffuse her body as if she had gulped down a whole packet of éclairs at once. This was proof that her sensation of a moment ago was real, and mutual. A minute speck of her consciousness had arrived within Geeta.

What is it? Anu asks.

Never mind, it's stupid.

Just a short while earlier, Anu would have agreed. Instead, she continues to press Geeta. You said, na, badminton is your divine activity, so your thoughts right now will be pure and inspired. Anu is taken aback by her own words and the caress in her tone, and she sees her own surprise mirrored in Geeta's expression, which is suddenly radiant.

I was thinking that if a few minutes of badminton can make me feel so utterly butterly like Geeta again, maybe if Mummy had lived a little longer and I would have made her play badminton with me every day, this would have healed all the bad blood inside her.

This time, Anu says nothing. What labyrinths were contained in that ‘if’ for her granddaughter. For Akbar, too, surely. For herself.

Anu tries to shake off the thought. ‘If’ belongs to the same landscape as tears—spokes in the wheel of time. Instead, she stretches further to return the shots. She puts force into the swing of her racket now, losing awareness of her feet as they gather speed through the grass and attempt a short leap.

Geeta, too, is adapting her game, seems to be playing faster, steeper shots. Anu feels her chest expand and contract, expand and contract, she follows with her eyes the motion of Geeta’s racket, but Geeta does something to the featherball, and it zooms off in the opposite direction.

I did it! Geeta shouts and Anu twists back, which makes her trip over her own feet as Geeta calls out, Reverse slice drop shot! and Anu falls like a heap of leaves on the grass.

Naniji!

The next second Geeta is there next to Anu, her face so close she can smell her granddaughter’s sweet breath. Geeta cups Anu’s cheeks in her hands, the child’s warm palms like band-aids on an invisible wound. As if this was a dance they had rehearsed together, Geeta expertly adjusts Anu’s face so that she can look straight into her grandmother’s eyes as she asks, Are you hurt?

For a long moment, Anu cannot breathe. How could she have known that she would find herself right in the middle of the labyrinth contained in that one word, *hurt*, just because she is asked a question she has never been asked before?

And that's when they come. Hot and dense like rays from the sun. Two wet streaks, tributaries running into nothing.

Geeta's eyes widen in alarm at her grandmother's unprecedented response. Oh no, that bad?

The girl wants to jump up, to call her father no doubt, but Anu uses her pain-free hand to pull her granddaughter back towards her. Without any prompting, Geeta enfolds Anu in her arms, and Anu shrinks into the embrace.

They sit like this for a while, Geeta containing Anu's trembling shoulders like a locomotive encasing the moving pistons inside.

There is no word for it, Geeta, Anu finally manages to say.

The pain?

Yes, the pain. There is no word for it.

Geeta is about to say more, but Anu makes sure she speaks first. A child who loses its mother is an orphan. A husband who loses his wife is a widower. But there is no word for—

Anu cannot finish the sentence. The convulsive gasp that leaves her mouth with a loud clap, renewing the downpour from her eyes, makes speech impossible.

For a mother who loses a child.

She feels her granddaughter's grip tighten as the words are whispered into Anu's ears.

Anu is not aware of her own wails that follow, does not notice Akbar arrive next to her, does not feel his hand stroking her back or notice the passers-by peeking through the gaps in the hedge.

I'm sorry, Sakshi, Anu says out aloud, so that her daughter may hear, I'm sorry I didn't take better care of you. I understand now. It's too late but I understand.

The next surge of tears erases her vision once more. She hears but doesn't listen to Geeta's narration of the events, after which Akbar asks Anu about where it hurts and, though Anu is eventually able to inspect her body to identify the single source of the throb in her right hand, hissing at the effort to be pulled up to her feet and guided to the parked car, she would not later remember being driven to the Pandara Road Dispensary, where the doctor puts her broken wrist in a cast and prescribes a course of painkillers, and Geeta admonishes no one in particular for not having thought of giving those to Naniji long ago, because there is no word for it.

Aunty! Aunty! Please let me in!

I have rung the bell and knocked on the door and banged the handle of the latch against its metal base multiple times. Still, no response. Bird Aunty almost never goes out—she says so herself, she doesn't have to, because she invites the whole sky into her house—so I know that she must be inside somewhere.

Aunty, it's me!

I know I should turn around and go home, but instead I initiate slippage down the door until my bottom hits the cement floor. First came termination of badminton. Then came official withdrawal of Faraz. Then last and least came cancellation of harmonium, because yesterday Naniji got a hairline fracture on her wrist and can't teach me anymore, and to boot Abba's only comment was, If that doesn't cure you of your badminton obsession, I don't know what will.

That is why I have come to see Aunty, who is the only person in toto whom I am happy to call Aunty inside my head and outside of it.

Suddenly, there is a burst of laughter from inside the flat, so I jump up and ring the bell once again. Because I have never heard Bird Aunty laugh, it is sincerely hoped that she and the brigadier haven't moved out. The sign next to the door still reads Brigadier Moses Philips and Mrs Benita Philips. Steps are approaching, and before I can wipe off the leftovers of my tears the door flies open.

Ah, if it isn't the absconding soldier herself, missing in action, our very own Miss Geeta Rahman.

I'm really sorry, Aunty!

Bird Aunty's bangles slide down her arm as she jams her hands into her substantial hips. Her short hair is curling in all directions around her head as usual, but it looks whiter than before, which makes me feel even more admonished than her furrowed brows, because it reminds me that I have not come to see her since the day before my birthday, the day Vicky joined my life.

Care to explain your unavailability? Were you leading an insurgency perhaps? Or building an empire? No, wait, you got promoted to oil magnet. Bird Aunty leans forward, which makes her nose look even more like it's melting and one drop of flesh is about to roll off its tip.

No, Aunty, I didn't, but I am in the process of being promoted to a badminton magnet, so I had to suspend all other activities in the interim.

A badminton magnet? Bird Aunty grins. A delightful idea, though unfortunately magnetism is like dandruff, Geeta—you either have it or you don't. You can't acquire it like onions at the bazaar. And taking care of living beings is not an activity, it's a moral duty, and—were you sitting outside my door and crying?

I really wasn't, Aunty.

Bird Aunty stares at me for a moment, then steps to the side and lets me into the flat, which is Number 199 and therefore all the way at the other end of Kaka Nagar.

Well, it's good you're finally here. Tinku has not been keeping well at all. After you stopped coming he didn't eat for days! So much trouble you caused me, disappearing like that.

I'm sorry, Aunty, I say again as I follow her into the flat, and I really mean it this time, because Tinku is my topmost favourite bird, even though Bird Aunty has many to choose from.

The bird clinic inside their flat is in the same room as mine is in ours. The wall by the window is lined with cages of different sizes, one row on the floor for the bigger ones, and one row of smaller ones on a shelf. Tinku, who is a small green parakeet with a sharp red beak, lives in a medium-sized cage on the floor. I can already hear him squawking, so I feel for the biscuit crumbs wrapped in newspaper in my pocket.

Luckily, someone else showed up who's been helping me every day—

I don't register Bird Aunty's words until I walk through the door and there is a familiar figure hunched over the largest cage on the floor.

Sitara! I pull the packet of crumbs from my pocket with a jerk and the next moment I am standing on biscuit sand beach. I don't look up as I collect the bird food in my palm and deposit it on the crumpled newspaper on the floor, because I don't want Bird Aunty to be angry with me twice in a row.

What are you doing here? I ask for the sake of distraction.

Same as you, I suppose. Salvaging my soul.

This makes Bird Aunty chuckle. I see you two know each other. I should have figured. One colony can only host so many misfits.

Tinku is hopping excitedly as I address his cage.

It was Sitara who made Bird Aunty laugh loudly a moment ago. From the corner of my eye I see her reaching into the largest cage, inside of which is a substantially ugly bird with a pink, wrinkly face and neck.

Who's the new patient, Aunty?

You know the silver oak on your corner? A vulture chick fell from its nest there, which I thought looked unstable, and broke its wing after the mother disappeared. Sitara here found it and has been tending to her with utmost care. We were just talking about what to name her, and Sitara suggested Icarus Philips, which I like.

Although I would very much like to know how Sitara found out about Bird Aunty and her clinic, I am even more negatively surprised that Sitara has already been granted naming rights, so I say, Why don't we rename Tinku Autonomous as per prior plan?

I told you before, Geeta, Tinku stays Tinku. You can't rename someone mid-life, he's already in a fragile state.

I like Autonomous, Sitara says. For a caged bird.

Sitara's praise is welcome but also not, because if she is on my side it makes it more difficult to be disapproving of her, and although I want to like her because of Faraz, she is also ipso facto the reason he is no longer my first and foremost friend, and now she is in the process of obtaining

Bird Aunty's primary friendship to boot. I therefore decide to give her a taste of my expertise in matters of birds and words.

Tinku is different. Tinku was born in captivity. We don't even know if he can fly. We've never seen him do it, but I know for sure that he could once we let him try.

With her typical non-smile smile, Sitara says, Sounds like we've both been thinking about autonomy.

Not me. Us.

Sitara and Aunty are both looking at me with puzzled faces, so I add, The word's autonomUS, and it means having self-government, at least to a significant degree.

Does the walking dictionary also know the meaning of irony? Sitara asks Icarus Philips, who doesn't respond.

Why don't you ask the istrywallah, I say, which makes Bird Aunty chuckle, so I pick up a fistful of crumbs just like Mummy, who was Bird Aunty's original friend—by making a cup with your hand—but I add a largish quota of triumph, and deposit it all around Tinku in a rectangle like a tiny badminton court for him to play in. Tinku starts eating it right away.

Bird Aunty says, I'll get their meds, and leaves the room.

The interim silence between Sitara and myself is so loud that I almost want to shout Thank you! when Sitara starts speaking.

Have you talked to Faraz lately?

Not since—

The pertinent words remain stuck to my tongue.

Since what, Geeta? Say it. Since I got branded a minx? Sitara's voice is like a shuttlecock that's spinning out of control, so I refrain from inquiring into the meaning of minx and write it into my palm with my finger for later reference.

Which is ironic, because most of my life I've been happily invisible to most people.

Last year there was one day in the calendar, which was sadder than the sadness of all the other days put together. It was the same day that Mummy died one year earlier. July 29. On that date and only on that date, Abba told me about the fire. He said though Mummy is no longer walking among us, her love burns in all of us. It keeps us warm but it also hurts a lot when we get too close to it and makes our eyes water when we stare at it for too long. I looked up 'love' in the dictionary, but there was no mention of fires or hurt or tears. And now a thought enters my head, that maybe Sitara, too, has a fire of love burning inside her for Faraz. Amply smaller than the one that burns for Mummy, of course, more like a matchstick with a tiny flame at its end.

In school they call me Shittlecock and Buttminton and Tubelight, because I don't like their childish games and don't do well in exams.

Sitara looks at me and then keeps looking, she is smiling but also not, and this activates a strange feeling in my belly, like being seen by Sitara for the first time but also seeing her for the first time. I quickly turn to Tinku, who has eaten the entire badminton court in the meantime, so I take another fistful from the newspaper and make an isometric circle around him. Then without checking to see if she is still looking, I push the newspaper with the remaining crumbs towards Sitara. I hear a rustling and watch her fingertips pick up a heap and letting them rain into Icarus Philips' cage, who flutters excitedly with his non-bandaged wing.

The truth is, most people are dumb like sheep, but unlike our woolly friends, they don't have a heart.

I think of my classmates and my teachers, and of the Greek Chorus and most of the grown-ups in Kaka Nagar and a substantial part of me wants to agree with Sitara, although I stop short of nodding, because I am afraid that she might also mean Vicky, and he is definitely the opposite of a sheep. Still, there is an urgent memo pending now stating that Sitara is not a public grievance per se. In fact, she displays unexpected potential as a future friend.

Have you talked to Faraz?

She shakes her head. I'm not allowed to talk to him, and he's not allowed to leave the house except for school.

I remember the harmonium, which will have to be returned to the Saleems later today, and say, I can give him a message from you.

When she turns from Icarus Philips to me, there is something on Sitara's face that I have never seen before: a smile, thoroughly and in full. Would you do that for me?

I nod.

She thinks about it for a moment. Tell him, The wetness of rain makes the monsoon worthwhile.

I repeat the words to Sitara, which augments her smile even more.

Behind us the door squeaks open. Bird Aunty stands in the frame with a metal tray bearing labelled bottles and syringes and bandaging material. She used to be a nurse in the army hospital, but she says she got tired of treating human beings, most of whom have a sickness called ego that she could not cure. When I asked Mummy later that day how you contract ego, she laughed and told me not to worry, because it's usually men who are at greatest risk of this particular disease.

Inside my head I say sorry to Bird Aunty one more time for my recent negligence, and then wait for Sitara to stand so we can help Bird Aunty together.

Even though the Greek Chorus comes to the Club House every day, it feels emptier than the mud room, which is still blocking the road in front of it in spite of Saleem Uncle's official complaint. Without Faraz it's as if the government meets every day but there is no Prime Minister. I saw him very briefly when I accompanied Abba to return the harmonium to the Saleems yesterday after my visit to Bird Aunty's clinic, but because Saleem Uncle did not leave me alone with Faraz even for just one second I had to deposit Sitara's message with Faraz verbally and disguised as sudden poetry addressed to Abba, but I think Faraz understood anyway, because when we left he said, Good you didn't lose your stinkato, Smalls, and his formerly tired-looking eyes now glowed like Naniji's prayer beads, which have been lying idly on her pillow now that her right hand is in a cast.

At the Club House we are all pretending to be busy playing and chatting, but the full truth is that the days of his absence already now feel like the hairs growing out of Shipwreck's nose: far too long and hard to ignore. The Greek Chorus just repeats Faraz's old jokes to keep giggling. And have been going without my red and silver Yonex ISOMETRIC, because I refuse to play badminton with imbeciles.

I am giving due consideration to the agenda of how to procure a bicycle, so that I can go see Tinku and Bird Aunty with more ease and frequency, but since my thinking is yielding no results, I am interim relieved when I hear someone call my name, so I that I can take a break from invisible-protesting badminton.

The voice is coming from the edge of the Club House and when I turn the corner I spot Vicky hunched in the cement spiral staircase that leads to the back door of their flat.

I have not seen him in two weeks, and am not sure if he is still angry with Abba or if I am allowed to be angry with him.

Hello, Uncle.

Vicky gestures for me to come up into the staircase and cower down on the steps with him in the middle of the spiral, so that nobody can see us talking.

I heard about your Naniji and the harmonium lessons. I'm sorry about her wrist.

It was my fault, Uncle.

Vicky considers this and then says, Don't mind me saying so, Geeta, but with great achievement comes great sacrifice.

I am not sure if he is referring to Naniji or Yours Truly, but I nod anyway because this is the kind of statement of facts that Abba would be in agreement with.

So listen, your tournament is on Sunday.

Oh. I thought my participation was cancelled due to aggravating circumstances.

Vicky sighs and mutters, I'm sorry, Geeta. I shouldn't have abandoned you like that.

I want to nod excessively, but decide not to.

After the frustration with your father, and the neighbours, and Anjana, I told myself it was not worth it. But in the end I couldn't help myself, so to address your concern: No, I'm not letting you miss this chance. Besides, your participation is still a condition for your school interview.

Does Abba know?

I've made sure of it.

I can smell onion on his breath and there's what looks like a pakora crumb hanging in his beard.

But today is Monday, Uncle. Sunday starts in six days.

You're right. We don't have much time.

My wrist is quite limber now, but the rest of me is not sufficiently trained.

That's why I cooked up an emergency plan for us. What time do your Abba and Nani wake up?

Abba's alarm rings at 6:45, and Naniji only gets up after I leave for school because of her insomnia.

Not before, you're sure, na?

Fully sure.

So we meet on my terrace for the next five days from 5 to 6:30 in the morning. I've arranged everything, the net, the light. Top secret.

Really, Uncle? Back to badminton?

Back to badminton.

I pinch my eyes close and shake my fists in the air, and then quickly retrieve them for the purpose of non-visibility. In the interim, Vicky's grin has grown wide like a breezy serve.

And every day after school you'll play a practice match

with Faraz. I'll watch from the terrace and give you my feedback afterwards.

But—I am not sure if Vicky is fully in possession of knowledge of what I am about to tell him. Faraz is not allowed to come to the court anymore, Uncle. Also my fault.

But Vicky does not seem surprised or upset. I know and, no, not your fault. Between us, Geeta, I was happy to hear about it just because it means my sourpuss daughter has finally found a companion.

But Saleem Uncle doesn't want that companion to be Faraz.

I told him, Let them be friends, show some faith and they will both still do well in exams. But he wanted to hear none of it. And all that happened was that Faraz got caught with a comic book Sitara had drawn for him—

The Smashing Confessions!

What?

Nothing.

And he was drawing one for her. It doesn't get more innocent than that! I knew there had to be more to it. Of course, given these times I assumed it's a religious objection. Well, it turns out I was wrong. But try getting a cop to talk, Geeta, it's no small feat!

Saleem Uncle never tells anyone what they want to hear.

Ha! Of course I got him to tell me everything. You can smell that self-made man scent on him from miles away. Always points to a deep vulnerability. Didn't you just say smashing confessions?

I nod, unsure now what exactly Vicky knows.

Faraz has an older brother, you see. He's a drunk and

lives in the gutter, and Saleem himself also had a brother just like that, and his father was like that, too, so the man fears nothing more than that his son will take after these bad eggs. Because it runs in the family. But I told him, it's not the leash that's important, it's its length. You have to give the boy the illusion of freedom or he will rebel.

You mean, be disobedient to some higher authority?

Vicky nods. Be that as it may, we made a deal. Faraz will come to the court for the next five afternoons accompanied by one of Saleem's men to play practice matches with you until your tournament, and in return I will put Sitara under indefinite house arrest, so she does not try to meet Faraz, at least until after the exams, because his teachers are worried about the recent dip in his grades.

But what about their friendship?

The truth is, Geeta, Saleem is right. I don't want them to get ideas beyond innocent friendship. It may sound romantic, but to have so much opposition in the end causes only resentment—Vicky pauses to scratch his beard, which releases the pakora crumb—and much worse. It's okay when you're young but soon that love becomes twisted and obscured and you do your very best to hide it from each other.

I no longer understand what information Vicky is trying to convey to me, so I say, Okay, but Uncle? How am I going to wake up every morning by 5?

Vicky presses his thick, hairy index finger against my lips and hands me an alarm clock, announcing: Vicky Uncle has thought of everything! It doesn't ring, it just vibrates, so only you will hear it. I've already set it for 4:40 a.m. Maybe we can even start a little before 5.

Thank you, Uncle.

Vicky nudges me. Coach Sir to you!

Thank you, Coach Sir.

Vicky's hand grabs my knee and he grins at me. Thank you, Geeta Ji. For letting me be that to you.

Coach Sir?

Yes?

What if my marks drop even more because of this and I fail the interview at SPV? Abba will be very angry with me.

Vicky pats my knee. Trust me, you won't fail the interview.

Because I will excel in badminton?

Vicky chuckles. Exactly. Because you will excel in badminton. He leans in to kiss me on the temple. Go now! And don't tell anyone!

I am awoken by a train rattling through my head. My eyelids are non-functional and I have to engage in a gargantuan effort to make them obey orders before I remember that this is a full-fledged undercover operation, with the vibrating alarm clock hidden inside my pillowcase. I find the right button and turn it off, and sit up in bed to avoid immediate closing of eyes. It might be advisable to introduce the official policy of afternoon nap-taking.

The train inside my head was so loud I am thinking it must have awoken Abba in the next room, but all is quiet. Should I be worried that I cannot hear Abba snoring? I slip into the clothes I have hidden in my bed and tiptoe into the front room with my racket. Is that light under Naniji's door or does she always keep a lamp on?

If I get caught, Abba will definitely cancel the tournament.

The only part of my exit that will make noise with absolute certainty is opening the multiple latches of the apartment door that Abba secures with due diligence every evening. Maybe I should rumble like a bus to absorb the noise? Or chirp like a cricket? I decide not to introduce addendum noises. Maybe I should peek into Naniji's room first to make sure it's just the night lamp. But if she's awake she will see me and I will have to miss practice, and we only have five sessions in toto as it is. I decide to go with the band-aid approach and quickly open one latch after another, stepping into the instant embrace of the dark air, which is neither cool nor warm but simply perfect. I close the door behind me and the next moment I am running up the stairs to Vicky's terrace.

The metal door is ajar and I slip through it. I can see the outlines of a net, two floodlights and the boundaries of a court shimmering in white chalk.

Coach Sir?

No answer. I want to explore the court and find the switch for the lights but it's highly dark all around me and I am substantially alone with no visual cross-references for what is around me, so I stay frozen in my place.

A feeling is pending inside my stomach, same like when you are about to walk into a trap. Vicky forgot our session, and now I am alone on his terrace in the middle of the night, where any ghost or dacoit or churail could find me with ease, and Abba would not even hear me.

I spin around, dart through the door and down the corridor, and just as I turn the corner onto the dark staircase I bump into something and a pair of arms grab me and I try to scream but a hand presses down on my mouth.

Shhhhhh!

I struggle but the arms only grab me harder.

It's me!

Once I identify Vicky's voice hissing into my ear I allow my arms to go limp.

He lets go of my mouth. For a moment, the only sound in the whole wide world is Geeta catching her breath.

Sorry, Coach Sir, I whisper.

No, I'm sorry. Not like me to be late but it turns out Anjana has insomnia now and spends her nights playing Tetris on Sitara's Game Boy in the living room. I didn't even see her sitting there in the corner. Try explaining to your wife why you're leaving the house in full sports gear at 4:30 in the morning without giving anything away.

So badminton is off again?

I'm here, aren't I!

Vicky nudges me back towards the terrace door.

Let's go. We've lost enough time already.

Shall we skip the warm-up then?

Why, you want to rupture your tendon?

I shake my head.

Anjana is leaving on a business trip tomorrow for four days, Vicky says as he locks the metal door behind us once we're on the terrace. So I'll be all yours until the tournament.

When the floodlights come on and my eyes have adjusted,

I see that the lines of the court are so straight Vicky must have used a ruler to draw them. When I pin my eyes to Vicky's I see that he is wearing the same look as a water buffalo after having spotted a pond at the height of summer. I quickly issue a full-scale smile, because I am sure now that my eyes are having the exact same point of reference.

And with that I let go of one of my underused new birthday shuttlecocks and swing my racket through the room of light that Vicky has built for us on his terrace.

Back to badminton! I shout as Vicky hushes me again and reaches to drive the shuttlecock and the whole world in the right direction.

Although having my first top-secret training session today made going to school afterwards almost acceptable, even the teacher noticed my non-stop yawning and sent me to the principal for information, guidance and compliance. I told her, of course, that my exhaustion is solely and in full due to excessive studying, but her eyes just looked at me as if to say, Don't bother, while her lips officially praised my commitment.

I am walking towards the metal gates for my bus line when I notice Faraz and Sitara in their respective school uniforms standing on the pavement outside looking for me among the crowd. I adjust my path towards them.

Smalls!

Hi, Geeta.

I thought you're not allowed to meet!

Though one of the best parts about the secret training is that I will get to play with Faraz this afternoon, I cannot think of another reason for their visit than to give me a belated proper scolding for having caused his house arrest.

And you also thought that would stop us?

Faraz is grinning at me just like before his Troubled Times began, and I grin back. Then he says, We don't have much time, so we're going to come right to the point.

Match point? My grin grows first in one direction and then the other like a reverse slice drop shot, which we practiced this morning on the terrace, and which Vicky has already started calling my signature shot.

Yes! It's match point for real, Smalls. Faraz is gripping my shoulders tightly in his hands and looking at me through his Gandhiji specs, which have smudges on them. The grin is suddenly gone.

Sitara and I—Faraz lets go of my shoulders and takes Sitara's hand in his. We're going to run away together.

I blink twice just like Mummy used to when Abba would do something leading to instant withdrawal of approval and say her ditto words: You're doing what, sir?

The response comes from Sitara.

We're running away together. Eloping. She winks at me. We're going to be autonomous.

Because I don't know what Mummy would have said in this situation, all I can think of is asking, Where are you going?

We can't tell you, Sitara says.

Why not?

Because if you spill the beans we'll get caught.

I won't tell anyone, I promise.

Sorry, Sitara says, but we can't tell you.

Clearly, our new friendship at Bird Aunty's clinic is already over again.

Oh, come on, Sitara, Faraz says, Why can't we just tell her that we're going to Chandigarh?

Faraz! Sitara rolls her eyes, but her lips are smiling incrementally.

I want to smirk at Sitara but my eyes notice that behind her the bus lines are very short now, the last children are getting on the bus. So instead I say to Faraz, Your father is going to send all his policemen to look for you! He's going to find you and then he'll be much, much angrier than that day.

I'm not afraid of his anger anymore, Smalls.

Even though as a general guideline you should only ask questions to which you want to hear the answer, my mouth is acting without prior approval. So once you leave we'll never see each other again?

Sitara and Faraz exchange a look. Not never, just not for a little while.

A long little while or a short little while?

Faraz's eyes remain stapled to me. A long little while.

The thought floats into my head that I am the only person on the planet who knows about this plan, which means I have the full and undisputed duty to change their minds.

But what if Vicky Uncle is right? You're getting ideas beyond innocent friendship, and though they sound romantic because of the collective opposition, in the end you'll do your best to hide from each other.

My father had better shut his big mouth!

He's just trying to help.

I know you don't want to hear it, Geeta, but my father's a liar. He put me under house arrest for nothing, only so he could make a deal about badminton with Faraz's father! That was the last straw! That's when we decided we've had enough.

He only did that because he wants to make me excel for the tournament! So that I get admission at SPV!

Your admission has nothing to do with badminton! The principal is Papa's oldest friend, he just has to make one phone call! Don't you see that he's a selfish ogre!

No, you're wrong! I'm going to be a fully professional badminton champion-cum-magnet, and Vicky is the only other person who knows it, too!

A horn blows sharply. I'm going to miss my bus! I turn to Faraz. When are you leaving?

Friday morning.

What, no! My tournament is on Sunday! If you leave on Friday then I won't be able to play! Plus you'll never know how I did!

The two exchange glances.

Please don't leave before my tournament! I'll keep your secret completely hidden, I promise! I won't tell anyone!

The glance turns into a long look, then they start whispering to each other very fast, but their voices are getting louder and louder until I can hear every word.

I'm telling you, it's a mistake!

It'll all go as planned, I promise.

But we already have our tickets!

We can change them. The tournament means a lot to her.

This is our life, Faraz!

Exactly, it's our whole life, so a few days won't make a difference. Faraz takes Sitara's hands in his as if they're about to start dancing together. I owe her that much.

Sitara sighs loudly. Fine, we'll do it as you say, only because she's your friend. She turns back to me first. We'll leave on Monday on our way to school.

Monday is Holi, I remind them.

Sitara sighs. Tuesday, then.

Tuesday, it is.

The bus's motor is roaring, another sharp blast of the horn.

Thank you! I say as Faraz nudges me. Run, Smalls!

I do, hopping onto the first step of the open door just as the wheels begin to turn and that's when I realise that I didn't even wave goodbye.

Objective assessment requires me to say that the implementation of top-secret early morning badminton training has not been without hiccups. Although it is highly appreciated that I get to play against Faraz again, there is something different about him being there now: he is on court but also not. His eyes follow the shuttlecock and his racket makes contact but there are no jokes, no comments and no time is allotted to teasing me, which makes our game efficient but also substantially boring.

This was the case on Wednesday and on Thursday, too. Now it is Friday morning, and Vicky has just informed me that we will not have a morning session tomorrow, because I seem exhausted and am meant to get adequate rest before Tournament Day. Vicky shoos me onto the court and from that moment on it feels as if Vicky cancelled training tomorrow morning only so that he can squeeze in two sessions today, because he forgets my water break and claps impatiently when I re-tie my laces.

No dilly-dallying, Geeta, we have a lot of ground to cover still!

I think that right now I could cover maximum ground by lying down on the floor and falling asleep on it but instead I stand up straighter and go through the motion of the reverse slice drop shot once more time.

When Vicky finally releases me, later than usual, I sprint down and run through the gate and open our door sincerely hoping that Abba has not awoken yet. He hasn't. I am so relieved that I collapse on my bed for an utterly brief break.

When I open my eyes and see the parent cadre looking down at me as if he is inspecting a particularly faulty tender, I know that a) I fell asleep and b) I did so forgetting to change back into my pyjamas and c) I am cuddling my racket.

Oh! I say, and then sit up straight in spite of my comprehensive tiredness so that I can supplement the facts without delay. Abba, I had the most commendable dream about winning the U-13 on Sunday, so I must have sleepwalked and sleepdressed. How funny, no?

Abba is not amused. Did you go outside at night? You're wearing your street shoes.

No, Abba! Of course not. Because of the dream I must have—

Geeta, if I find out that you have been—

She's telling the truth, Akbar.

Abba and I turn to find Naniji on the threshold. I have never heard Naniji use Abba's name.

I heard a noise about an hour ago, so I got up and saw her dressed like this dancing through the room with her racket. I asked her what she was doing, but she kept whispering, I will win! I will win! And that's when I realised she was doing all this in her sleep. I watched over her till she went back to bed and that's how you found her.

Although I can tell that Abba finds my sudden bout of sleepwalking highly questionable, he has no choice but to believe Naniji, because under no prior circumstances has she been known to side with badminton and tell a direct and unambiguous lie.

Fine, he states. Just promise me that this is going to be your first and last tournament. We're only doing this for your admission.

Before Abba can go into the details about how the dictionary defines badminton not as a career but as a pastime, I state, Promise, Abba! because after my first tournament the whole stadium will be chanting my name—Geeta! Geeta! Geeta!—which is when Vicky says Abba will come around.

I quickly get ready for school and before I take my bag and leave for the bus stop, I quietly slip into Naniji's room for a substantial Thank You.

She is sitting as usual on her cot with the television on, though it is quite dark in her room, and I am not sure if she is awake or not. I sidle up to her but before I can say anything, she mutters in my ear, Don't worry, I understand.

Today is the terminal day of school before my tournament, so the feeling is like going on holiday to a highly objectionable place. Still, I have the last match with Faraz to anticipate in the afternoon, and when the decreed hour finally arrives, I am already on court with my high-sugar smile. But Faraz doesn't even say hello to me, and I want to ask him whether he is angry with me for postponing their elopingation plans, even though I promised I won't say anything, because anyone could be listening, so I just go through the shots like Vicky told me but somehow my heart is not in it, and neither is Faraz's and I can all but hear Vicky's voice in my head shouting, If you're both trying to lose is the loser the winner or the winner the loser? I want to share this joke with Faraz, but he is not looking. When the three games are finally over, he takes a beeline to my side of the court, looks me in the eyes and says, You know that you and I are the same, no? We're both perfectionists who dare to be imperfect.

Before I can ask him what he means, he just turns and leaves and for the first time it feels like a bona fide fact that Faraz is about to leave me for a long little while and for a few moments I can't breathe only.

With the imminence of Holi, the sun suddenly has teeth. I am picturing the colourful blotches that will decorate my knees and elbows on Monday, even though it's still only Saturday now, the last afternoon before the tournament, and Vicky has arranged for us to meet on the terrace for a final strategy meeting. He is kneeling before me and has been non-stop speaking since I stepped through the metal door.

Isn't it fascinating, the amount of time it takes to bring the racket up in comparison to the distance a shuttle will travel in that time? So remember to keep your racket up, or you will miss many opportunities of killing the shuttle, which is the only reason you're up at the net to begin with. Geeta, are you listening to me?

Hm.

On my elbow there could be a purple blotch having a thorough resemblance to a cat with a broken tail.

You're not listening to me. Is something on your mind?

My main impediment: Because of top-secret training, I shall have to leave behind my coach and rely on my inbuilt flexibility to internalise his guidance. After a few moments of waiting in vain for my response, Vicky picks up the shuttlecock lying between us.

Do you know what feathers are used to make the professional ones?

A shuttlecock's?

Vicky chuckles. I mean which specific feathers of a goose's are used?

I didn't know that geese have specific badminton feathers, so I say nothing.

Six, maximum seven feathers from the goose's left wing.

Only these have the right curvature, weight and length. Takes about one year, from pluck to production.

What happens to the goose's right wing?

For amateurs. You see, the feathers on each wing are curved differently. The feathers on the left spin clockwise. That's why you can't mix the two wings on a single shuttle.

Because then it'll fly in a zigzag.

Vicky inspects me like there is an invisible magnifying glass between us. Then he nods. That's correct! Not a zigzag that you could spot yet, but a pro knows. And each goose is different, so each shuttle is a bit different. A pro can tell with a single shot whether it's a fast or a slow shuttle, or a high-spinning one.

So my shuttles are right wing?

They'll be duck feathers, I'm afraid. Goose shuttles are expensive.

Oh.

Vicky spins the cork bottom between his fingertips.

I'd like to see a zigzag that no one else sees.

Vicky smiles. Maybe tomorrow you will.

And what if I lose tomorrow?

You won't.

But what if I do?

What I can't tell Vicky is that I'm not just referencing the tournament but also the fact that Holi is Faraz and Sitara's last day in Kaka Nagar. A substantial part of Geeta wants to inform Vicky that he will not see his daughter for a very long while. I happen to be in possession of knowledge of the fact that Abba at least would be excessively sad if I were to suddenly disappear, and I don't want Vicky to experience the selfsame. But I also promised to comprehensively avoid bean-spillage, and it may be remembered that promises are not exchangeable like wrong sizes or broken antennas. Besides, he and Sitara seem to want this more than anything else, so as their primary friend it is my duty to assist them.

Well, then maybe you don't have it in you after all.

What, Uncle?

Coach Sir.

What, Coach Sir?

To be a true champion.

I commit there and then to being a true champion, not just in badminton, but also in the maintenance of promises.

I do!

So then you won't lose!

I temporarily adopt my high-sugar smile, even though Vicky's answer is not fully satisfactory and the pink blotch I picture on my knee looks like a bursting light bulb.

Vicky's hand lifts my chin, so I raise my eyes to meet his. Look, Geeta, I'm not going to lie to you. Most players tomorrow will be older, stronger and taller than you, and their names will not be Faraz. There will be four other matches going on around you, there'll be shuttles zipping around like bacteria in a hospital. Coaches and onlookers will cheer for your opponent as you play. They'll make it very clear to you that they want you to lose. On those courts, your will to win will be easily matched by that of every single other player there. Tomorrow is going to be not about your wrist but about your nerves. Vicky taps my temple with his index finger. Can you handle it?

I think so.

No, Geeta, that's not good enough.

Yes, I can.

Tell me you're ready.

I'm ready. Saying it makes it feel true. After all, sometimes a long little while can be a lot less long than expected. But this only makes me think of Mummy's illness. If I am having to be fully honest, I don't know how I'll play the tournament tomorrow.

Again. Are you ready?

Ful-ly ready! Saying it louder makes it substantially truer. What if there is a way to make saying goodbye be not like losing, but more like winning—you miss the other party so much that you suddenly see the fire burning for them in your interior, which you couldn't even see before you had to say goodbye. Still, this logic is faulty: I don't know what I won by losing Mummy.

I look back up to Vicky, who is staring at me like I'm a word missing from the dictionary, then he puts his hand on my shoulder and states—nothing.

Even before Abba and I enter the indoor section of the stadium, my dutiful ears hear shoes whistling against wood, voices flying around, catgut whipping cork, which in toto is happening not in isolation but seems to be coming from all corners around us. It sounds like we're about to enter a railway station.

We push through the door—not one, two or even three

or four but five matches are in progress simultaneously: Leaping calves, curling fingers, tumbling knees, squatting feet, soaring arms, twisting torsos; mouths groaning, lips cursing, hands clapping, chins muttering; and all around the courts is a ring of helper ants—Coach Sirs and Coach Ma'ms, Uncles, Aunties, brothers, sisters, didis, bhaiyyas—crawling over each other to deliver this snack, that towel or such and such message. At the Annual Kaka Nagar Badminton Tournament, every onlooker has a name of which I am in possession of knowledge. With the exception of Abba, this stadium is completely anonymous.

We stand in line at the registration table, and I try to block out the noise exploding behind me. The whirr and crack of shuttlecocks drives my pen as I sign my name on the roster.

Don't be nervous, Abba orders as we walk to Court 2, where my qualifying match is due to begin as soon as the ongoing one concludes.

I say nothing but find Abba's hand as we walk. Maybe because I haven't done that in a long time, Abba looks at me.

And don't forget that your admission depends on your performance today.

Since all the present U-13s desire to become champions like myself, it is deemed useless to explain to the parent cadre that thinking about my school admission to boot is not exactly assisting me in the achievement of said goal.

That must be her: Gitanjali Gil, age 12, from Ludhiana.

Geeta vs. Gita.

One look at her notifies me that she did not have undercover training with a secret coach. She might say she is twelve but she could easily pass for a fifteen year old boy: her short hair is oiled down on both sides of her head, she is wearing a white Polo shirt with open buttons hanging over black shorts, and her thick wrist is gripped so tightly by a silver kadha that a handcuff may be remembered.

Her coach is looking very coachlike in his gym suit unlike Abba, who is wearing office clothes. The coach is nodding in my direction and talking into her ear. She nods back slowly, looking at me as if I am not made of Geeta but of excessively thin glass.

Go introduce yourself to your teammate.

She's not my teammate, Abba.

Abba takes up a squatting position and seeks out my eyes through Vicky-like chin-liftage. Someone will have to lose today, Geeta, and it cannot be you.

I want to tell Abba that I prefer him to say it's just a game and that he wants me to have fun instead of focusing on the school admission.

Think of it as a battle you have to win.

It is deemed likely that none of the other players have a school admission tied to their performance, or that anyone else here has to secretly say goodbye to their best friend this weekend.

Stompage of left foot occurs before it can be prevented. Facial expression of opponent spells A-M-U-S-E-M-E-N-T.

My eyes are suddenly two magnets for tears; before I am fully in possession of knowledge of events, my cheeks are soaking wet, and I haven't even started my warm-up as per Vicky's instructions. Because now I am wishing Mummy were here so that I could say out aloud that I really, truly and in full do not want Faraz to leave with Sitara on Tuesday morning, and that I need Vicky to be there instead of Abba, even though I am availing of his neck and shoulder for disposal of salty water and snot.

All right, Geeta, listen. Take a deep breath.

The umpire says, Geeta Rahman? You're up next.

Just give us a moment, sir, Abba tells him. He cups my face in his hands and scans my eyes. I'm not going to force you to play, okay?

I *want* to play! Just not with all these people around.

Well, baby, that's how tournaments work. If that stupid Mr Bhabra hadn't filled your head with all this instant champion nonsense, you would be on court already fulfilling your admission requirement, not crying on my shoulder.

This statement only enhances the magnetism of my eyes.

We're on a tight schedule, Mr Rahman, so perhaps she should try again next year.

The umpire and Abba are looking at me with expectation-filled eyes. They are both forgetting that next year I will not be U-13 anymore.

You want to forfeit?

Just think about your future, Geeta.

I do as I am told, but all I picture is a bag hanging from a nail with all my badminton gear stuffed into it, gathering dust like Naniji's harmonium at the Blind School.

I forfeit, I say, but nobody can hear me, because my statement has been absorbed by the sound of a whistle so piercing it could burst open the tightest knot on the most confidential file, and it only stops once I look up to locate its origin, abandoning Abba's shoulder in the process and finding myself looking straight at a light-blue banner in the top row of the stands, hiding its bearer:

ALWAYS A TIGER!

NEVER A MOUSE!

I swerve my tears away with the base of my palm, like Mummy shifting gears in our car. I think of Vicky hiding on his terrace only so he can observe me on court.

Wait, I'm playing! I shout. I'm playing!

The coin toss goes in my favour.

Geeta Rahman to serve. Love all. Play!

Is it my imagination or is the umpire's voice quivering with excitement? Only a few hours have passed since I beat Gitanjali Gil in straight sets, and then I beat Salma Abidi in the quarterfinals, and then I beat Priyanka Modgill in the semi-finals and now I am playing my last match of the day—the finals of the U-13 against Ragi Pasricha, who is a tall, excessively thin girl with a ponytail down to her waist and also the reigning tournament champion from the previous year.

I close my eyes for a second and focus just on the grip of my racket—reminding myself of torn terry cloth and chipped wood peeking out from underneath. I ignore the sting at the base of my index finger where a blister has formed, and adjust my grasp: Firm enough so the little bird doesn't escape, but not so tight as to crush it. I picture Tinku inside my palm. If he was here, I am sure that today would be the day where he would show us all that he can really and truly fly.

My other arm is raised, bent at the elbow, fingers curled around the shuttlecock. Although I am playing with my back towards ALWAYS A TIGER, NEVER A MOUSE, I can sense that Vicky is in attendance. I can feel his eyes following my every move. This is it. This is the moment we have been waiting for. And yet—no matter whether I win or lose, tomorrow Faraz and Sitara are leaving. The thought staples itself to my mind like the most pointless memo. It sticks and becomes entangled in my head.

Quickly, I kneel down before the audience to re-tie my laces before anyone can check whether they're really loose. This silences the memo. I push my thoughts all the way down to my feet and tie them up in double knots, so they don't float back up into my mind. Then I stand, adjust my position and open my fingers to hit the shuttlecock hard.

It sails straight into the net.

Service over. Love all.

Cheers like paper tearing everywhere. Without my advance notice, the stadium has suddenly filled up. Ragi has brought her fan club. They are waving banners reading RAGI NUMBER ONE FOREVER and CHAMPION OF RAGIMINTON and WE LOVE YOU RAGI. I am having the impression that not just her whole school but the whole country is in attendance to support her.

I raise my hand to signal to Ragi and the umpire that I am not ready. I check to make sure that Abba is there to applaud my points but I don't see him. Did he have to choose this moment to go to the loo?

Rahman, play! the umpire scolds me. I get in position and Ragi serves. It's a shot fully lacking all kindness: fast, hard and on the mark. The shuttlecock flashes across the net just an inch above it and yet it falls towards the court lightly—with God's grace, I hear Naniji's voice inside my head—before I manage to lift it at the last split second. Ragi is already waiting, pelting me with the shuttlecock. She scores the point, and I am relieved that the rally is over.

One—Love.

Another thought arrives neatly typed in my head: Maybe Ragi deserves to continue as champion, because her shots are having a deadly combination of speed and precision that I cannot match.

The next serve is low. In the full sense of the word. Ragi hits it an instant before I take position and I barely manage to drive it across. There is a slight drift in the stadium. It picks up the shuttle slightly—enough for Ragi to smash it across court and beyond my reach. We play an almost identical rally, like a victory dance Ragi has ordered me to perform for her again and again.

Three—Love.

Hah! Ragi cries every time she scores. I jump on the spot to shake the contents of my brain into my feet. Is it too early to re-tie my shoelaces again?

Rahman, play!

Is it the certainty that Ragi will win? Or the fact that badminton without Faraz is like trying to read without knowing the alphabet?

Rahman!

A collective boo goes through the audience in support

of the umpire's scold. Vicky explained to me that delaying on court is a fault and that an umpire can disqualify you if you overdo it. But rather than weakening Ragi through this tactic, I feel my own knees quivering.

Ragi serves low again. I barely manage to sustain a four-shot rally before hitting the shuttle into the net. Again. The crowd's cheers are deafening.

RA-GIIIIII! RAAA-GI!

RA-GIIIIII! RAAA-GI!

I try to drive the shuttle across in an effort to keep up with Ragi's speed but she is immediately on to my strategy, using the faster pace to make me run more. I am doing my utmost to restrict the game to the front section of our courts and making my drops less easy to read but Ragi seems to have some kind of special dictionary for my game and, shot by shot, she pushes me back towards my base line, where it happens more than once that I drop a shuttle in the hope that it's out. It never is. Within minutes, Ragi has achieved an eight-point lead.

In the short pause before the next serve I hear the crowd's chant clearly: Nikal de, Ragi! Throw her out, Ragi! Kehech ke le, kehech ke! By her ears!

Vicky's words float back to me like the gentler shuttlecocks of Kaka Nagar: Badminton is chess for the body. Tennis and cricket you play with your arm, but badminton you play with your mind. It is most difficult for me to break out of her clearing game without taking too many risks. The rallies are getting shorter and shorter. I hit a wide. Ragi scoops up the shuttle next to her baseline—and already she spins around preparing to serve. Net shot. A collective moan runs through the audience.

Service over! The score is 4-13.

The crowd is serenading Ragi's impending victory: Jeete gi, bhai, jeeti gi, Ragi jeete gi!

Within seconds, the serve is Ragi's again. Then it's match point. Ragi aims her deadly shuttlecock at my heart. A shot like this is not only impossible to return, it makes the opponent look like a fool as she tries.

Game Pasricha.

It may be noted that I have never lost a game by such a large margin but more than facing this highly deficient crowd I am fully dreading talking to Abba, who will remind me of my need to avoid losing and tell me that there is no shame in having a full stadium sing songs about my negative performance. I unglue my throat with a sip of water from my bottle.

Abba does the only thing worse than saying something: not saying anything.

I swallow and take the banana Abba hands me, which he had gone outside to buy, and am taken by surprise by Abba's hand suddenly gripping my chin. I glance up at the parent cadre, and there is a look on his face that he normally wears only when he is reading his favourite poetry: calm and content.

I'm sorry, Geeta.

Although I don't want to hear him say that he is sorry for having to witness my substantial and thorough and utmost failyourownlife, I know I will be unable to defeat his words with mine without triggering a stream of tears, which I want to avoid at all costs in front of Ragi and her very own Greek Chorus.

Your passion, your talent, your will—I'm stunned.

I want to ask whether he is joking or still being fully serious but the umpire's whistle is calling us back to the court. I quickly turn back to him.

I'm losing badly.

I'm in awe of you, Geeta. All I can do now is ask for your forgiveness.

What about my admission?

It doesn't matter. What I am seeing today is worth so much more to me than that.

Abba's words are like the glasses he puts on to read his poetry: All at once, I see things clearly. I was afraid of Ragi because she is the reigning champion and I have never even played a tournament before. But if Abba, the number one champion non-believer of badminton, is suddenly converted to believing in my courtly talent regardless of a school admission, then I must be the superior player, because winning against many odds is more difficult than winning without them.

I return to the court. We have changed sides. It was beneficial for Ragi to play against the drift so she could push the shots, but now I will have the advantage, because, as Vicky informed me, drift is harder to control than friction.

Ragi serves and immediately scores two points in a row. Then she serves into the net. I run for the next point, miss it, but win the serve back right away and score my first point of the game.

This time, Ragi serves wide and I quickly equalise. We slap the shuttlecock back and forth, I return with a deceptive net shot, which Ragi lifts—into the net. That's when I am having my realisation thanks to Abba's re-evaluation: Ragi is in a hurry to win, and she is unable to keep up with her own pace, which is why she is beginning to make mistakes. Vicky's voice is in my ears: Greed for power is punished. There are no shortcuts in life and in badminton. Don't lose patience.

Because when you rely on speed as heavily as Ragi does, once your speed starts dropping even just a fraction you begin to feel weak, which in badminton means you are weak. All I need to do is slow down the game, and that will break Ragi.

One fierce rally now follows another. There is no opening, no room for deception. I lose patience, drive the shuttle, aiming at the spot between Ragi's eyebrows. Cross-court smash—her signature shot. The crowd booms.

Then, finally, I make the next rally extend like one of Saleem Uncle's qawwals. I stop counting at 23 shots. There are long lifts and aborted smashes and powerful drives, and in the end I take the point to limited cheers with a reverse slice drop shot—my first of the match!

8–7 for me.

I glance at Abba, who is making the thumbs up sign at me for taking the lead.

Ragi stalls, clearly trying to make me nervous and overthink the upcoming rally. She walks to the edge of the court and stretches her racket arm.

Pasricha, play! comes the warning from the umpire.

I jump on the spot to indicate that I am far from nervous, perhaps even a little bored. Ragi is suddenly back on court, signalling for me to serve, and she takes the point with a backhand net shot that I did not anticipate.

Service over.

My whole life plan is to win the serve back at the next point. I will not let Ragi take the lead again. Her serve cuts the air like Naniji's knife slicing open an onion. I rush forward as if to play a delicate drop shot but at the very last moment, with a flick of the wrist, I toss the shuttle over Ragi's head. Slightly more applause than last time.

Ragi returns my serve. We rally back and forth. She is playing badminton but I am intending to play chess with Ragi. I set up my disguised net shot three rallies in advance, so that when I stretch my arm, swing but stop as the racket is about to make contact and deposit the shuttle just over the net with a soft touch, Ragi cannot make it in time.

10–7.

My lead is growing, and with every point, I am having more and more chances to expose the heaviness of Ragi's legs. But Ragi knows that a match is won point by point. All you have to do is win the next point. Then the next one. And so on. Again and again, Ragi manages to speed up the game. She comes close to taking the lead—but doesn't. Another wide from her and the serve is mine again. I feel the utmost power in my wrist when I drill the shuttle into Ragi's shoulder. One after the other, I tear points from the court and throw them onto my side of the scoreboard.

And yet the game is faster than average and my eyes dance from side to side. My breath runs as fast as my legs. Neither are granted more than a moment of rest between rallies. Ragi and I have both already played three matches today, and she probably has blisters on her hands, too. But at least I am now fully capable of forcing Ragi to resort to defensive clears, which I then convert into commendable net shots finished off with a smash.

13–9.

I prepare to serve, then raise my hand to indicate a pause. I feel for Naniji's pendant around my neck. She asked me on my birthday whether I could shoot through seven palm trees at once with my shuttlecock, just like Ram did with this very arrow. That day my dutiful response was Not yet. Today, I will win the next point with a maximum of seven rallies, and each of my shots will have the power to pierce one palm tree in full. Like Vicky, I aim my serve at Ragi's neck, which she barely manages to return. I give her one of Faraz's powerful backhand clears. Still, Ragi is fighting back. She hits the shuttlecock deep into my backcourt. I fire a fully compliant drive to Ragi while facing my own back boundary line, the riskiest shot I have ever seen and that only once, when Sitara performed it on the court in Kaka Nagar. Ragi returns again. Next is a preparatory shot so straight and orderly that Abba could write a whole file about it. Ragi obliges and I make Naniji's wrist pain stop with another perfect drive that Ragi returns exactly to the designated spot. The last step is a reverse slice drop shot so precise that it could easily steer the whole world in the right direction. I dedicate the shot to Mummy as Ragi races towards the net—in the opposite direction as the shuttle.

Match point Rahman.

Shabaash! comes Abba's voice from the sideline.

When I look up, Ragi no longer has the eyes of a hungry wolf but those of an ant whose breadcrumb has just been moved to the other end of the table. She is a firecracker on court, but she burns out fast. She knows that there'll be a third game, and suddenly, I, too have a special dictionary that helps me read my opponent: Ragi Pasricha is scared of Geeta Rahman. She's leaning on her racket, which can only mean one thing: she is exhausted, fully, thoroughly and in toto. Although I feel like doing the same, I force myself to stand even straighter as if I am receiving the most pertinent new details about Mummy. I decide not to pay for a point Ragi is giving me for free. Before I can say interim relief subject to terms and conditions, the umpire is announcing:

Game Rahman.

And suddenly, the applause for me is loud like the beginning of monsoon. It's as if the audience is punishing Ragi for disappointing them, and I grant myself permission to look around and see the roar in the stadium, which leads to automatic chin liftage.

We change sides again.

The next game isn't really one.

Ragi scores a point here and a point there but she's little more than an audience to my game. And then it is my match point already. A part of me wishes that Ragi would put up some resistance so that this final rally could amaze everyone one last time. But a few seconds later, the shuttle falls limply at her feet.

And, just like that, I am promoted to undisputed winner of this year's U-13. I am going to have a trophy just like Sitara's in her glass case. Before I can turn around to share the news with Abba, he is right behind me, hugging me so tight I have trouble catching my breath that is still racing. When he lets go, I see that Abba's eyes are wet with tears.

He wants to say something, but the karela in his throat is not letting him. It doesn't matter, because I can hear the words deep inside my heart even without his voice: I am so proud of you. I wipe the drops from his cheeks with my thumb.

I did it, Abba! I shout, even though his nose is touching mine. I'm a champion! Officially and bona fide, I am a champion!

Abba's red eyes tell me that he is in full agreement. The umpire is calling my name for the handshake. I wipe more tears from Abba's face. He kisses my hands, again and again, and I do the opposite of stopping him.

Geeta Rahman, please come!

Abba nods at the voice behind me and wipes his eyes on his sleeve. Then he smiles and says as he nudges me back onto the court, Go, na, my official and bona fide champion daughter has a trophy to receive.

Benita lowers Icarus back into his cage and rolls off her rubber gloves. At least he drank all the glucose water today—a definite sign of impending recovery. Today must be an auspicious day, with Geeta winning not just the tournament but also a spot in Prakash Padukone's new badminton academy in Bangalore, which means that Geeta's days in Kaka Nagar are now numbered.

She leans her hand on the edge of the steel tray, wiping sweat from her brow. Did spring turn into summer at this very moment? She steadies herself and glances at her watch. The brigadier would enter with his Dessert of the Day in 5, 4, 3, 2,—

The door swings open.

There you go, love. Gajar ka halwa with roasted sesame. No nuts, just raisins.

Icarus finally stopped whimpering, she says and takes the spoon from him.

She feels his eyes pinned on her as she makes the rust-coloured pulp disappear into her mouth.

Love the sesame, don't like the raisins. Carrots chunkier please for more texture. Also, add a smidgen of ginger, and what happened to the honey we talked about last time?

Noted. And I told you, didn't I, Icarus has the soul of a soldier.

Benita places the blanket over her favourite bird's cage. For tomorrow I'd like something more solid, like cake. Something fruity, please.

And you shall have it.

They stand next to each other as Benita empties the bowl.

That was delicious, darling.

The brigadier smirks and whispers, I know.

Benita takes one last look around the clinic. All the birds are asleep under their cloths. She then turns to the brigadier, who nods at her, the cue to leave the clinic for the night.

All right, I'm off, she says, as they enter the living room.

The brigadier walks her to the front door and hands her the torch from the hook next to it.

Did you change the batteries? she asks.

You wander alone, but I provide the light.

Benita nods and smiles at her husband, slips on her shoes and out of the door.

When she was younger, Benita thought his complete acceptance of all her principles, which others readily dismissed as whims, was due to his instant and complete love for her, but over the years she understood that he is only able to love in such a manner, because his innate grace allows him to see all living beings just as they are. It had been this way from their first encounter at the barracks in Panjim, where her father, the original brigadier, had given the young Lieutenant Philips a dressing-down for reporting to duty with mud plastered all over his shoes. Little did the lieutenant know that this was the brigadier's traditional welcome, with Benita commissioned to dig a shallow pit right under the mat in front of the brigadier's doorstep and fill it with muddy water whenever there was a new recruit. Little did the brigadier know that Benita had observed the lieutenant the previous day as he nursed an abandoned rabbit kit and decided for the first time to omit the welcoming ritual, so that when the brigadier finally glanced at the lieutenant's spotless footwear and stopped mid-rebuke, the lieutenant quickly bent down and polished them with his handkerchief to spare the brigadier the embarrassment of apologising, which, being the man that he was, he did later that evening over a glass of Old Monk.

Benita shakes her mane and takes a deep breath of night air. It is that perfect blend of crisp and soothing, like a peacock's cry. So summer has not arrived after all. The thought makes her chest constrict for a painful moment. She misses the summers of her childhood in the south, which were so dense with heat and moisture you had to think hard every morning whether last night's dreams hadn't been the previous day's events, and vice versa. Delhi summers are dry like cardboard and taste of dust.

Unlike her morning walks, her nightly wanderings are not so much about the birds (though she did once discover a sparrow barely twitching on the road, probably having flown against a windshield. She took it home and injected a painless death into its veins, and then the brigadier buried it under their bougainvillea shrub). Nighttime walking is for mentally preparing for the next day, which may very well be your last.

The dimension of the walk is one round of Kaka Nagar,

which takes her half an hour. The brigadier is aware of this figure, of course, and it is an unsaid contract between them that she will never be gone longer than this duration, or he would have cause to, as he always says in situations that warrant alarm, bring in thc army.

Out on the dark road that evening and for reasons Benita cannot quite fathom, she spontaneously decides on an anti-clockwise circumnavigation of Kaka Nagar. At this hour even the digestive walkers have returned home and she has the narrow street to herself. She is surprised by the vigour in her step, as if her feet are conducting a secret mission that the rest of her body is not privy to but has blind orders to assist. At this rate, she might even make it back sooner than the thirty minutes.

Her favourite part of the walk is to imagine behind every window a specific act of kindness unfolding in the moment of her passing by. In 189, a moth decides not to chew through old Mrs Ahluwalia's muffler but sits still on the closet rod a little while longer; the ants in 182's kitchen are clearing the counter of all crumbs; in 176, Snoopy the Pomeranian lies by the side of his owner, suffering from a migraine, until he's asleep; in 168, the gecko eats the mosquito before it can suck the baby's blood.

In this manner she reaches the ditch in front of the Club House and finds herself staring at number 11, drawing a blank on what act of kindness might be unfolding therein. Though Geeta was a special girl, no doubt, the family has been steadily continuing its path to self-destruction since Sakshi's death. Not a day passes in this colony without a blatant reminder of this fact playing out right in front of

Benita's eyes. Take just this afternoon: first she sees the grandmother eating half a packet of éclairs on her way home from the temple, even though she is telling everyone that she has given them up after fracturing her wrist. Of course, everyone knows she only goes to the temple to harangue the young people and cleaning staff. Meanwhile, that scheming secretary Pushpa is loitering in front of their house with a bouquet of flowers (always using poor Geeta as an excuse!), so obviously in love with Geeta's father, I wonder Geeta's mother never saw it. And you would think a victorious Geeta would be dancing and celebrating, but instead barely an hour after their return she is leaning against her champa tree, forehead against bark, tears streaming down her face, no longer climbing up like she used to with her legs hanging free. And how many times has she seen Geeta's father during her nightly walk curled up in his car, motor running, crying himself to sleep?

This family is not unique for lying to themselves, of course, but Benita knows that at least some families manage the occasional U-turn. Here, it's been a long one-way street, and, frankly, it started even before Sakshi's diagnosis: Sakshi, whom everyone thought such a rebel, but Benita always found her rather conservative, tame even. She sounded just like your average fanatical Aunty when she spoke to Benita about getting Geeta into the best school or fostering her 'true talents,' whatever those were. The hard truth is, Geeta blossomed when the fostering stopped. Her heart might be broken forever, but at least she knows who she is now. She has found her way. And it turns out that it is Geeta who is the truly impetuous one.

Benita shakes herself from her reverie in order to, as she has been doing every night, shine her torch into the ditch to make sure that no living being has fallen in. When she looks up, she finds another torch's beam being shone straight into her eyes through the Club House hedge.

Who's there?

The light is averted, followed by a chuckle, then silence, then another chuckle before she realises that the chuckles are sobs.

Who's there? she asks again. Are you injured or just upset?

A throat is quickly cleared. I am injured, but my wounds are invisible.

Man, middle-aged, self-important, with a predisposition for sentimentality likely born out of a frustrated childhood and an unfulfilled marriage. Benita smiles: that description fits about every other man in Kaka Nagar.

All right, I'll leave you to it then.

No! Don't go. I know you. My daughter speaks of you. Highly. Not to me, of course.

There are only two girls in this whole colony who speak to me at all. And since you're clearly not Geeta's father, you must be Mr Bhabra.

Instead of an answer, there is just another sob, leading Benita to wonder if Sitara's mother has finally asked her overbearing husband for that divorce. And if so, how will this impact Sitara's elopement plans? Why exactly the girl is so smitten with Faraz Benita cannot fully grasp. The boy weighs less than the brigadier's elbow, imagine eloping with him! That said, who doesn't want to run a mile when they see his father? Of course, it's nice of Faraz to take pity on grieving Geeta, though the degree of condescension in his kindness towards her is hard to stomach sometimes.

Benita feels sweat on her brow again and the need to sit. She climbs through the gap the Club House children have manufactured into the hedge. Vicky Bhabra is sitting on the rusty swing set, a pile of papers in his hands. Benita hesitates for a moment, then sits down on the other swing. This makes a sound like a donkey wailing.

Do you know what this is?

No, but I suspect you're going to tell me.

A letter. From my father. To me.

Of course, Benita thinks. It's not the impending divorce that will make someone so domineering break down on a swing set. It's a grubby old letter.

His mother was murdered! While he was competing at the All England in London in March 1947.

Poor timing, Benita says, meaning both father and son as she checks her watch.

He didn't know that things would get so dire so fast in Lahore. And how could he have known? They cheated us into Partition!

Benita regrets engaging. She stands, making the donkey wail again, and says, I don't have time for political discussions, Mr Bhabra.

No, you don't understand! He found out about his mother on the morning of the finals. That's why he lost! That's why he wanted nothing more to do with badminton! Don't you see how twisted it all is? He returned to Lahore and then had to flee to Delhi, he stayed just down the street from here, at the refugee camp in Purana Qila, a stone's throw away from the very court on which Geeta, with my help, evolved into a champion today—don't you see? My father's Partition is my alienation, which in turn is the catalyst for Geeta's success.

Vicky sits so perfectly still staring at the sheets bracketed by his hands that Benita, too, feels the need to be quiet for a few seconds. Could it be that Vicky did not yet know about Padukone and the badminton academy? His pride would be encased in a hard shell of sadness to see Geeta go—the daughter he never had.

Benita retrieves an army green metal flask from the pocket of her dress, part of her mobile clinic, and hands it to Vicky, who unscrews it and takes a long gulp as if he was expecting it in just that moment.

I knew there had to be a reason for why he lost. I never saw him play but in my heart I always knew that he was the best player of his time. This is what I've been searching for all my life. A look inside my father's soul. So why do I now wish I had never seen this?

Because of the timing, of course. Why do you think your father chose to reveal all this to you now?

He didn't. He wrote the letter shortly before his death years ago and slipped it into the sleeve of his racket, probably thinking that I'll find and read it right after he passed. You see, he wanted me to have his racket! But why didn't he just say so? Why did he have to avoid me most of the time?

Doesn't he say in the letter? Final redemption and all that.

He says he wanted to protect me. From the madness raging inside his head. But he never let on and after his death I kept the racket in some corner and never took it out until today.

Because Geeta won the tournament today and you wanted her to have the racket to remind her that fathers don't always know best.

Bhabra turns to look at Benita, clearly wanting to smile but somehow unable to.

I want her to have the racket so that she'll never forget that it's not because of her parents and grandparents but because of these other people, her badminton forefathers—including a certain Prakash Bhabra from Lahore—that she is who she is.

Geeta, the underrated orphan from Kaka Nagar?

Geeta, the future of Indian badminton. But to find her way there, she will have to remember where she came from. The racket will remind her of that.

Benita wants urgently to go but in the end she doesn't move.

I was always angry with my father, Bhabra says. I was addicted to being angry with him.

A part of her wants to tell Bhabra that whatever sense of loss he's experiencing is about to swell exponentially. His daughter is eloping tomorrow morning, with the parents set up to find out—with her help—only later that evening. Then she remembers what Sitara's mother told her recently when she came to pick up her daughter from the clinic: Seeing a man disappoint as a husband is one thing, but when your husband fails as a father it is impossible to ever respect him again.

So instead Benita says, You know what they say in the

army? Pain and hope are two sides of the same coin. And the coin's currency is self-respect. My advice to you, Mr Bhabra, is, move on.

Benita hears another sob, then realises that this time it's a chuckle.

The irony is, of all the things my father writes here, what makes me the saddest is the first line: I am writing to you from the loneliest place on earth, an empty badminton court.

Well, he's wrong. The loneliest place on earth for a man is a hospital. And for a woman it's motherhood.

Benita says these words knowing what Bhabra will say in response: How would you know? Is that why you have birds instead of babies? She resents it, of course, when people say to her, as they so often do, that her birds are like the children she and the brigadier never had. She resents it because the prevailing notion that she would and should have preferred a human baby to an avian one is precisely *why* Benita decided before she even met her husband that she would never put children into this twisted world, children who would inevitably grow into adults with prevailing notions. The particular genetic cocktail of insolence and dimwittedness brought to perfection in humanity means that most people could not even see—and probably wouldn't want to—that we routinely take all that is sublime and precious about this planet and karate-chop it to dust.

Benita was eleven when she finally understood that motherhood was one of humanity's biggest PR hoaxes. It was the day her parents told her that she was adopted and, baffled by their anxiety-ridden faces as they told her about how her biological parents had died in a flood in their ancestral village shortly after her birth, she responded by saying that love was transferrable beyond blood and that loneliness, greed and sadness of all kind would immediately be cured if people would stop treating children who came out of their own bodies better than others.

Benita looks up to find Bhabra staring at her with a curious mix of perplexity and amusement.

I just realised that you're also wrong, he says. The loneliest place on earth for a man, too, is motherhood.

Benita holds his gaze for a moment, just long enough for a breath of recognition to pass between them, delicate as a moth's nest.

Good night, Mr Bhabra, she says, and, turning away, involuntarily adds, Good luck to you.

Only then does she check her watch.

Benita has never run anywhere as an adult. Even as a child she was rarely in a hurry, stopping to observe the downy red stigma and countless bright yellow stamen of a hibiscus blossom, as her classmates dashed past her, tearing the flowers off in passing to suck the nectar from its ovary. She would collect these butchered and quickly discarded flowers from the dusty street, withered in her palm by the time she reached home.

Benita runs. She feels the pull of gravity on her bouncing flesh and brings her arm up to support her breasts. Her nostrils feel like two collapsed tunnels, and she opens her mouth to ease her breath. Soon she feels a sting in her side, but she forces herself to breathe through it, and accelerates her step. Her torch's zigzag leads the way.

When Sitara came over to confide her elopement plans in

her, Benita's admiration and support for the girl was intact and Benita didn't even press the girl on revealing to her their destination. She didn't approve of the elopement, of course, and told Sitara that she would almost certainly come to regret this move, especially if she hadn't even finished her exams for the year. Yet even more than in the futility of teenage elopements she believed in treating children not like unformed, bite-sized adults but as innately wise human beings able to make their own choices and bear full responsibility for them. The girl came to her needing moral support and Benita was not her mother to try to discipline or educate her—or to worm more information out of the girl. It was, ultimately, none of her business where she and Faraz were heading on Tuesday. She acted as a friend would: offering honest advice but showing unconditional support once the decision was made. Talking to Vicky Bhabra made her realise the gravity of her mistake. For her reasoning neglected one important factor: we all drag behind us our personal, invisible fisher's net of grief and regret, and the people who get caught up in it accumulate with age. Vicky Bhabra's net is heavy, and adding the full weight of Sitara to it now will shred it irreparably. And however bullheaded and egotistical he might be, the man did everything he could to save Geeta, and he deserves a second chance for that alone. As always, life is about getting the timing just right, and while for Geeta the moment is overdue already, she is now sure that Sitara's timing is off. She will tell Sitara in the morning, she will take her aside on the pretence of wishing her happy Holi. She will bring a thermos of the brigadier's tea and talk Sitara through it while the others are busy slinging colour.

There will be no need to force her or withhold anything. Sitara will listen and understand. Not like an unformed, bite-sized adult but as innately wise human being.

Benita runs faster. There is a tingling in her arm now that would feel almost pleasant if it weren't for the nausea spreading in her gut, which is suddenly strong and pervasive, and flips the lightness in her head into a thumping pain. But she does not stop. The brigadier will take care of her as soon as she reaches home. There's nothing a steaming cup of his tea won't cure. She is not far now, just a few more rows of houses, then one last turn—the fire alive in Benita's chest seizes her so abruptly that she stumbles and lands on the edge of the road as the darkness of the night blends unhurriedly into the more complete shade of black glazing her eyes.

The news of Faraz's and Sitara's elopement the day after Holi has spread through Kaka Nagar like a gas leak. Abba says that Vicky and Saleem Uncle expected them to come back after a night or maximum two, but they didn't and now everyone is excessively worried, and not only because missing all their exams next week will mean they will have to repeat the year.

Apparently, Sitara went to Bird Aunty's house to study there after school on Tuesday, but when she didn't come home in the evening, it turned out that it was a lie, because Bird Aunty had a heart attack on Sunday and has been busy recovering in the hospital since then.

The last time I saw Faraz was right after the tournament, when I went straight to his house to tell him about my trophy. Abba tried to convince me to go the next day, what's the hurry? But I told him that I wanted to be the first to tell him rather than him hearing through the neighbourhood grapevine, which Abba admitted is faster than speedpost, so he let me go. The truth is I also wanted to tell Faraz about how sticking things out at home can sometimes be excessively rewarding, so I didn't even go with the exclusive intention of saying goodbye but with the hope of welcoming him back.

As soon as Faraz saw my face beaming at him, he shouted, I knew it!

His mother was crocheting a hanky in the other room but had positioned herself so she could watch us sitting on the sofa through the open door.

I've been waiting around all day to hear about your victory! I didn't even go to the loo, I was so nervous for you. Oh, what a beautiful rhyme. I should have written that into a card for you. Or a song.

Don't lie, you were not waiting for me all day.

I couldn't say why exactly but suddenly I felt excessively angry at Faraz for always turning everything into a joke, including Yours Truly, even when he was about to go away for a very long while and leave me behind to deal with everything by myself. I wanted to fling my anger at him like a ball of mud, but I kept the rest of my thoughts to myself: you were NOT waiting to hear from me all day. You were secretly packing. You were daydreaming of exchanging dearness allowances with Sitara. You were counting the minutes. You can't wait only to get away and forget all about our matches and that teasing me is always number one on your agenda.

I wanted to stand up there and then and leave but Faraz asked me about the tournament and I didn't dare to start a fight with him when his mother was watching, so I kept going into more and more detail to infect him with my anger, wanting to make him say to me, Smalls, ya, did you really win by playing or did you just talk all your opponents into the ground?

But he didn't. In fact, he asked more questions, which brought me very close to shouting, Stop pretending like you want to know!

Instead, when he asked, So at that point did Ragi go for the cross-court smash a second time or not? I simply stood up, ready to let go of Faraz, formerly known as Best Friend.

At first, I thought Faraz did not notice me, because his eyes were pinned on his bouncing knee, but then I heard him mutter, Stay.

And with that one word, all my anger was smashed out of the court and I sank back onto the sofa.

Stay.

I wanted to say it back to him. Could it really be that just for that one moment, Faraz needed me as much as I needed him?

Do you remember the first time we met? he asked me in a small voice and then his eyes began to dart again like he was watching an obstinate mosquito.

Ya, we had just moved here and you were feeling sad and Mummy cheered you up with a joke and then—

Do you know why I was sad?

I realised that I had never asked Mummy, or maybe I had but could not remember. It was only later that the boy became Faraz for me. I shook my head.

I ran away from home that day. Didn't get very far, obviously.

Why? I asked him.

I snuck out to play in the rain and got completely drenched and when I came home I realised I had forgotten that my father's boss was coming for tea, and so not only was

I absent when he arrived, everyone saw me enter the house like that. When the man left, my father called me to his desk and handed me a knife and said if I ever dared to disappoint him like that again, he would put the knife in my hand and plunge it straight into his own heart, so that next time I could watch him bleed to death for real and not just on the inside.

Faraz nods in the direction of the desk, above which a carved knife sits on a shelf.

I couldn't bear it: the idea that one wrong step, even by accident, and my father would make me kill him.

That's what you told Mummy?

Not all at once. That day I just told her I never wanted to go back home ever again.

And what did she say that made you change your mind?

You are not alone.

Right, because Mummy was there with you now.

No, that's not what she meant. She told me that she, too, ran away from home many times as a child, but that she was always caught, but it didn't matter after a while, because she knew that one day love would set her free.

She was telling you about me!

Well, you weren't born then, Smalls. That's when Faraz gave me his sideways grin. You did, however, step out of the car while she was telling me this.

I smiled back and thought: This is the best farewell present Faraz could have gifted me. And though Faraz was being in denial, I still think she had me in mind when she told Faraz this story. That's when I asked him, Do you remember what she was saying to you that made you smile when I came out of the car?

His grin widened. She said to see this not as a Greek tragedy but as a fully desi chutkulla.

I could not help but smile more. When Mummy got sick, I explained to him, she wanted me to see that also as a chutkulla only.

It's almost time for dinner, Faraz's mother called from the other room.

I nodded and said loudly for her to hear, I should go home, Abba will be waiting. I was expecting Faraz to ask me to stay again, but he just stood, so I did, too, and then I waved bye to Faraz's mother and was relieved that she followed us to the front door only with her gaze.

Faraz said, Congrats again, Smalls! Celebratory hug?

He wrapped his arms around me. When he released his grip I looked up and saw that his eyes were swimming and before I could stop them, tears began to slide down my lashes, too.

Faraz quickly cleared his throat and straightened his back.

Don't go, Faraz, I whispered from across the door's threshold.

Don't ever lose your stinkato, Smalls, he whispered back and quickly closed the door between us.

And so Faraz did leave with Sitara as planned, but I think there was something about staying to see me win that freed him to go. Or at least that's how I want to think about it.

And so I have decided to see Faraz's departure as yet another chutkulla as per Mummy's directive and to instead focus on the other items on my agenda: I hope Bird Aunty will come back home soon, so that I can go see Tinku. And maybe Bird Aunty will let me take her and Tinku for a spin. Because: Abba finally taught me how to drive! When we got in the car after the tournament, before I went to see Faraz, I pleaded and pleaded with Abba to just once show me how to start the car since he was so proud of me and all, and in the end he gave in and explained everything to me step by step, even though he made me double promise not to try it out myself.

But now it's Friday, and Bird Aunty is still not home.

Yesterday, Day 3 of the elopement, Saleem Uncle and Vicky came to talk to me. Abba led me into our living room, where they were sitting at opposite ends of the sofa set. Vicky said, Hi, Geeta, and Saleem Uncle firmly attached his eyes to mine like a leash onto a dog's collar but to my surprise they were the opposite of angry.

Come sit with us, he said and pointed at the chair adjusted so it was standing in front of him. I did as he asked.

How is your exam preparation going?

Excessively—I glanced at Abba, who was looking at me expectantly—well.

I heard about your tournament title. Congrats. Well done.

I found myself staring at Saleem Uncle to see if he was being serious, but there was no indication in his face that he was joking.

You know I can be strict at times, but I've always thought that you're a brave girl, Geeta.

That's when my eyes flew to Abba for a detailed memo on how to respond to this new Saleem Uncle, who at that moment was doubly confusing, because not only was he saying substantially friendly things, he was saying them even though he should have been comprehensively furious about Faraz. But Abba looked just as perplexed.

I said, Thank you, Uncle, and meant it also, because who would have thought that Saleem Uncle has so much untapped potential for being officially designated a Friendly Uncle?

Saleem Uncle leaned towards me. As you know, Faraz and Sitara left home on Tuesday morning. I know Faraz is like a brother to you, and he's my son, my boy. We're worried out of our minds, they're just—

I thought you said there's no reason yet to be—

Mr Bhabra! Kindly don't interrupt my... my chat with Geeta.

The look Saleem Uncle hurled at Vicky made him stay silent. My eyes got caught in Vicky's, and I saw something I never saw in there before: Vicky looked comprehensively scared. He turned away. I wanted to run to him then and tell him about how after they gave me the trophy, they took Abba and me to a room and then in came a man who said he watched me play and wants to offer me a full scholarship to come to his new badminton academy in Bangalore and that he would personally be in charge of my training. It was Prakash Padukone! Every day I'd been meaning to tell Vicky this Truly and Fully Extraordinary News, but our post-tournament analysis never happened because of the elopement, and of course now was not the right time. And

I didn't even tell Faraz about Padukone either, because I didn't want him to conclude that if I was leaving, he also had no reason to stay.

Saleem Uncle continued, I'm here to ask you, to plead with you, as my son's best friend and a trusted, brave member of our little community here in Kaka Nagar, did they tell you anything about this?

My hands were stuck under my thighs and my eyes pasted to my knees with superglue. If I stayed like this long enough would they all go away and believe that I was not withholding any secrets, leads or other pertinent information?

Silence is often a sign of complicity, Geeta.

Abba put his arm around me. I'm sure she will say if she knows anything. Give her a moment.

I heard Saleem Uncle taking a deep breath and for a moment I was not sure if it was a sob, but when he spoke again, his voice was not shaking, Young people like my son believe they are immune to bad luck, to sin, to danger. But you, Geeta, you were forced by fate to learn early on that life is fickle and unreliable. The only thing that God leaves entirely in our own control is our conscience.

Silence flowed outwards from Saleem Uncle. And just when I thought I would have to drown in it or tell him the truth, he started speaking again. Did they mention any upcoming plans? Any preparations you noticed? Any unusual behaviour?

I have since revised my prior assessment and determined that Sitara was right: it would have been preferable if they had not told me anything. Faraz must have known that Saleem Uncle would come to question me like this, pretending to be a Friendly Uncle, which is somehow much scarier than if he had stayed his usual self, because I don't know whether it means that this time he will definitely arrest me.

Imagine this scenario, Geeta: Faraz and Sitara are sitting together somewhere right now, you know exactly where they are, so you can picture it clearly. They're laughing, they're having fun and they made you promise not to say anything. So you don't. But then night falls and they don't have any money and—

Saleem Sahab, don't mind me saying, but I don't think this is helpful. Abba quickly turned to me before Saleem Uncle could object or continue, his face directly in front of mine as he spoke to me in his imploring voice: Jaani, if you don't know anything about this, then it's fine, nobody is going to be angry and it's not your fault, but if you do know something, anything, you have to tell Saleem Uncle. We all miss Faraz and Sitara, and they need to come home soon. Do you understand?

I wrenched my eyes from my knees and glanced up into Abba's two black inkwells staring back at me, waiting to be written into the truth by Yours Truly.

C-H-A-N-D-I-G-A-R-H.

That's what Faraz had let slip against Sitara's wishes. If I broke it down into harmless, impartial letters, could I protect Faraz and release him at the same time?

C—, I said and from the corner of my eye noticed Saleem Uncle and Vicky swoop towards me like two crows about to pull a worm from the earth.

And that's when I remembered Faraz's words: I am a perfectionist who dares to be imperfect. Although I felt scared together with Vicky and sad for Saleem Uncle, who had to twist words around with me only because he wants his son back and is afraid that he will end up in the gutter like Faraz's brother, whom Faraz never once mentioned, I determined in that moment that Faraz, Sitara and I are all birds that should be granted permission to fly. Didn't Sitara say, Autonomous is a good name for a caged bird?

See? Saleem Uncle repeated.

Sitara, I said. And Faraz. I don't know where they are. They didn't tell me anything. They didn't even say goodbye.

I hear the sizzle of something liquid being poured onto hot oil. Soon the smell of uttapam, my topmost favourite lunch item, fills my nose and I sit patiently at the dining table, writing my Truly and Fully Extraordinary News into the coconut chutney with the tip of my spoon for Vicky to read telepathically. My thighs still feel like two wrung-out towels, even though it's been five days since my bona fide championhood. The chatter from the kitchen informs me that Abba, who has taken the week off to be my official assistant in this pre-exam period, and Naniji are cooking together.

It was on the morning after Holi, before the news of the elopement became public knowledge, that Abba squeezed me against his chest and whispered, I'd never thought I'd say this, but you're in a win-win position: Padukone is serious about you, and he assured me on the phone just now that he can get you into a top school in Bangalore, so we can afford to take the pressure off a little on these exams.

He then proceeded to notify Naniji and me that on Friday

after school he would take us both to Appu Ghar, where I used to ride the toy train and the bumper cars and the Columbus Jhoola with Mummy and Naniji while Abba stood on the side with a giant pink beard of our three respective candy flosses. But that was before Mummy got sick, and we have not been back there since then.

I am wiping up the last streaks of Naniji's sambar from my plate with a piece of buttery uttapam when Abba taps his watch with his finger and says, How is it two o'clock already! Come, come, let's hurry up now! Appu Ghar closes at five thirty.

Just then the phone rings, and Abba stands to answer it. Although we cannot hear his words in the other room, there is something unusually brief about his tone, so that Naniji and I automatically exchange a look. The next moment Abba rushes back into the living room and turns on the television. Only then does he say, There's been an attack.

We are all standing now, and I am too scared to ask what kind of an attack and if that means we are not going to Appu Ghar, even though I made up my mind that this time I will not be chicken-hearted and try The Roller Coaster. The screen is showing smoke rising from a crumbled building. I glance at the parent cadre, whose fist is covering his mouth.

What happened, Abba?

He doesn't answer, just puts his arm around me and squeezes me into his side, which is somehow even more worrying. The newsreader announces two separate blasts in Bombay, damage and number of dead as yet uncertain.

Abba says, Four-By-Four called to say we should stay indoors today, in case they are targeting Delhi, too.

Who's they?

We don't know yet.

Then the pictures stop and the newsreader is back. She looks at us for a moment, then swallows what looks like a karela and announces that reports are now confirmed that another bomb went off a few minutes ago next to the Shiv Sena Bhawan in Bombay.

Abba says, I guess we know who they is now.

How, Abba?

Because the Shiv Sena orchestrated much of the riots in the last months. Their goons played a role in the demolition of the Babri Masjid. This is revenge.

Why isn't the newsreader telling us this?

As if this serves as an adequate answer to my question, Abba just shakes his head and says, There is no end in sight now, Geeta. It's going to be Beirut in Bombay.

I am about to ask Abba why Beirut would come to Bombay, but he puts his finger on his lips as the newsreader announces that the number of dead is still unclear, though it is now confirmed that the first blast at the Bombay Stock Exchange was the most powerful of the three and that the building is in severe danger of collapsing. She speaks to a reporter on the site, who says more bodies are being recovered by the minute and many of the injured are in critical condition.

Then she interrupts the reporter.

There has been another blast.

Again in Bombay.

At the Air India Building in Nariman Point.

Four blasts in one day! Abba mutters. Those animals.

What's going to happen now? Naniji asks the newsreader, whose fingers have taken hold of the sleeve's seam of her dark red sari blouse as if to turn off a hidden switch.

Divide and rule, Abba says.

The newsreader announces that buildings are being evacuated pre-emptively, people don't know where to go, there is chaos on the streets of Bombay. So far, it looks as if all the bombs had timers and were hidden in parked cars or scooters. New pictures show a man being carried away by three other men, blood criss-crossing all of their faces like masks.

As Abba goes to call Pavan Uncle in Bombay, I wonder if Faraz and Sitara are watching the same images on a screen in Chandigarh, and if this means they will want to come back now.

He's safely at home, Abba says as he returns to the living room. The newsreader comes on again, her sleeve untouched but she is leaning into the camera, as if she is going to climb through it and go straight to the bomb site.

We have just received confirmed reports from Bombay of two more bombs—

Hé Bhag!

Six!

Naniji turns and runs out of the room, and I hear her putting up all the latches on the front door before she returns.

Make it stop, Abba. Can't we go just to Appu Ghar?

Abba says nothing, but presses me against him so hard I can't keep my face aimed at the television.

For a fraction of a moment I feel at once light and prickly as if too many hands are trying to pull me away and no matter how hard I try I cannot seem to free myself of them.

Abba, are there going to be bombs in Delhi also?

Abba lets go of me and pulls up a chair and slumps down in it. I go stand next to him.

I don't know, Geeta. I told you, didn't I? The country is on fire but nobody wants to see the flames. It's the end of everything, and soon U-turns will no longer be possible.

I go sit with Naniji on her cot. She offers me another éclair. She has stopped eating them herself ever since the accident, and is always trying to feed them to me with the wrapper still half on, because the cast slows down her éclair hand. I take the candy but it's as if my tongue has been unplugged from my mouth and I can't taste anything. We sit like this through bomb number 7 and then bomb number 8, and by the time they announce bomb number 9 the too-many-hands are prodding and poking me not just from outside but in my belly also, so I quietly go to the bathroom, because of the vomity feeling in my stomach, but all that comes out of my mouth is a long string of saliva like a leash I have swallowed, and it wraps itself around my tongue as I try to rid myself of it, so I have to pull it out with my fingers. Afterwards I wash my hands once and then again, but still they seem to smell bitter as if there is a whole mountain of karelas piled up in my stomach.

While I was in the bathroom a tenth bomb went off, and I think it will never stop now. We will see bomb after bomb going off on television until the one meant for our house explodes, and that will be The Official End of Everything.

After bomb 11 and bomb 12 the Chief Minister of Maharashtra comes on the television and says there was a thirteenth bomb in a Muslim-majority area, so we must not make any premature assumptions about who carried out the attacks.

He's lying, Abba says. But who can blame him? You can see the panic in his eyes, fear of the clashes to come. And it'll be the poorest Muslims, of course, not those brainwashed criminals, who'll be slaughtered in retribution. This cycle cannot be broken now.

When there have been no new blasts in over an hour, the number of dead is estimated at well over two hundred, with many more injured. Reports are contradictory as to whether there were twelve or thirteen bombs in toto, but they were all in Bombay.

It's dusky outside when we turn off the television. Naniji goes to the kitchen to prepare dinner, and Abba sits down at his desk in his room, staring at a book. I go back into the living room, which is soaked in darkness now like a teabag left in hot water for too long. Something stops me from turning on the light. I sit cross-legged on the floor, running my palms over the rug and making crumbs and grains of dust jump around. Soon there are pins and needles pricking my fallen asleep foot. Instead of stretching my leg out, I squeeze my heels into my buttocks until my other foot, too, feels stiff. This is exactly how I was sitting on July 29, 1991, in darkness and with feet gone numb, as I was waiting for Abba to come home from the hospital. When he finally did, he sank down on the floor in front of me and said once and then again and again and again, She's gone, and we sat like this for a very long time, the constant movement of my toes necessary and unbearable at the same time. When I stood up my feet could almost not hold my weight, and I hobbled over to the television on what felt like a path of crushed glass. I switched it on. Abba didn't move at all, so his back remained turned to the screen, which was showing two women with badminton rackets facing each other on a court. The black and white image was so grainy that I couldn't make out the shuttlecock, but their movements were implemented with such precision that they were evidently able to control this invisible force.

The glass shard floor had long turned back into the rug when I curled up in Abba's lap, a single question on my mind: What happens to the invisible force when the rackets stop moving? That was the moment it hit me that I would never see Mummy again.

The night of the day of the twelve bombs minimum, March 12, 1993, I am incapable of falling asleep. The watchman goes on his rounds tapping his stick and blowing his whistle as if everything is normal, but I think all of India must be lying awake right now. Surely, Faraz and Sitara are lying awake, and Bird Aunty and the entire Greek Chorus are lying awake, and even Prakash Padukone is lying awake, not to mention Vicky and Saleem Uncle, who have probably not slept since Monday.

Of course, if Mummy were here, she would be the most awake of us all. And, suddenly, I am in receipt of a memo incapable of misconstruction, informing me exactly of what

I have to do: talk to Mummy, who is the only person at this juncture not affected by the bombs or by Faraz and Sitara's elopement and who will be willing, utterly and in full, to speak to me as if the whole world is just as it should be. Availing of my recent expertise in sneaking out of the house, I open all the latches with utmost care and noiselessness, but only after taking Abba's car keys from the designated hook.

Even though I promised Abba on Sunday that I would not apply his driving instructions to practice until I was eighteen, this is an emergency situation that even Abba could not have foreseen, and I really need to talk to Mummy right now.

I am sitting in the driver's seat of our Maruti, which is still parked on the street, where Abba left it when we came home from school in anticipation of a quick departure for Appu Ghar. I resist the temptation to honk to avoid parental notification of my absence from bed: No number of bombs can stop Geeta Rahman from being an independent young woman! Since I could still not tell Vicky my news, I am going to tell Mummy about it myself.

I close my eyes and remember what Abba told me after the tournament. Then I complete step one: releasing the handbrake. When I look up through the windshield, I notice that the car has slowly begun to move. I sit up straight and stare ahead. Yes, the car is definitely rolling at a non-advanced pace. I sway on the edge of my seat, running my hands in a circle around the steering wheel. Even though I did promise Abba that I would not implement the driving lesson, even he understood after the tournament that it's not always the best course of action to stop when you're told by a superior authority to stop. Champions don't become champions because they slow down, and if Geeta Rahman is on a roll, she should not be asked to give that up. I can steer the world in the right direction, too!

I'm coming, Mummy! You'll never believe what I have to tell you!

And before I can say subject to revision without notice, my feet are on the clutch and the accelerator, and I have turned the dangling key in the ignition. The motor groans and suddenly the car is alive. I feel the vibrations tickling the tips of my fingers on the steering wheel. The car is already pointing away from the mud room, so all I have to do is shift the gear and—SLOWLY, baba! I hear Abba say in my head—release the clutch in order to begin my first ever solo round of the park as an official and bona fide champion. My reward for all the early mornings and sleepy afternoons and aching calves and parental scoldings!

I am rolling past the Club House gate and then past our Ashoka tree hedge.

Bye bye, Club House! Bye bye, Abba! Bye, bombs! Just try and stop me now! Mummy, are you listening to me?

And then, suddenly, just like Abba promised, there is Mummy's voice in the most deepest, warmest room inside my heart: Yes, jaani, I'm listening.

Mummy! You're here! I can't help but bounce up and down in my seat as I twist the steering wheel to turn left onto the small road that goes around the park.

Can I tell you my Truly and Fully Extraordinary News?

I can't wait to hear it.

Prakash Padukone is going to be my Coach Sir at his new badminton academy in Bangalore!

That is truly and fully extraordinary, my darling.

Then I'll be a badminton magnet not just of Kaka Nagar, but of the whole world!

Although I have to do my tortoise neck to see the road ahead, in toto being a champion driver is much easier than I thought.

And, Mummy, there's more!

Even more?

Yes, because after the tournament Abba was talking non-stop like I've never seen him do before. It was like a rain of shuttlecocks that some people like to draw. And you know what the bottom line was?

He said yes, didn't he?

Yes, Mummy! My foot is slowly pressing down on the accelerator. The car is smacking its lips like former Naniji eating an éclair. All I have to do is steer. He said he's ready for a change. That this is a sign and that he's going to request a transfer to Bangalore. Mr Padukone is going to get me admission in a top school there, so that I can be a champion in academics also and—Mummy? Are you crying?

I'm just so moved, my jaan. I wish I could have been there with you and Abba today.

Me, too, Mummy! But please don't cry! Then I remember something. Mummy, is this how Vicky is feeling now that Sitara is gone?

He must be very sad, yes.

And is it going to be The End of Badminton for him when I go to Bangalore, just like his father always said?

Tell him to think of it as the Happy End of Badminton.

That's a commendable idea, Mummy! I turn right. The

yellow streetlamps are guiding me into the future, because the car lights are off, and I am not in possession of precise knowledge of how to switch them on.

Another right. This is almost too easy. My ride is beginning to feel less and less like match point and more like playing knocks, so I increase the pressure on the accelerator. As I lower my foot, I can almost feel Mummy sitting next to me.

Can I ask you something?

Anything.

Before Abba said yes, he told me that so far he was afraid of leaving Kaka Nagar. Are we going to lose you a second time if we go?

You never lost me, jaani. I will always be with you.

Promise, Mummy?

Promise. I'll be by your side wherever you go, even if it's the North Pole.

When I turn right one last time to arrive back on the road that leads straight back to our house I realise that I have been pressing down on the right pedal a little too firmly, because it is suddenly becoming difficult to stay in a straight line. Mummy, I'm going too fast!

Was that the door scraping against the edge of the pavement? It is hoped that there are no scratches and that Abba won't notice tomorrow that the car is pointing in the opposite direction than where he left it. Now our building comes into view and I realise that I forgot to ask Abba about the exact procedure on how to make the car stop once it is going at full speed.

Mummy, help me!

But Mummy doesn't answer.

I try to pull the handbrake again but I can't do it without letting go of the steering wheel. The car seems to be going faster still. There is the dark outline of the Club House up ahead and then I see a flash in front of me like Faraz's bicycle and then it's gone again, and I'm trying to get my thoughts in order—what am I forgetting? Foot on clutch? SLOWLY, BABA!—but then I note the mud room up ahead, and the car is shrieking and I'm screaming for Mummy, and I tear both my feet from the pedals and prepare to fall deep but instead the car makes a big jerk and stops and when I open my eyes all is quiet.

Only my breath impacts the silence. The car is not broken. The bombs did not go off. I didn't chase Faraz into the ditch on his bicycle.

I open the door and cool air rushes in and I wipe something from my forehead and step outside. That's when I start shaking, because the Maruti stopped at the very edge of the mud room. Something inside me says that when I peek over the rim, underneath a wheel that's spinning very slowly, as if the floor of the mud room sprouted a ceiling fan, I will see a Faraz-shaped figure with one leg twisted outwards like the arm of an octopus, but when I look down into the mud room it is empty. I look again, just to be sure, and breathe out with interim relief and say a quick Thank You to Chandigarh.

I leave the Maruti where it is. Another drop of blood has gathered on the scrape on my forehead but I am not otherwise hurt. I turn to go home, where I will wash my face, lie down in bed and fall asleep immediately. Tomorrow a suitable explanation shall be found about the car's location for Abba's appeasement.

But even before I open the door, I can see through the window that the lights are on in Abba's room. Of course he was awake, and of course he heard me sneak outside to break my promise, and now he will cancel Bangalore and take away my racket and it will truly and fully be The Official End of Everything.

Abba is standing over the telephone, his back turned towards me. His fingertips are hovering over the receiver.

I'm sorry, Abba, I say, because when Abba is so quietly disappointed it is much worse than when he is loudly angry. He glances up and I see that he is crying a complicated network of tears that seems somehow purposeless and lost, like tracks leading down a blind alley.

I run towards him, wanting only forgiveness, and he squeezes me so tight that the burning sensation on my forehead multiplies, and then he pulls back and touches my face, and though his lips are moving his voice sounds as if it's coming from elsewhere.

He's dead, Geeta. They eloped to Bombay, and now he's dead.

I tell Abba that he's wrong, that they're in Chandigarh but Abba starts talking of a hospital and that he died in it this evening from the injuries sustained in the blast and that Sitara was there with him but that she is unhurt by some miracle, so I tell him again that they are both in Chandigarh and Abba says, Maybe that's what they wanted you to say, and I tell him that I didn't, that I didn't give them away, just like I promised.

Abba hushes me and that's when I feel excessively tired. Abba's arms are there to catch and cradle me.

I remind myself that I won a trophy like Vicky said I would and that I spoke to Mummy today and that I'll be in Bangalore soon. But the next moment I remember that I made them stay. I made them stay. And then Faraz is in my head, saying what he said to me on the court that day. I push my fingertips deep into my ears but still I cannot stop his voice from telling me over and over again: Never forget that we are born to lose.

ACKNOWLEDGEMENTS

This novel has been my shelter and my storm. Thank you to all the people and institutions who stood by Geeta and me:

Bill and Brenda Andrew, the curators of the National Badminton Museum in Milton Keynes, for giving me access to their fabulous archive and sharing with me their boundless knowledge of the sport.

The writing residencies at Sangam House, the Toji Cultural Centre and Hedgebrook, where parts of this book were written.

Eleanor Birne, my agent and my biggest champion.

Ayesha Pande for representing the novel in the US.

Sayantan Ghosh, the perfect teammate for Geeta and an editor who just gets it.

The PR team at Simon & Schuster India, Abhay Singh, Shobhita Narayan, Mridu Agarwal and Shadab Khan, for their enthusiasm and dedication.

Bani Abidi, Sarnath Banerjee, Chandrahas Choudhury, Touché Gafla, DW Gibson, Sam Miller, Michelle Sterling and Madeleine Thien for your inspiring and uncompromising writing and work, your unquestioning support and for your vast, unfading friendship.

My parents, Jutta and Jyotindra Jain, and my brother Rumi Julian: the words 'thank you' cannot express the depth and density of gratitude that I feel every day that we spend together on this earth.

Christopher Kloeble, my co-conspirator and favourite writer: We've come this far and my love for you just grows and grows. You and our children are my home.